"I follow the facts, Ms. Fitzpatrick."

"I wish more people did. Maybe then they'd let me have a place here. And it's Faith." He tipped his head.

She figured he needed to stay professional where she was concerned. If he thought she was guilty, he'd continue calling her Ms. Fitzpatrick. Wasn't that what detectives were supposed to do? Keep their professional distance with suspects in a criminal investigation? Yes, she thought, stepping closer as a challenge of sorts. If he continued to call her Ms. Fitzpatrick, he would continue to see her as a suspect. It wasn't a solid conclusion, but she figured his next words would tell her everything she needed to know about where she stood in his book.

His expression fell serious. The moments ticked silently between them as she waited for a response.

"There's a place for you here," he said softly. "Even if it doesn't feel like it right now."

Dear Reader,

While writing *Where the Heart May Lead*, I fell a little in love with Detective John "Tully" McTully. As Charlie's fiercely loyal best friend, who was so determined to do the right thing, I knew Tully could handle a heroine with a little edge and a lot of heart.

Like so many of us, Faith Fitzpatrick carries deep wounds from her childhood. After years of searching for belonging in other places, she returns to her hometown of Roseley, fearful that others won't let her make the fresh start she deserves. In Tully, Faith finds a person who sees through her defenses and admires her heart. May we all be seen for the good that resides in us; what a love story that really would be.

I hope some part of Tully and Faith's story resonates with you. If it does, I would love to hear from you. Consider following the Elizabeth Mowers Author page on Facebook or find me at elizabethmowers.com.

Wishing love to you and yours,

Elizabeth

HEARTWARMING

Her Hometown Detective

Elizabeth Mowers

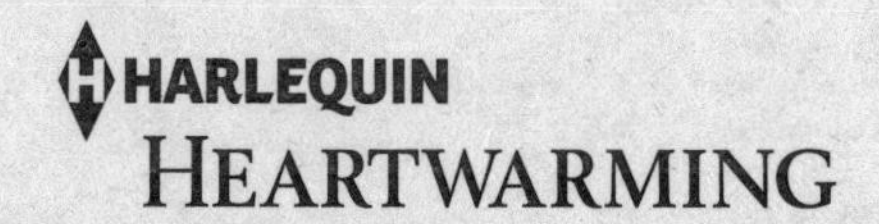

ISBN-13: 978-1-335-17972-2

Her Hometown Detective

This edition published by arrangement with Harlequin Books S.A.

For questions and comments about the quality of this book, please contact us at CustomerService@Harlequin.com.

Harlequin Enterprises ULC
22 Adelaide St. West, 40th Floor
Toronto, Ontario M5H 4E3, Canada
www.Harlequin.com

Printed in U.S.A.

Elizabeth Mowers wrote her first romance novel on her cell phone when her first child wouldn't nap without being held. After three years, she had a happy preschooler and a hot mess of a book that will never be read by another person. The experience started her down the wonderful path of writing romances, and now that she can use her computer, she's having fun cooking up new stories. She's drawn to romances with strong family connections and plots where the hero and heroine help save each other. Elizabeth lives in the country with her husband and two children.

Books by Elizabeth Mowers

Harlequin Heartwarming

A Promise Remembered
Where the Heart May Lead

Visit Harlequin.com for more Harlequin Heartwarming titles.

To my husband, Kevin

Steady, loyal, honorable, and true

The original John McTully

CHAPTER ONE

DETECTIVE JOHN "TULLY" MCTULLY lowered his truck window and hung an arm out, allowing the humidity to smack him in the face. The wooded two-lane highway leaving Roseley was bursting with bright green foliage thanks to the frequent rains of May and June. The heat and humidity that followed in Michigan did nothing to deter the summer tourists who flooded the charming lakeside town every year for the long Fourth of July weekend. For a few days more, Tully savored the quiet drive out of town for the break it was.

He'd lived in Roseley for most of his life. Aside from a few years of schooling and then police work in Grand Rapids, he'd stuck close to home and near the people who had supported him since childhood. Like his best friend, Charlie, who had recently returned to Roseley and married. There was Tully's father, now living quietly alone on the outskirts of town. And Samantha, his sister, who had been his opposite in nearly every possible way since they'd been children. Samantha always added a bit of drama from time to time.

After cruising for a while, Tully reached for his cell phone vibrating in the center console.

"Hello, Samantha," he said.

"Are you still picking me up from the airport?"

"That was the plan." He accelerated at the tone in her voice. Samantha hated having even a moment of downtime on her hands.

"Perfect. We touched down."

"You're early."

"Don't I know it. The pilots are my kind of people." She laughed, her gregarious voice most likely carrying throughout the entire pressurized cabin. "Is Dad with you?"

"No."

"Thank goodness." Her sigh of relief was all too common when Dad's absence was mentioned. "I really can't take him right now."

"I know, I know. See you soon."

For the longest time, Tully had tried to remember what his baby sister had been like when they'd been children and their family had been a family of four. He couldn't recall a time when Samantha hadn't been so…much.

He knew losing his mom at a young age had changed the trajectory of his life, but for Samantha, he thought it had changed her trajectory most drastically. The only person who could corroborate his theory was his father, but in the old man's own words, some things were better left unspoken.

When he finally arrived, Samantha flagged him from the curb as if he would have a hard time spotting her. Dressed like the jet-setter she was, in designer threads and a fancy hairstyle, she stuck out in town like rhinestones on work boots.

Tully helped her throw her suitcases and gear in the back cab of his truck.

"New equipment?" he said, jostling her satchel. Samantha rolled her eyes.

"I had to replace a few things on the road."

"Between all your travels and expensive photography equipment, I don't know how you save a cent."

"Who said I ever do?" she said with a laugh. "When I die, I want to skid into my coffin penniless and happy."

Tully climbed into the truck and studied his little sister. Her youth kept the wear of a long flight from showing too much on her face, but it was her forced smile that made him pause.

"Are you happy?" he said, starting the engine. Samantha dodged the sincerity of his question, sliding on her aviator sunglasses with flair.

"I had the time of my life in Cape Town, John. Wait until you see the followers I've accumulated since I uploaded my photos." She scrolled through the pictures on her phone as Tully pulled onto the main highway, aiming them in the direction of town. "I'll bet you didn't know your sister was doing *this* last week." She held up her phone to show a picture of herself in a giant steel cage.

"Don't tell me…" Tully said, glancing between the phone screen and the road. "Diving with sharks?"

"*Great white* sharks to be exact."

"Why on earth would you want to do that?" He wasn't surprised by Samantha's choice of vacation excursions, but he didn't see the appeal.

"It was exhilarating. And I got more hits on a handful of these pictures than I got over the last six months."

Tully chuckled. "I'm glad you had fun."

"How's dad?"

"He's still kicking around."

"Have you seen him since I left?"

Tully had to think. He didn't keep track of how often he drove out to visit his father, instead sensing by osmosis when a visit was due.

"It's been a few weeks," he said. "Do you want me to drive that way?"

"Ugh. And get the *you're just like your mother* sneer for the millionth time? No, thanks."

"But you're going to drive out there soon, right?"

Samantha shrugged. "It would be a lot easier if he lived in his house instead of that shack in the middle of nowhere. I still don't get why he moved there in the first place. I understand wanting space, but geesh. Have you made any headway on convincing him to move home?"

Tully shook his head and pulled into Elmer's Gas Station. Elmer, a crotchety man in his eighties, sat behind the counter, a lump of chewing tobacco tucked in his lower lip.

"Need anything?" Tully said, shifting gear into Park and stepping out of the cab. Samantha shook her head, engrossed in her smartphone.

"Not unless Elmer's started selling cappuccino."

Tully no sooner began to pump gas when Elmer came shuffling out.

"Pump is slow," Elmer called. Tully glanced at the other pumps, but they were all closed.

"How slow?"

Elmer shoved his hands in his front pockets and made a clicking noise with his tongue. "Dripping molasses."

"It's all right, Elmer. I have the time."

"How's your dad?"

"Same."

"He stopped here last week looking for bait. Said the fishing was good."

"The lake is high." Tully tried for polite conversation whenever his father came up as a topic.

"Sure is. We're gonna have a lot of tourists for the Fourth, I suspect."

"Always do."

"Tourists," Elmer said with a grumble. "Can't live with 'em, can't do without 'em. I guess their money burns the same as locals'." He shuffled back into the station as Tully watched the meter. Elmer wasn't fooling; the fuel pump dispensed gas at about one cent a second.

Tully leaned back against his truck, taking a minute to relax and enjoy the sunshine. He needed only enough gas to get him through the long weekend before the Fourth of July holiday sent the price climbing. His old Boy Scout motto to "Always Be Prepared" rang in his head.

He had begun wondering what plans Charlie and his wife, Paige, had for the holiday, when the rumble of a motorcycle turned his attention.

A little Sportster with midnight-black paint pulled up behind him and dropped the engine to idle. Tully noted that the motorcyclist was a young woman, not only because of her petite stature, but because he knew every rider within a twenty-mile radius. She had slipped past his radar and, no doubt, the radar of the local, ahem, busybodies. Otherwise, Tully concluded, he would have heard about her before now.

Tully had a few folks around town who kept him up-to-date on Roseley's current events. He didn't enjoy getting involved in the gossip or petty politics, but as Roseley's only police detective, his job required that he always be "in the know." When there was a case to solve, he knew whom to reach out to for leads and tips.

As Roseley was landlocked on three quarters by a lake and a state park, it wasn't on the way to anything. Rather, it was the very definition of being out of the way. This young woman was most likely not passing through. As she didn't have any cargo or travel bags strapped to her Sportster motorcycle, she was most likely visiting friends for the upcoming holiday and had ventured out for an afternoon cruise.

She removed her helmet and shook out a head of dark messy cropped hair. When she removed her leather jacket, Tully made note of the heart tattoo on the back of her shoulder. She was attractive, from where he stood, but when she bent over to check the straps on the bike's saddlebags, he quickly turned his attention away to maintain his professionalism.

Checking the pump's display screen, Tully thought the meter clicked slower than before, as if aware another person waited in line. He took care of a few maintenance things to pass the time: checking his oil, washing his windshield and windows, and cleaning dead bugs off his headlights. He'd just returned the squeegee to its container when a voice called from behind him.

"Why don't you give it a coat of wax while you're at it?"

Tully turned to find the motorcyclist squaring off with him, clenched fists planted on her hips. Her eyes were hidden behind dark sunglasses. Her rosebud mouth puckered in a scowl.

"Excuse me?"

"I'm not waiting here for my health, honey." Her voice, dripping with sarcasm, purred in his ears. How she managed a smart remark that could make him stand up and take notice, and yet tantalized, was beyond him.

Before he could form a response and point toward the meter, she strode past him and into Elmer's shop. He couldn't decide if she was irritated at him or just plain irritable in general, but something about how she moved, like she was charging onto a battlefield, made him want to offer a memorable reply.

When the pump clicked that it had finished, he returned the nozzle and swung his truck around so he could watch the motorcyclist emerge. He worked hard to resolve conflict in his town and felt no obligation to explain that the wait was the fault of Elmer's slow pump, not him. However, he also didn't mind watching people who'd just lipped off to him have to eat a little crow.

"What was that all about?" Samantha

asked, angling in her seat to see what he was looking at. “Do you know that woman?”

Tully shook his head as the motorcyclist returned and pulled her bike up to the pump. She squeezed and released the nozzle a few times, noticeably frustrated. When she looked his way, he tipped his head in a nod. The small gesture managed to infuriate her. Though he watched from a distance, he was sure she muttered a curse word or two as she stormed back into the station, most likely to complain to Elmer. Tully chuckled. He knew Elmer wouldn’t respond too kindly to a harsh word from an out-of-towner. In fact, if Elmer had any say, he might try to make the pump go slower.

Tully put the truck into gear and was about to drive off when she exited the station. He couldn’t help a quick glance since she was now striding in his direction.

“Here we go,” he said to himself.

Tully was used to dealing with all types of personalities. His kind demeanor could shift to fierce intimidation in two seconds flat when he sensed danger or deception. It made him both respected and beloved by the townspeople, who could always count on Tully to do what was right.

Was she coming over to offer an apology? She made no motion to indicate she had made any mistake. "Good afternoon," he said once she'd drawn near. Her mouth spread in a sarcastic smile, an audible *hmph* vibrating in her throat.

"Some welcome committee, you are."

"You're new, then?"

"Did I say that?" She glanced to either side of her as if checking for eavesdroppers. "I can hear you gloating from across the parking lot."

"What about?"

"You know very well," she said. "People in this town never change."

Tully frowned, noticeably confused. He had been enjoying their encounter right up until the moment she'd tossed some prior emotional baggage into the equation. He leaned out his window, letting the midday sun highlight his face. "Have I offended you in a past life, ma'am?"

She whipped off her sunglasses. Her eyes were gray, like a storm brewing over the sea. By the way they narrowed on him, he knew they matched her temperament perfectly.

When he removed his sunglasses, her breath caught. It was quick, something most people would miss, but he was not most people. He had spent years studying every flinch of a person's eyebrow, every hesitation or redirection when a person was caught in a lie. He'd knocked her off guard, though in what way exactly, he couldn't say.

"I—" She blinked rapidly, grappling for words. He struggled to place her, wondering if he'd arrested her during his short stint working in the city. His mind drew nothing but a blank. He was good with faces, heck, names too, but he didn't know her. As sure as he was about that, he was also sure that he wanted to get to know her.

"I'm Detective McTully," he said. "I don't believe we've met."

"Detective," she said, the word drawn out slowly as if she had to readjust her perception of him. "You became a detective."

He waited, patiently as always. In his line of work, he found that the less he spoke, the more information people gave him. He felt perfectly comfortable idling in the awkward silence that most people despised. Because of this, folks tended to run their mouths, usually to their own detriment and to the benefit of a case solved.

Unfortunately, his sister, the famous orator of Little Lake Roseley, was riding shotgun.

"Hi, honey!" Samantha called. "I love your motorcycle. Harley-Davidson, isn't it?" The woman tore her gaze from Tully to nod, but quickly returned to studying his face. Samantha continued, "I haven't been on a motorcycle since one of my college boyfriends took me for a spin. I never regretted dumping him, if only I could have kept his bike." The woman almost smiled at this. He hurried to place her. The rounded pale cheeks sloped to a delicate chin. Her entire face resembled a heart, and it brought his thoughts to the tattoo on her shoulder. Her features were distinct and breathtaking but in no way familiar. She peered back at him like an alley cat, skittish to see what he'd do next. If she was waiting for him to remember her, they could be here all day.

"Are you visiting family for the weekend?" Samantha asked, leaning over Tully's lap to get a better view of her target. "Our fireworks are the best in a hundred miles, you know. Who are you staying with?"

"I'm not."

"Not what?" Samantha pressed. "Staying with anyone? Did you move here? Tully knows everyone in this town, but I can tell he doesn't know you." He wished Samantha would seal her lips for a moment, as her comment made the woman blink awake, alert. She frowned.

"I'm sorry about earlier," the woman said, backing away. "I thought you were… I don't know what I thought. You obviously weren't…"

"We've all been there, honey," Samantha shouted after her, causing the woman to offer a friendly wave as if an afterthought. She sped off, fired up her Sportster and zipped out of the parking lot, heading toward town. "She can certainly handle herself on that motorcycle."

"She didn't get more than a couple bucks into her gas tank."

"Then she won't be able to get too far." Samantha smirked. "Go on. I know you want to."

"What?"

"Give chase."

"Excuse me?"

"Don't you want to see where she's going and where she's staying? I saw how you looked at her." When Tully shot his sister a look, she giggled. "And how she looked at you."

"I didn't notice."

"It was pretty difficult to miss, Tully, and it's okay to notice, you know."

"I might say the same thing to you." Now it was his turn to chuckle as Samantha shifted uncomfortably in her seat. "You're as averse to relationships as I am."

"If I ever find a man who can keep up with me, I'll pick out china place settings with him."

"No, you won't," he said, finally pulling out of the parking lot. Samantha laughed hard.

"Nope! I probably won't, but that'll never stop me from trying to get *you* settled down. It's bad enough I have to worry about Dad when I'm traveling. One of these days you'll turn into an old man too, and I'll have to check in on you both."

"Sis, I'm not the—"

"*—marrying kind.* How many times have I heard that?"

"Yet you're still ready to fix me up with a random woman on the street."

"All I'm saying is I can tell you're interested in her or else we would have left the parking lot ages ago."

"I was hoping for an apology."

"Is *that* what they're calling it these days?"

"My day goes better when people acknowledge when they've done something wrong."

"I didn't realize she'd done anything wrong."

"Never mind. She's not my type."

"What, intriguing? She looked like a lot of fun to me."

"You think everyone outside of Roseley looks like a lot of fun."

"Yeah, and I'm usually right."

Tully turned on the radio. "Let's drop it, or I'll blindside you with a fix-up as payback."

Samantha smacked him on the arm but turned her attention to the view outside her window. Tully was grateful for the silence. And, he thought to himself, it didn't matter if the motorcyclist had managed to get under his skin. By the sound of it, she didn't think too highly of the folks in town and was probably passing through. He figured it was unlikely he'd ever see her again.

CHAPTER TWO

FAITH FITZPATRICK HAD spent her first few days back in Roseley getting the lay of the land and cleaning out her newly leased shop. The rental unit had been empty for nearly a year, so cleaning and moving in hadn't been as difficult as she'd expected. She'd also enlisted the help of her cousins, Caroline and Trig, although Trig had taken off to check his work email as soon as the heavy lifting was done.

"Don't you want me to open up the front door and let some fresh air in here?" Caroline asked, dragging a wet mop along the linoleum floor toward the entrance. The front window and door had been covered with butcher paper and Faith was happy to leave it in place for as long as possible, even if the space stayed dark.

"Absolutely not." Faith hustled to block her cousin from the entrance. "Not yet."

She and her cousins had grown up together

until just after high school, when Faith had escaped town and all the drama that had come with it. Being back with her cousins had given her the confidence boost she needed to tackle the obstacles over the next few days.

"Faith, you're going to have to announce your presence eventually. That is, if you have any intention of earning a living."

Faith had daydreamed of more than earning a living in Roseley. She hoped to make a life here. She had never wanted to leave in the first place, not really. But after what had happened with her father, leaving had quickly turned into her only reasonable option if she didn't want to continue hanging her head in shame every day. Ducking around corners to avoid her meanest critics had been awful.

"I'm not worried about that, Caroline. I don't care what people in this town think of me." Caroline's face smoothed in skepticism.

"It's okay to be nervous."

"I'm not nervous." She fiddled with a tub of plaster. "I don't want to open the shop until it's ready. A grand opening is supposed to be grand, right? It's a big reveal."

Caroline wrapped an arm around Faith's

shoulders. "We'll have this place looking fabulous for its big reveal in no time."

"Are you sure you can stick around to help me?"

"Sure. You really need to open before Fourth of July to build some buzz."

"I should have opened months ago to better establish myself before riding season." She'd always wanted to open her own motorcycle repair and detailing shop, but her husband, Kyle, had squashed her dream every chance he got. She'd stayed in their marriage hoping for the best but tolerating the worst. The day she had finally packed her bags and walked out of their house for good had been anticlimactic compared with the rest of their relationship. She now wished she'd left much sooner.

"Don't look back," Caroline told her. "Just think of this opening as a head start to next summer's riding season."

Faith nodded at her cousin's encouragement. She hoped the summer was a head start to the rest of her life's happiness, finally. "Do you think I should paint?"

They looked around at the red brick walls. It wasn't a place that needed much decor, at least not for what she needed it for. The space was tidier than any repair shop she'd ever worked in.

"I doubt anyone cares what the aesthetics are. They'll only want to know you do good work. You might need to reconsider if you start *selling* motorcycles too."

"True. I'm a long way off from being a distributor and opening a showroom. Repairs and detailing will have to be my bread and butter for now. Once I know I can make the rent, I can think about expanding. For now, I have to keep my overhead low. I also need to see how many guys are comfortable with me working on their motorcycles. If their egos don't get in the way..."

Caroline smiled. "Egos always get in the way. Look at Trig."

Faith's cousin Trig had come home to Roseley for a long holiday to support her return. But she knew he was itching to get back to Detroit and to his fast-paced sports journalism career. He was one of the most driven, competitive people she knew.

"The one thing I do need to do, perhaps tomorrow, is paint this front window. I love how everyone decorates theirs, and I want to hold up my place on the street."

"Ah, the pride of being your own boss,"

Caroline said. “You also used to be a good artist when we were kids. Any chance you kept up with that too?”

Faith tipped her head thoughtfully, considering the size of her front window. “I’m sure I could do it justice. Heart Motorcycles needs a beautiful new logo right about here.” She peeled away a tiny piece of the brown butcher paper covering. When she found an eye peeking back at her from the other side of the window, she yelped.

“Who’s in there?” a voice from outside called. “This place is closed, you know!”

Faith backed away, motioning to Caroline to stay hushed. She wasn’t ready to talk to anyone, face anyone, explain to anyone why she should be here. She’d been sneaking in through the back door for a week, grateful to stay undetected, but now…

“Hello!” the voice squawked. “Show yourself or I’m calling the police. If you’re in there doing that graffiti or stealing copper pipes—”

“Hang on,” Caroline called, throwing up her hands in an apology to Faith. “It’s like ripping off a bandage,” she whispered. “Just get this first encounter over with, and then we’ll get back to work.”

“This wasn’t the plan,” Faith said, her voice

cutting. She was ready to order the woman to get lost, but her sweet cousin had already moved to unlock the door. Faith crossed, then uncrossed her arms, finally whipping on a pair of lightly tinted sunglasses and widening her gate to exude as much confidence as she could.

The adage *Don't give the devil a foothold* crossed her mind as Caroline opened the door only a few inches before a short woman with bright peach lipstick pushed the rest of the way in. The woman's determination to know what was going on had certainly overshadowed any concern she might have had for her safety. She stopped short once she got a good look at them both.

"Caroline," the woman gasped, noticeably taken aback at not finding hooligans running amuck. "What are you doing in here? Are you renting this place? Mark didn't mention he'd leased the unit yet."

"Why, no," Caroline said, a polite smile spreading. "It belongs to—"

"Ms. Fitzpatrick will do just fine," Faith said.

Caroline nodded in understanding as their guest stepped closer for a better view. Faith yearned for a few more days before she announced that she, formerly known as Faith Talbert, was back. She could only imagine how that news would spark a wildfire of gossip. She wanted only a little peace and quiet.

As the electricity had not been turned on and the windows were still covered, the woman had to strain to make out Faith in the dim light. Faith, however, recognized the woman immediately as CeCe Takes, one of her family's loudest critics. When her father had been arrested for orchestrating an investment scam, CeCe had been at the forefront of reporting it to the town. She was sure CeCe had not thought of her once over the years, but Faith had, unfortunately, thought of her neighbor many times. On her way out of town as a frustrated seventeen-year-old kid, Faith had taken satisfaction in smashing CeCe's storefront mailbox and flowerpots. Her anger had spurred her on, wanting to make CeCe pay for her gossip, which had worsened the Talbert family crisis. It had felt good at the time to hear the crinkle of metal and to imagine the look of horror on CeCe's face when she found the ruined mailbox and flowers strewn up and down the sidewalk. She'd blazed out of town right after that rather pleased with herself, but during the ten years since then she'd come to regret her actions, felt ashamed any time she thought of what she'd done.

If CeCe recognized Faith, she certainly didn't let on, curtly making her introduction as she glanced about the place. "CeCe Takes. My husband, Angelo, and I run The Sandwich Board a few stores down."

"Ms. Fitzpatrick has moved here from out of state," Caroline said. Faith squared her shoulders. She knew she was noticeably different-looking now. At least, that was what she had hoped during the long drive to Roseley. Over the last decade, Faith had put on the curves of a woman, cut her long, wavy hair to a short crop and darkened the sandy blond shade to the darkest brown. She'd also traded in her preppy, conservative clothes for an edgier style that screamed *don't mess with me*. But as much as she knew she'd changed, something about being back reminded her too much of the upset little girl who had skidded out of town as one of Roseley's disappointments.

Faith dug deep for a pleasant response. "Nice to meet you."

CeCe's brow lifted as she made a study of Faith's appearance. She could tell her low-slung faded Levi's, tight black tank top and old leather riding boots didn't impress. "What kind of business are you opening here, Ms. Fitzpatrick?"

Faith glanced at Caroline before answering. "Motorcycle repair and detailing."

CeCe's face soured as if she'd deep kissed a lemon. "*Motorcycles?* Heavens, why?"

"There's a need for it, Mrs. Takes," Caroline said.

"Really? Hmph. Well, if you say so." CeCe wandered around the shop, running her fingers over the various mechanical tools. "Do you have a fella?"

Faith nearly gagged on her reply. "Excuse me?"

"I assume you're running the business end and your fella is running the repairs."

"You assume wrong." Faith settled back on her feet, enjoying the look on CeCe's face as she worked out whether she had been insulted. Her cousin's jaw shifted askew, warning. "No," Faith said. "I don't have a fella. I don't need one either."

"If you say so," CeCe muttered before wandering to the front door. "What's the name of your shop?"

"It's not open yet."

CeCe spun around. "What am I supposed to tell people?"

Faith swallowed hard. CeCe hadn't changed a bit. She still thought everything was her business and her news to share.

"You can tell people that I'll be ready for a grand opening later this week."

"Hmm." CeCe frowned in disapproval. "Welcome to the neighborhood..."

"Ms. Fitzpatrick."

"Ms. Fitzpatrick. I suppose your first name isn't ready yet either?"

Before Faith could piece together a smart reply, Caroline had ushered CeCe out the door. "Thanks for stopping by, Mrs. Takes!" she called and speedily locked the door behind her. She spun and collapsed as Faith wiped the beads of perspiration that had formed on her brow. Starting a new business should be the most nerve-racking thing she would have to do this week, yet talking to CeCe was coming in at a close second. Caroline let out a long sigh that climbed into a laugh. "Hey, not to worry, you know what they say. One down—"

"Two hundred more to go?" Faith removed her sunglasses, now feeling foolish for having hid.

Caroline crossed over to her as if reading her mind and said, "She's going to figure out who you are eventually, you know. Everyone will."

"But I want that to happen on my terms."

"I know, I know, but you can't control everyone. You certainly can't control Mrs. Takes."

It could have been the truest thing she'd ever heard her cousin say.

"Thanks for backing me up."

Caroline touched her shoulder. "I'll always back you up, cousin." There weren't many people in Faith's life who would do so, but Caroline was one of the good ones whose words she believed in.

TULLY HAD JUST claimed his desk chair and tipped his coffee mug to his lips when Charlie, his buddy and fellow police officer, answered the phone at the station house. Dolores Mitchell, a lifelong resident and shop owner, was on the other end of the line. Her normally sweet, low voice had a slight shrill to it this morning, and Tully could hear her end of the conversation from a desk away. The facts were simple. Her storefront window had been vandalized sometime in the middle of the night. She wanted to file a police report, and no, she didn't know who would do such a thing.

Roseley, despite its friendly charms, was not immune to petty crimes. Occasionally, Tully got reports about smashed mailboxes, busted locks on shed doors or foul-language graffiti on the giant rocks at Roseley State Park's entrance. Infractions like these tended to be a rare occurrence in recent years, likely the drunken antics of bored folks looking for something to do on a Saturday night.

Occasionally, more serious misdemeanors cropped up. The summer before, teenage boys, looking to go on a joyride, had stolen a speedboat and careened across the lake endangering others and nearly killing themselves.

The worst scandal in memory, felony on several counts, had involved Ray Talbert, an investment broker who had swindled several people out of their life savings over a period of nearly seventeen years. Talbert had moved to town and married one of the local girls, setting up shop immediately. His good looks and thick charm had made him well-known and had also helped make him a very wealthy man, or so the FBI said. The day they'd arrested Talbert, Tully had been away, completing his second year of college, but his father had kept him updated. His dad had been one of the few not to invest with Talbert, but that made him no less interested in the story. Given the way his father lived, Tully assumed his dad had hefty savings squirreled away in a coffee can buried in the backyard.

News of Talbert's arrest and the scope of his fraud had shook folks straight out of their front porch rocking chairs. Over the last ten years, his name or the name of one of his victims would crop up in conversation, usually accompanied with a sad shake of the head and a word of warning. Talbert's case became a cautionary tale to trust a little more slowly than what Roseley residents had preferred.

This sentiment about being careful resonated fine with Tully. He knew who his genuine friends were and didn't let too many people into his inner circle. Charlie had in fact become the brother Tully had never had but had always wanted. Charlie's relations also felt like his second family.

"Are you heading over there now?" Tully said, curious to see the damage to Dolores's storefront. He followed Charlie out of the station.

"I bumped into Emily Peaches yesterday," Charlie said once they'd climbed into Tully's truck. "She looks great."

Tully had gone on a few dates with the dimple-cheeked beauty and had half expected news of their relationship to make the front page of the local newspaper. Now that Charlie was happily married, he was almost as bad as Samantha when it came to meddling in Tully's love life.

"I'm sure she does." Emily was a knockout, although Tully knew he'd never had a problem attracting beautiful women. Dating had never been a problem, period. It was when his date brought up the notions of exclusivity, marriage and the future did he kindly, but firmly, wish them well and return them to a cordial "just friends" status.

Charlie chuckled as they pulled up in front of The Cutest Little Tea Shop. They sat in the truck for a moment, taking in the sight. The tea shop wasn't cute any longer.

The two-foot-long window box had been ripped off the front of the storefront wall and had been banged up pretty badly. The flower baskets and ivy adorning the entrance had been torn apart and kicked along the sidewalk. Someone had emptied a can of black spray paint on both the storefront window and mauve bench in front of it. The ugliness of it all stood in contrast to the beautiful morning sunshine warming the sidewalk.

"I know people are people—" Charlie said as they emerged from the squad car.

Tully finished his sentence. "—but it's always a surprise to find something like this here."

"Thanks for coming so quickly," Dolores said, popping out of the shop. Her violet-gray updo frizzed in the morning humidity. "I didn't want to start fixing anything until I filed a police report. I'm glad you got here as soon as you did, because I have to get this place cleaned up. It'll take me all day to scrub this black paint. What a shame. Those flowers were finally blooming too."

"What time did you find the place like this?" Tully asked. Dolores gathered pieces of the strewn flowers and motioned down the block.

"CeCe saw it first."

Tully spotted CeCe Takes hurrying up the street, two hot coffees in hand.

"Yoo-hoo! Detective! I'm sure I can answer your questions." She handed each man a coffee and settled back on her heels, pleased with herself.

Dolores scowled at her friend. “I could have gotten them something to drink, CeCe. I run a tea shop, for heaven’s sake.”

“They prefer coffee, not tea. Don’t you, Detective?” CeCe’s face smeared into a wide smile. CeCe had wanted to fix Charlie up with her niece a couple of summers before he’d married Paige. When that prospect fell through, she had aggressively turned her attention to Tully, eager for him to be her new nephew. Tully could think of nothing worse than getting roped into a relationship that would place CeCe as a more integral part of his life. He’d ducked and dodged the anxious matchmaker for months before her niece had decided not to move to town for at least another year.

“What time did you find this mess?” he asked, motioning to the black spray paint. CeCe tipped her head thoughtfully, trying to remember.

“I’m an early riser. Even when our walking group takes the morning off, I still like to power walk on my own. At my age, it’s important to keep moving. Anyway, I was out about a quarter after five when I found this.”

"Did you see anyone leaving either by car or foot?"

"No one. But I did see a light on—" CeCe lowered her voice considerably *"—next door."*

Tully sauntered over to take a closer look at the adjacent property. Brown paper covered the inside storefront window with only a few skinny pieces ripped away. He cupped his hands around his eyes and pressed his forehead to the glass to get a better look inside.

"Someone was in here this morning?" he said. "I didn't know Mark had leased it."

"Some woman is opening up a—" CeCe flicked an eyebrow in disapproval "—motorcycle repair shop."

"Really." Tully caught a glance at some tools, but no motorcycles. He'd ridden a little in college and found his curiosity piqued.

"Have you met the owner?" Charlie asked.

"Unfortunately."

Tully turned, considering the negative undertones. "Why do you say that?"

Dolores huffed and crossed her arms, her annoyance at her friend rather than at the new resident. "CeCe *said* the woman had a bit of an attitude, Detective."

"She did!"

"You think everyone has an attitude." Dolores picked up a handful of her crushed flowers. "Especially outsiders."

"That's not true." She turned to Charlie. "I thought Paige was the loveliest girl when I first met her, didn't I, Charlie? She told you how welcoming I was, didn't she?"

Charlie grinned as CeCe turned her attention to Tully.

"It's worth noting that the only light on so early in the morning was coming from this new shop next door, isn't it? I banged on the door for several minutes and hollered at her to open up, but she didn't answer. Isn't that a bit suspicious, Detective? Like she's hiding something?"

"Was your shop light on also?" Charlie asked. CeCe's brow furrowed before easing into an amused smile. She winked at him.

"My light is always on, Officer." Dolores bellowed a laugh as the rumble of a motorcycle snagged their attention. Cruising up the block before coming to a stop in front of them was the same black Sportster from the gas station and the same rider.

"Well, I'll be damned," Tully muttered, softly enough for no one else to hear. The rider cut the engine and sat for a few moments, as they all stared at her. Finally, after heaving what looked like a deep breath, she slipped off her helmet and ran a hand through her shiny locks. She had one of those haircuts that looked like she'd rolled out of bed, spiked some gel in her hair and didn't give two cents what anyone thought about that. He liked it more than he ever expected he would.

She slid her sunglasses off in one cool movement, briefly shifting storm-gray eyes his way. Eyes that could cut a hundred men in one swift slice. She nodded curtly to everyone else standing on the street.

"Good morning, *Ms. Fitzpatrick*," CeCe said. The corners of the rider's mouth rose slightly, politely, but her eyes remained unchanged.

"Is everything okay?" Ms. Fitzpatrick asked, easing off her motorcycle. CeCe pointed to the mess in front of Dolores's shop.

"Not if you call smashed mailboxes and ruined benches okay."

"Simmer down, CeCe," Dolores said. "That wasn't what she meant." She turned to the woman. "Good morning, dear. We haven't met yet, but I'm your shop neighbor, Dolores Mitchell."

Ms. Fitzpatrick moved forward to shake hands before turning to Charlie.

"Officer Stillwater," he quickly supplied. "You've already met CeCe. And over here is—"

"Detective," she said, accepting his offered hand in a shake. Her petite hands had a faint smear of grease on them, the residue that most likely still lingered after several minutes of scrubbing. It was nothing he minded. If anything, he found this dichotomy about her to be fascinating. Delicate hands, working hands. Fair skin, dark hair. Feminine features, bold attitude. When she squeezed his hand and her eyes met his, she managed a polite smile. "Nice to see you again."

"You as well," he said. "And..."

Her eyes flashed, making him the first to release his grip. She spooked easily even if she tried to hide it.

"Pardon?" she said.

"He wants to know if you have a first name, Ms. Fitzpatrick," CeCe supplied, her condescension making everyone cringe. The woman's jaw tightened, but Tully was certain that no one had seen it but him.

"Faith," she said.

"Did you just arrive in town, ma'am?" As usual, Tully worked to keep his voice calm and steady, as if he was negotiating a hostage situation at the bank. Still, she shifted on her feet as though he had accused her of a heist.

"And if I did?"

Tully noticed a strange charge hung in the air. He set his gaze steadfast on Faith, patiently letting the silence draw her into more of an explanation.

"No," she finally said, as if reconsidering her tone. "I moved here a week ago to get my shop prepared for opening."

"What kind of shop?" He already knew the answer, but he wanted her to relax a bit, wanted her to know he wasn't there to accuse her of anything. He would lob a few easy questions over the net and affirm her answers with every response.

"Repairing and detailing."

"Excellent. Is this your Sportster?"

"Of course."

"It's a nice bike."

"Thanks."

"How's it run?"

"It serves me well."

"Glad to hear it. Is anyone else working here with you?"

"Why does anyone else *need* to be working with me?"

Tully surveyed her stance: shoulders back,

chin tilted, eyes defiant. Without warning she'd crushed the ball across the net in a return that baffled him. He wondered where the hostility came from. Their first encounter at the gas station had started off on the wrong foot and had then fizzled out when she had seemed to recognize him. Maybe getting her away from CeCe and the others would help him figure her out.

"Based on our brief encounter yesterday, ma'am, I'm pretty certain you don't need anyone at all."

Her face flinched in a smile before turning to Charlie and motioning to the notebook he held.

"I didn't see anything, Officer. I've been putting in long hours to get my shop ready for the holiday weekend. I was out early this morning, but I didn't see any of *this* happening." She strode to the doorway and picked up Dolores's smashed mailbox. "I could hammer this out, if you'd like. You'd need to repaint it, but I could get it smoothed out a bit and—"

"She doesn't want some banged-up mailbox," CeCe said. Dolores shushed CeCe before smiling at Faith.

"Yes, I'd appreciate that, Faith. Thank you for offering."

Faith smiled before moving toward her shop, mailbox under one arm and store keys in hand.

Charlie turned his attention to Dolores and CeCe, asking them to show him around inside. Meanwhile, Tully followed Faith.

"How long have you been repairing motorcycles?" he asked. Her entire persona from her outfit to her Sportster to her edgy attitude conveyed a message that she had something to prove. But the fact that she could repair motorcycles and open a business on her own made him think she didn't have to.

She fiddled with the key in the lock. "My uncle taught me years ago."

"Does he live in Roseley?"

"Not now. Anyway, working on bikes is all I've ever wanted to do."

"You're in the right place." She paused at his suggestion.

"Why do you say that?"

He gently reached for her keys. "May I?" She eased her hand away, letting the key ring hang in the lock. He worked the lock as best as he could. "A lot of folks around here ride."

"Not according to Mrs. Takes."

"Did she say that?"

"No. But she has some negative biases about people who do."

"Oh?"

"It's apparent she doesn't like riders…or, I guess, me."

He shrugged. "She has a lot of negative opinions about a lot of things and always has. I wouldn't take it personally." He continued, keeping his tone light, "Where are you staying?"

"If business is good, I'll be here most of the time."

"And if business is bad?"

She leaned against the door frame, arms crossed tightly over her chest.

"I haven't found a permanent place yet. Gonna wait and see how things go."

"With your shop?" She nodded, but the tone in her voice clued him in to something else. "It's always wise to be prudent." Tully made his way to his truck, retrieving something from the cab. He returned with a spray can of WD-40. After a few squirts, the lock clicked easily. He pushed the door open, motioning for Faith to enter first.

"This is it," she said, flicking on the overhead lights. The fluorescent bulbs cast few shadows around the room as there wasn't much in the shop aside from a short counter, tool chest and a handful of cardboard packing boxes.

"Are you still moving in?"

She breathed a sigh of pride. "I don't need much."

It qualified as the understatement of the year. The place was spotless and the few things she did have were well organized.

"Does this place have a name yet?"

"I haven't decided."

"When do you open?"

"Fourth of July."

"Then you need a name."

She tipped her head thoughtfully. "I was thinking of calling it Heart Motorcycles."

He recalled the heart tattoo on her shoulder, though it was currently covered by the leather jacket she was tucked into.

"Any special meaning behind that?" he asked. Her lips parted in surprise. He could tell she was piecing together an answer instead of recalling the truth.

"Why do you ask?"

"Your heart tattoo made me curious."

"Do you have x-ray vision, Detective?" He could sense amusement in her expression. As she wiggled out of her jacket to give him another look at her tattoo, a sexy thought crossed his mind as he sadly shook his head to convey he didn't. She hung her jacket on a hook. "You were paying more attention yesterday than I thought."

"It's not every day someone around here yells at me." Faith frowned as if misunderstood.

"I didn't yell at you."

"I wouldn't call it flirting." He strode to her tool chest. The polished chrome tools were laid perfectly in the open drawer. Faith followed behind. From the corner of his eye, he could tell she watched each one of his movements like a hawk. "Who did you think I was yesterday?"

She stopped short at his question, redirecting her attention back toward the counter.

"I didn't think you were anyone. I've only just moved here."

"Have we met before?"

"Gee, that's a strange question."

"Yours is a strange answer."

It bothered him that he still couldn't place her. He was normally so good with faces, names too for that matter. Nothing about her triggered a memory. He knew she was certainly someone he would not easily forget, but still he could recall nothing.

She moved around the counter, putting the Formica surface between them. It was a classic maneuver to distance herself from his question. Most people did similar things subconsciously when they wanted to escape a conversation, but good manners prevented them from doing so.

He slid his hands into his front trouser pockets and strolled up to the counter. She swallowed.

"I think Heart Motorcycles is a good name."

"You do?" He could tell she wasn't sure if she believed him. He nodded. "Thanks," she said.

"You're welcome."

The silence expanded between them like a balloon filling with air. A flicker of light caught his attention, pulling his focus to a delicate heart charm dangling around her neck. It was tiny, almost something no one would notice, except the light streaming in from the front window had caught it. The dainty necklace was out of place compared with the rest of the edgy apparel she wore, and for reasons he couldn't put his finger on, he thought it was something worth noting.

"Tully?" Charlie rapped lightly on the door. "I took down Dolores's statement, and I have to get over to The Copper Kettle. Gemma locked her keys in her car again."

Tully faced Faith. "It was nice to meet you, Ms. Fitzpatrick."

"Faith," she offered and walked him to the door. "Thank you, Detective."

He paused on the curb. "For what?"

She contemplated his question with a shrug. "For fixing my lock, of course."

"It was my pleasure." He knew he meant it. "Good luck with your grand opening, Ms. Fitzpatrick."

"Faith."

He smiled. "Welcome to Roseley."

CHAPTER THREE

FAITH PULLED INTO her uncle's driveway, slowly easing her motorcycle to a stop. The loose gravel and small potholes brought a scowl to her face every time she had to drive her motorcycle over them, but she'd have to tolerate it until she found an apartment of her own.

In the backyard, Caroline lay sprawled out in a lawn chair as Trig flipped burgers at the grill.

"You'd think Uncle Gus would pave this driveway at some point," Faith said. "Those tiny rocks are going to do a number on my paint job by the time summer is over."

"Nah. Dad would never spend money on something like that. Not when he could spend the money on new fishing lures." Trig smiled the same devilish grin as his dad's. "How's the shop?"

"I need to paint the logo on the front window but I'm close to being finished."

"Are you still going with the name Heart Motorcycles?"

She grinned. "You both know how important the heart logo is to me."

"Even if it's too girlie for you?" he chortled. Faith rolled her eyes. "Why not name it something tough or cool?" Trig asked. "You want something that will make guys check it out."

"Guys will like the name just fine, thanks." She really wasn't so certain. Aside from Trig, the only other guy she knew in town was Detective McTully, and he had seemed to like it. He didn't strike her as a man who said things only to say them. Nor did he seem like a man who would tell a lie to make her feel better. She appreciated the honesty.

Caroline rolled a cold soda can along her forehead, chanting, "I love my brother. I love my brother."

"She's cross because I was teasing her before you got here," Trig said. "It's my brotherly duty to give her a hard time any chance I get. Although, Faith, I hear *you're* the one I should be teasing."

"What's that supposed to mean?"

Trig flashed his wicked smile again. "I heard you saw your old crush today."

The temperature of Faith's cheeks rose ten notches as Trig chuckled.

"What are you talking about?" Caroline said, noticeably confused. "What crush? Faith, who did you see today? Not..." Her cousin sat upright, a wide smile spreading in realization. "Did you see *John McTully*?"

"I don't... What?" Faith scrambled to piece together how Trig knew about their encounter.

"Oh, she saw him all right," Trig continued. "I heard it over the radio."

"You and that stupid police scanner," Caroline said. "Why do you listen to that thing? You're not even a cop."

"I like to know what's going on in my town. Plus, it's interesting. This morning, I was on my way out when I heard the call about The Cutest Little Tea Shop—"

"*That* came over the police scanner?" Faith said. "It was a few smashed flowers and a dented mailbox."

"Remember where you are now, cousin." Caroline laughed and tossed her a cold soda. "That's considered big news around here."

"I forgot. And, Trig, why is this any of your business?"

"Can't my cousin's new motorcycle shop

be my business? I wanted to make sure your place was okay. I swung by in time to see you and Tully heading inside. Is he as dreamy as you thought he was back in high school?"

Faith considered chucking her soda can at Trig's face.

"Trig Waterson, I swear to all the heavens and the earth—"

He laughed. "Oh, simmer down. I'm only joking with you. It's been a long time—"

"A *long* time."

"I'm sure you don't have feelings for him anymore. Right?"

"I absolutely don't."

"Of course not."

"My days of fawning over John McTully—"

"Secretly fawning," Caroline noted. "He didn't know you existed back then."

"Thanks for the reminder." Faith scowled, considering how true it was. "Back then *no one* knew I existed...before you know what."

Her cousins nodded solemnly, as Faith considered life back then. John McTully was one of the very few people she'd hoped to see on her return. John had always been so kind to everyone, understandably making him somewhat of a hometown darling. The teachers adored him, the coaches favored him and nearly every girl in school had been half in love with him. She'd been in good company for crushing on him.

What made John McTully even more endearing was the fact that he'd graduated and left for college before the news of her father hit. She was certain he knew all the nitty-gritty details now, but at the time, she was glad she'd never had to face him when the details were fresh. Since she didn't have a memory of him looking down his nose at her because of her father's crimes, he seemed even more endearing today.

"Earth to Faith." Faith snapped to attention and Caroline dissolved into giggles. Caroline handed her a plate with a burger. "*I said* what did the two of you talk about in your motorcycle shop?"

"Nothing."

"Nothing? Were you too busy staring deep into his eyes—"

"Oh, you two are the worst!" Faith said. "It's a wonder I ever decided to move back here."

Trig shrugged. "We're family. This is what family does."

Faith drew a deep breath. "Family, huh?"

She sighed. “It’s been so long I forgot what one looks like.”

“You’re the one who left,” Trig said. He glanced up as if to see how his comment was received. It was true, unfortunately, and ever since she had, she’d been daydreaming of returning.

“Can you blame me?”

“*Nope.* I’d have done the same. We’re glad you’re back though.”

“Tully’s single, you know,” Caroline said. Faith ran a fingertip around the edge of her soda can, wondering how on earth that was possible. He had been the greatest catch when they had been teenagers, and from what she’d seen since moving home, he had gotten better-looking with age.

If she had been out of his league in high school, having a family scandal and a quickie divorce on her record certainly didn’t sweeten things.

Faith asked, “If you’re keeping track of his relationship status, why don’t you make a move?”

“I’m not his type.”

“What? Beautiful, kind and successful?”

Caroline twisted her long red hair into a

messy knot on top of her head. She hoped her cousin knew how terrific she was.

"He keeps to himself mostly," she said, looking at Trig. "I can't think of the last time he dated anyone for more than a few weeks. Can you?"

Trig shook his head. "There have been a few ladies who have swung and missed. Most recently I saw him out with Emily Peaches."

"He dated Emily?" Faith asked, swallowing her disappointment. If Emily Peaches was his type, she didn't stand a chance. Emily had been sweeter than a bowl of strawberry shortcake and in high school had been voted the person most likely to brighten up your day.

Trig continued, "He's dated a bit, but no one has come close to taking him off the market. He and his sister, Samantha—"

"She's a wonder," Caroline said. "I follow her online to see what kind of dangerous adventure she's up to next."

Faith recalled how friendly Samantha had been at the gas station. Samantha also hadn't recognized her, although recognition required knowing the person well enough in the first place. Samantha had run in a different circle in high school.

"It's only a matter of time before everyone eventually figures out who I am."

"And once they do…what?" Trig said, settling into a chair beside her. "Do you think they're going to hold you accountable for your dad? You were a kid back then, Faith. What would they have expected you to do?"

It wasn't what they expected that had her on edge. It was how they sneered behind her back that made her cringe. The last few years had toughened her up, sure, but was she ready to be remembered again as Ray Talbert's daughter?

"I wish I'd had a brother or sister to help me shoulder this," she said. "I wouldn't mind spreading out the judgment a little." Trig squeezed her shoulder. He and Caroline had run into some trouble after Ray had been arrested, but they were a few more degrees removed from it all than she was.

"Can you settle for a couple of well-meaning cousins instead?" he asked.

"I'd be glad to if you'd cut out your teasing, Trig."

Caroline chuckled. "Count yourself lucky, Faith. If he had been your brother, he'd have crashed your first encounter with Tully at the shop, instead of just driving by."

Faith was about to correct her. About to tell them about the gas station and how she'd yelled at John McTully before she'd realized the man hidden behind dark sunglasses was the same man who'd given her the only thing to look forward to sophomore year.

She settled into her chair, resigned to keeping that little incident to herself like a tiny treasure she'd found washed up on the shore. As with every desire of her heart, she'd keep it hidden where no one else could find it or taint it, because in her experience, people always managed to do that.

TULLY HAD HEADED home for the day when Charlie texted him with a dinner invitation. Charlie's sister, Mara, was a stickler about having family dinner on nights she didn't have to work until closing at Little Lakeside Sports Shop, the store she owned with her husband, Peter. Tully appreciated his honorary place in Charlie's family and rarely turned down an invitation, no matter how last minute it was offered.

He'd arrived at Mara and Peter's house and had finished fixing a plate of food when Paige, Charlie's wife, arrived. Charlie and Paige had married the year before after a very short engagement, and Tully thought Paige had been an excellent addition to the family.

She smacked a kiss on everyone's cheek before embracing her husband. "What was this I heard about Dolores's shop getting vandalized?"

Tully had spent the day thinking a lot about Dolores Mitchell's shop, but not because he was worried about a little vandalism. The woman who had moved into the shop beside Dolores had hijacked his thoughts ever since she'd spouted off to him at the gas station the day before.

"Nothing to get worked up over," Tully said. Lucy, Mara and Peter's preteen daughter, scooted onto a chair and frowned up at him.

"I want to know what happened. *Details*, Tully. Did someone break in?"

"Nah. It was most likely some kids running around at night, bored in the summer heat."

"Do you remember the trouble we used to get in as kids?" Charlie asked. "Everything in this town used to close by nine o'clock at night. There was nothing for us to do except night swim or tear it up in the woods or—"

Mara shot her brother a scowl, motioning toward twelve-year-old Lucy.

"Not everyone needs to hear about your shenanigans."

"Or what, Uncle Charlie?" Lucy said, bypassing her mother. Charlie glanced at Tully for help.

"Or staying up all night," Tully filled in, taking a seat. "I heard you had a slumber party last weekend and didn't get to sleep until…"

"Until *seven* in the morning," Mara said. "I had the headache and four cups of coffee that morning to show for it. Giggling girls kept me awake most of the night."

Lucy smiled. "It was so fun, Mom. We saw the sunrise."

"What do you and your girlfriends talk about all night?" Tully couldn't imagine having enough to say to another person that would warrant missing out on precious sleep or precious silence.

"Tully has a daily word limit he doesn't like to exceed," Charlie said. "Been like that since forever."

"Why change a good thing?" He smiled. Paige finished fixing a plate and settled in across from him.

"I heard Samantha made it home in one piece."

"Yes."

"Good. She'll be here for the Fourth."

Tully offered a hesitant nod. His sister might agree to stay in town for a few days or a few weeks even, but once a new idea popped into her head, holding her back was like trying to rein in a hurricane. They'd have plans one day, and she'd be off jet-setting to Kilimanjaro the next.

"The Fourth at least. We'll see what the next few weeks hold after that. You can never say for sure with Sam."

"*Speaking* of new arrivals," Charlie spoke up. Tully immediately recognized Charlie's playful tone and set a death stare on him. "What did you learn about that new woman? Faith, was it?"

"What new woman?" Mara asked, turning her attention to her husband, Peter. "Babe, did you know there's a new woman in town?"

Peter stopped midbite, contemplating. "Is she the one who's renting that empty store lot?"

Tully settled into his most professional tone. "She's turning it into a motorcycle shop—detailing, repairs. She hopes to open by the Fourth."

"Wow," Mara said. "I didn't hear anything about someone moving in that quickly."

"I did," Paige said. "I stopped into The Sandwich Board today—"

"CeCe Takes," Tully said, biting back a groan. He wasn't surprised. There was a telephone, a telegraph and a teleCeCe when it came to news in this town. He usually worked CeCe's gossip to his advantage as much as he could. There was no use beating the pavement to get leads when CeCe already had a pulse on every small happening in town. She was always so eager to keep him informed too.

"Do you know anything about this new shop owner, Tully?" Mara asked, leaning to get a closer view. "Is she nice? Attractive?"

Tully focused intently on his food and shrugged.

"No?" Charlie's face spread into a lopsided grin. "She's nice enough. She offered to help Dolores fix her broken mailbox."

Tully quieted his chewing, waiting to hear what else his friend thought of the new woman.

"Is that it?" Mara prompted. "What does she look like, Charlie? I want to say hello if I pass her on the street."

"Black hair—"

"Dark brown," Tully said, jabbing at his plate. Charlie cleared his throat.

"*Dark brown* hair. Blue eyes—"

"Gray."

Charlie leaned an elbow on the table. "Maybe you should take it from here, buddy."

Tully leaned back in his chair. "There's nothing to tell. She hopes to get her repair shop off the ground and seems pretty intent on keeping to herself. I don't blame her if the first person she met in town was CeCe Takes. Fielding her questions is like dodging a firing squad."

"I'll introduce myself tomorrow," Mara said. "Maybe we can do some cross-advertising if she's interested. Does she have a name?"

Tully let the name roll softly off his lips. He liked the alliteration. He liked how the sweet first name was in stark contrast to the tough exterior of a woman he'd encountered twice. "Faith Fitzpatrick," he said. "She needs a soft approach."

"Why do you say that?" Mara asked.

"Trust me."

THE NEXT MORNING Tully pulled up in front of Grandma's Basement, Roseley's favorite antiques shop, as Betty Jenkins, the owner, waved from the front window. Miss Jenkins always moved about her shop with a studied charm. Tully had a lifetime of memories visiting her, the 1950s-style dresses she wore always swishing as she glided to greet him.

Today, however, Betty's shoulders slumped, her bright pink lips drawn in a thin line.

"Tully, sweetheart," she said, drawing him in for a hug. He wrapped a protective arm around her shoulders, the full volume of her dress fabric doing little to disguise her frail frame. "I only arrived a little while ago. Isn't it a shame?"

Tully glanced around at the spray paint and broken glass. The damage was more considerable than what had been done to The Cutest Little Teashop. If the same person was responsible for both crimes, he or she was getting bolder. Someone had shattered all the glass in the front door. In the same shiny black paint as before, they'd spray-painted sporadic paint swipes along the exterior brick wall. There were no messages, only random blotches.

Tully took a few pictures with his cell phone and texted them to Officer Allison White at the station. Before moving back to Roseley, he'd seen his fair share of gang tags.

The black-paint swipes looked sporadic, not signifying a gang was operating in Roseley. Still, it didn't hurt to have Officer White do a little research for him.

"What time did you get here this morning?" he asked, squatting to examine the broken glass. Whatever had been used to break the door had been taken away with the assailant.

"Dolores called me at about six thirty, after she called you. She's a sweetheart, isn't she? Everyone is always looking out for each other on this street."

"Don't you normally rise early?"

"I pop awake at five thirty." She sighed, staring off into a distance that expanded farther than the door frame. "Sandy has been dead for ten years, but I still startle awake at five thirty to get her medicine ready."

Miss Jenkins had spent her adult life taking care of her sister, who had suffered with a chronic illness before her passing.

"Old habits die hard," he said.

"Sadly, they sure do."

Tully glanced up at the aging profile of the woman he'd come to adore over the years. Not every little boy found a surrogate mother figure when he most needed one, but after

Tully had healed his physical scars of losing his mom, Miss Jenkins had been there to dry his eyes as he attempted to heal the emotional ones. His friends had always loved coming to her antiques store for the free candy samples, but he'd had other reasons.

"Do you know of anyone who is angry or annoyed with you? A disgruntled customer, perhaps?"

Miss Jenkins tipped her head thoughtfully. "I can't think of an angry soul going back twenty years, Tully."

"This looks like the stuff of amateurs. Are any kids giving you trouble?"

"I get the typical stuff from time to time." Tully raised his eyebrows. "Oh, it's nothing to worry about. You know how little kids are."

"Little?"

She smiled. "Well, I occasionally get some teenagers in here with sticky fingers but offering them a peppermint stick when they first come in seems to change their minds. My granddad always used to say that if you talk to the kids when they're little, they won't egg your house when they're teenagers. He was right about that. In fact..." She strode to the front counter and returned with a red-and-white-striped peppermint stick. "I always keep your favorite in stock." Tully accepted the candy in the same way he always had as a kid, with a warm smile. "How's detective work treating you?"

"Just fine."

"That's you," she said, her eyes crinkling in a knowing way. "Always fine. Whenever you visited as a boy you always said you were fine."

"I always was," Tully said. She watched him for several beats, and he knew he wasn't fooling her now, like he hadn't fooled her when he was a kid. "How's your dad?" she finally asked. Tully shifted on his feet.

"Holding steady." Things rarely changed much for his dad, but the mention of him reminded Tully that he needed to make a trip out to visit him sooner than later. Why did later always seem so much more appealing?

"Have you met the new store owner at the end of the street?" Tully opted for a topic that didn't involve his father or the past. Miss Jenkins's mouth pursed in confusion.

"No, I haven't. All I know about her is what Dolores relayed. What's your impression?"

"She's opening a motorcycle shop—"

"I heard. I bid recently on a Triumph Speed Twin. I thought it would look lovely at the front of the store, but the price rose too steeply for my budget. I'll have to mosey down and introduce myself."

"Her first encounter was with…" Tully cleared his throat. Miss Jenkins's face relaxed in understanding.

"Oh, dear. I'd better get down there this morning. We don't want her judging Roseley based on our dear CeCe."

Tully smiled. He could always count on Miss Jenkins to understand things without much explanation. She'd always seemed to know how he had been feeling as a youngster too, offering a well-timed hug without him having to ask or articulate anything at all. A lot of healing had happened in this place over a peppermint stick. More healing than had ever happened at home.

CHAPTER FOUR

FAITH DIPPED HER brush into a small can of ruby-red paint and glanced at the heart logo she'd sketched. Heart Motorcycles needed to make a statement, not just to brand her store, but to rebrand her own image. If the people in town could get to know the real her before they remembered her as Ray Talbert's daughter, maybe she'd have a chance to stay in Roseley and be happy. Maybe.

She outlined the red heart on her window and quickly began filling it in with paint. She wasn't aware of anyone watching her work until she heard a voice from behind her.

"It looks promising."

Faith needn't turn around to know Detective McTully was checking in on her. The thought that he was visiting again so soon made her heart somersault.

"Good morning, Detective," she said, choosing to focus more intently on her painting.

"You need some white and black to offset so much red," he said. She turned and frowned up at him.

"Excuse me?"

"Too much red is a bit overwhelming and—"

"I heard what you said. I don't agree."

"Take a step back and look at it from here." He tipped his head, encouraging her to join him. She shuffled a few steps backward to stand next to him and gazed at her heart logo. The red was too much all on its own.

"The lettering will be in black," she said, quickly. "It'll look great."

"I take it you decided on Heart Motorcycles for the name." He motioned toward the giant heart sketch taped on her window.

"Putting your detective skills to work, I see."

"I've been known to do that from time to time."

"That's good."

"Getting a repair shop in town is good. I'm glad to see someone using this lot."

She nibbled a serious hole in the side of her cheek to keep from smiling. He had no idea what it meant, especially coming from him.

"What are you doing here?" she said. Her question flew out of her mouth more as an accusation and not at all how she had intended.

Her father had always accused her of not minding the tone of her voice. As it turned out, he should have been the last person to educate her in getting along better with others.

"There was a vandalism call from down the street."

"Another one?"

He nodded, studying her intently. "Are you keeping your shop door locked at all times? Even if you step away during the day?"

"Yes, but I'll make sure to do a better job."

"Good." He glanced down the street as CeCe Takes hustled toward them. "Making friends yet?"

Faith shot him a scowl, nearly bringing a smirk to his perfect lips. "No friends are better than—"

"Good morning, Detective!" CeCe sang once she'd reached them. "Are you investigating Betty's break-in?"

"I am."

"Is your sandwich shop okay, Mrs. Takes?" Faith said, trying for kind concern. CeCe forced a smile.

"No one in this town would dare touch my sandwich shop. There was a little incident years ago with my mailbox, but I knew who did it and sought out his father to pay for the damages."

Faith's stomach tightened, recalling the delight she'd felt at defacing CeCe's mailbox. She had known back then that CeCe would never catch her, but she hadn't considered that CeCe would pin it on someone else.

"Betty is fine," Tully said. Something about how his dark eyes locked onto hers made her stomach twist tighter. She desperately wanted to keep him from looking at her the way everyone else in town used to. She wouldn't fess up about that stupid mailbox if a team of horses tried to drag it out of her. "She's cleaning up some broken glass and might need a little help scrubbing the spray paint off the brick. Dolores somehow managed to clean it—"

CeCe nodded furiously. "Angelo helped her power wash it. I'll send him down to Betty's this afternoon."

"I'm sure she'll appreciate that."

"What about you?" CeCe said, turning her focus to Faith.

"What about me?"

"Are you worried someone will target your shop?"

"I don't have much to steal or destroy yet, so…no."

CeCe moved her head in a bit of a bobble. She passed judgment as discreetly as she might a kidney stone.

"I'm going to check on Betty, Detective. She'll need my moral support after this ugly little incident." Once she'd scurried down the block, Tully faced Faith.

"Don't let her get under your skin," he said.

"I'm not. She doesn't bother me at all. I don't even think about her." Faith realized she'd protested too much when Tully cracked a smile.

"Yes, I can see that," he said.

"Why should I be worried about CeCe Takes?"

"There's a heart of gold buried beneath all that…"

"What?" Faith cocked her head, interested at what Tully thought.

"Fussing."

"That's a gentle way of putting it. Is that what you call it?"

"In public."

Faith smiled this time and found Tully's face mirrored hers.

"Take care, Ms. Fitzpatrick. And keep that door locked."

Faith pretended not to watch him walk to his truck, but it was difficult to tear her attention away from a man like Detective McTully. As she recalled, it had always been difficult.

FAITH WAS SECURING an advertising poster to the back of her motorcycle with zip ties just when she heard a light rap on the front door. She turned to find Mara Selby.

"Hi, neighbor," Mara said, coming into the shop. Faith admired Mara. Mara looked like she hadn't aged a day since high school. Her skin was still a gorgeous bronze and her long silky brown hair hung in a soft curtain over her shoulders. They hadn't been friends in high school, but Mara and Peter had been dubbed the golden couple. Everyone knew them.

"Welcome," Faith said. "I'm not open for business yet but—"

"No, I came to welcome you to the block." Mara held out a flyer. "I'm Mara Selby. I own Little Lakeside Sports Shop at the opposite end of our street."

"I saw that. It's right on the water."

"Nearly. It's a good place for a water sports shop, don't you think?"

Faith examined the flyer.

"Tully said you were new in town. Faith, isn't it?"

"John told you about me?" Faith bit back a smile.

"Officer Stillwater too, though he's Charlie to me. He's my big brother."

Faith nodded as if learning this information for the first time. Charlie Stillwater had been friends with John McTully in high school.

"Anyway, I thought you and I could do some cross-advertising. I'd be happy to post a flyer for you in my shop."

Faith sputtered; the offer was more considerate than she had expected.

"Really?"

Mara considered her response. "Of course. We're not competing, are we? I don't do anything with motorcycles, but maybe our patrons would be similar. Why not help each other? What do you think?"

Faith nodded. "I don't have any flyers yet, but I'll get you one as soon as I print them. Maybe some of my business cards too."

"No rush," Mara said. She admired Faith's motorcycle. "I've never been on one of these.

I imagine it's the same feeling as bicycling though, huh?"

"Riding clears my head when I..." Faith smiled, surprised to have stumbled over her words.

"When you have a lot on your mind? I understand. Two years ago, I put more miles on my bicycle than the prior three years combined. Nothing but me, the road and the wind on my face."

Faith moved around her motorcycle, tightening the last zip tie. "You do understand. Rough year?"

"You could say that."

"Business, family, health?"

"All of the above."

"Those things are usually intertwined, aren't they?"

Mara agreed. "Where are you from?"

Faith squatted behind her motorcycle, pretending to attend to something under the rear saddlebags. She liked Mara immediately, considering she'd never talked to her in high school, but she didn't want to divulge too much too soon. "I've been all over. I graduated high school and took off to see what was out there."

"What did you find?"

"A terrible husband."

"Don't you hate those?"

They both chuckled. "Yeah. Marrying him wasn't my finest decision."

"I take it he didn't come here with you."

Faith shook her head. Their divorce and the move were supposed to be the clean break she needed. Kyle's surprise calls were making it a lot harder for her heart to set and heal.

"Do you have family around the area?"

Faith tried for a response as close to the truth as possible without giving a lot away. "My parents live out of state. No siblings, unfortunately."

"Where are you staying?"

"I've known Caroline Waterson for a long time so I'm crashing with her until I find an apartment."

"I know Caroline. I haven't seen her in a while, but she and I went to high school together."

"Roseley High."

"That's right. She's a great gal. So, you're living in Gus Waterson's house. Have you met him yet? He spends the heat of the summer fishing in Canada."

Faith's unease at the direction the conversation had taken was causing her fingers to shake. She fiddled with the tiny gold heart hanging around her neck. Mara continued, "Trig and Caroline's dad is one of a kind. He's been a staple in this town for many years. I don't know if Caroline has mentioned any of the things that went down with her aunt and uncle though."

"She doesn't talk much about it."

Mara nodded. "That's understandable. She'd most likely prefer to forget she was ever related, even if only through marriage, to Ray Talbert."

Faith turned away from Mara, pretending to organize her toolbox to hide her face at the mention of her father's name. Moving back was a mistake. There was no way she could keep her resolve when all it took was one mention of Ray to send her pulse racing. She'd no sooner grabbed a socket wrench and turned back toward her bike than her grip failed her, sending the wrench clanking to the floor.

She and Mara both squatted and reached for it, Mara beating her to the tool.

"Careful, honey. You almost clanked it on these chrome pipes." She leaned closer to hand the wrench to Faith, and as she did, her expression fell serious, noticeably doing a double take.

"Thanks," Faith said. She staggered back to her tool bench.

"This might sound strange," Mara said, stepping closer. "Maybe it's because I was thinking of Ray Talbert but..."

Faith turned, her eyes meeting Mara's. She saw the recognition come over Mara's face and hurriedly moved for damage control.

"Please don't tell anyone," Faith said. "I'm not ready to...to... I wanted a clean slate here. I'm not ready for people to know."

Mara had to forcibly shut her mouth to keep from gaping. She stood still for several moments while Faith's pulse beat in her ears.

Finally, Mara spoke. "Honey, I am so sorry. I was jabbering on and on about Ray Talbert and all this time... I apologize for even bringing it up. I didn't recognize you until now."

Faith winced. That was her desire. Few people from her past recognized her since she was mostly known as "Ray Talbert's daughter," not a young woman with a name and identity of her own. She thought that if she could distance herself from a connection to her father, people could look past any resemblance she still had to the scared, insecure girl she'd been.

After years of being on her own, and then worse, being married to the wrong man, all she longed for was a place to call home. She'd spent the last few years changing her physique, her style and her skill set. But as Mara fumbled to apologize, she was now looking at her the way some folks in this town had in the past.

"It's fine. I'm used to it."

"What brings you back?"

"Family," Faith managed. "I wanted to be near—"

Mara slapped her forehead as she must have connected the dots. "Right. You're staying with Caroline because she's your cousin. Darn it, I really put my foot in my mouth this time."

"Mara, I'd appreciate it if you didn't tell people that I'm…Ray's daughter."

"You won't be able to hide that for very long, Faith. You do look different, but people will figure it out soon enough."

"I know but…"

"You want that to happen on your terms. I get it."

"My dad's notoriety made me leave before

I was strong enough to fight for my place here. Maybe it's wishful thinking to hope people will give me a second chance but—"

"I know all about wishful thinking," Mara said. "Peter and I had problems with our daughter, Lucy, not too long ago. Outrunning your past can be difficult but…"

"Yes?"

"It's possible."

"Knock, knock!" CeCe called from the front door. "Mara, I thought I saw you on this end of the street."

Mara glanced between Faith and CeCe. "Faith and I are planning to do a little cross-advertising."

"Heavens, why? A motorcycle shop isn't really your speed, Mara, dear."

Faith held her tongue to keep from snapping at CeCe. The woman didn't even realize who she was, but was still looking down her nose on her, and why? All she wanted to do was tell CeCe Takes to hit the road, but if she did, Mara might turn on her. She prayed Mara wouldn't.

"I'm so excited for the opening of your shop, Faith," Mara said, ignoring CeCe. She squeezed Faith's shoulder and made her way to the door. "By the looks of it, I take it you're riding your motorcycle in the Fourth of July parade?"

Faith motioned to the advertisement poster on her motorcycle. "Putting on the finishing touches now."

"I'll see you at the parade. Don't forget to bring me flyers when you get them. CeCe, walk me out, would you?"

Faith froze as CeCe followed Mara out to the sidewalk. She imagined Mara spilling the beans about who she was, but after less than a minute of chitchat, the two women parted ways, CeCe not looking any the wiser.

Faith leaned back against her tool bench and took in the little shop that was supposed to be her fresh start. She was operating on borrowed time and needed to do more to make friends in this town before everyone realized who she was. She had no doubt that life would change drastically once they did.

CHAPTER FIVE

TULLY SAT ON the roof of his house, admiring the view of town from afar. He had settled for a place on the far side of the lake not only for its spectacular view of the sunset, but because having a little distance from the folks in town, especially after a long day on the job, was more of a necessity the older he got. He loved the residents, just not all the time. He didn't want to end up like his father, living alone in the woods without much contact with anyone, but having his own space was paramount.

His cell phone vibrated on his hip. A message from Officer White came through. The black paint swipes outside Grandma's Basement weren't affiliated with any known gang tags.

Tully considered if there was any special meaning behind the spray paint. It could be as insignificant as a few bored teenagers getting their hands on a half-empty can and using it up for fun.

"How's it going up there?" Charlie called, shielding his face against the setting sun.

"Never been better. Come on up."

Charlie managed the ladder, a six-pack of soda in one hand, and settled on the severely pitched roof more clumsily than Tully would have liked.

"Careful, buddy," Tully said, ripping off a can of soda. "I don't feel like rushing you to the emergency room tonight."

Charlie sat beside him and cracked open a can. He scanned the spectacular view.

"I can see why you like to come up here. Better perspective."

"It's good for thinking."

"Really?" Charlie said. "What about?"

"Work and fishing. What else?"

Tully had a few things on his mind these days, but he was not one to share, even with his best friend. He needed to drive out to check on his father before the holiday. He needed to convince Samantha to visit too. He needed to think about a lot of things including…

As if reading his mind, Charlie said, "Mara said she met Faith this morning."

There had been her too.

"Is that right?" Tully tried his best to sound unfazed by the mere mention of her name. "How'd that go?"

"She said she's a nice woman."

"Nice?" Tully could think of a lot of adjectives to describe Faith, but *nice* wasn't one of them. "She probably didn't talk to her very long."

"Well, she isn't mean."

"No."

"She's probably a little defensive."

"A little?"

"You could do a lot worse."

Tully let a laugh escape. *"What?"*

"I like her. So does Mara."

"And?"

Charlie shrugged nonchalantly, taking another swig of soda. "You've got a solid job and this big house—"

"It isn't that big."

"It's too big for just you. Despite that full kitchen of yours, you're always coming over to Mara's for dinner…"

"I don't cook much."

"Not surprising since all you have in your fridge is beef jerky and pickles."

"Good enough for me."

"I'm not the only one to notice..."

"Notice? What?"

"Even Paige picked up on your reaction at dinner the other night. You might try to hide it, but Faith got to you."

"Ha!" Tully said. He snapped the tab off his soda can. "Is that what you think?"

Charlie's face broke into a wide grin.

"We think she's pretty great."

"We?"

"You know Mara and Paige want to fix you up again. Why not Faith?"

"I don't need help finding a date."

"True, but you need help keeping a woman longer than two weeks."

"I suppose now that you're happily married, you want me married off as well. You've been friends with me long enough to know I'm not interested in being tied down."

"I don't feel tied down. Paige is the best thing that's ever happened to me."

"I believe you, *but* you almost married Crystal, and she was the poster child for what the wrong partner looks like. She broke your heart with one of your best friends—"

"And a good thing too or I wouldn't have met Paige."

"I'm glad you can find the silver lining in that, but I'm not interested in—"

"—putting yourself out there?"

"Look, man. I've said it before, and I'll say it again. I'm not the—"

"—marrying kind. Yeah, I remember," Charlie said, staring at him. "Still..."

Tully huffed, finishing his cola in a few giant swigs. There were plenty of fine single women in town. He enjoyed the flirting, but casual dates were more his speed. He'd learned a long time ago that loving someone long term was the easiest way to get hurt—deeply hurt. It was never worth it.

"Why date down there when I'm content up here, thinking about fishing? It's a moot point." Tully punctuated his statement with a light chuckle to put a friendly, but firm, end to Charlie's line of questioning. His friend nodded, as if the message was received loud and clear.

"Speaking of people who need to settle down, where is Samantha heading off to next?"

Tully released a groan. "Who knows. At the rate she's going, she'll have to fly into a war zone to get the kind of pictures her so-called fans demand. Tell Mara and Paige to set their matchmaking sights on her for a change."

"And your dad?"

Tully turned his face away, staring at the tree line in the direction of his dad's cabin.

"I ought to drive out there. I really ought to."

"Want me to come?"

"No. It's better I visit alone. You know how he gets." He crushed his can, compressing it to a thick disc, and tossed it off the roof. It clanged when it hit the open trash can near the garage.

"Nice shot. Double or nothing." Charlie crushed his can and handed it to his friend.

"I didn't know we were betting."

"I want to see if you can make it under pressure. Miss this shot and Mara will put out feelers to see if Faith finds you attractive." Tully twisted his mouth. He knew how to handle pressure in all matters. Well, *work-related* matters anyway.

"And if I make it?"

"You won't hear a peep out of me about Faith again."

"Are you sure you can restrain yourself?"

"I will do my best, but just so we're clear,

if you miss this shot, I'll always wonder if it was on purpose."

Tully snorted and tossed the crushed can. It clanged around the inside of the can, ringing a successful shot.

"And that's why you were a high school all-star," Charlie said. "Tell me again why you're still single?"

Tully peered at him from beneath hooded eyelids. "Do you want me to help you off this roof?"

"I'm only kidding." Charlie held up his hands in apology. "I'll drop it already."

Tully nodded. He watched a speedboat skimming over the lake, at least a hundred yards in the distance. It reminded him of a case he'd had two summers before.

"I think I might make a trip out to Harrison's place tomorrow," Tully said.

"Heath Harrison?" Charlie looked off in the direction of Heath's house. Heath had graduated high school a couple of years ahead of them. After he and his wife had split, his son, Oliver, had gotten involved with Cody Ward, a troubled teen who had been more than happy to cause his fair share of trouble in Roseley, including vandalism.

"I know what you're thinking, but I'd suspect Cody long before I'd suspect Oliver."

Raised by his grandparents, Karen and Moody, Cody had a reputation for pushing boundaries at home and at school.

"Me too, but I'll have an easier time talking to Heath than Moody or Karen. Perhaps Heath will have some insight on Cody," Tully said, reaching for the cell phone vibrating on his hip. "As it turns out," he continued, reading the text message that had come through, "I might have to run out there sooner than later."

"Why?"

"Are you familiar with The Gypsy Caravan?"

"The new antiques shop on Third Street? I don't think it's opened yet."

Tully nodded and stepped carefully toward the ladder, motioning his friend to follow. "It hasn't, but they just had a break-in."

"The sun isn't even down yet."

"Yep. Whoever our suspect is, he's getting bolder."

FAITH HAD ENJOYED dinner at The Nutmeg Café with Caroline. Her back ached a bit from all the moving and cleaning she'd accomplished over the last few days, but it didn't keep her from treating her cousin to dinner. It was a gesture of thanks for all of Caroline's help.

The Nutmeg Café was one of the few new additions in town. She cruised the narrow side streets admiring all the cute storefronts and felt happy that not much else had changed.

Years ago, she'd roamed these streets alone on her bicycle. Riding was a happy respite from her parents' arguing, but after her father had been arrested, she'd needed the freedom to escape the silence that fell over the house whenever her mother disappeared to her room to hide away from the world. Aside from Uncle Gus's home, the open road had been her only refuge. The road didn't judge her or criticize her or suspect her of being like her father. The road was always forgiving.

But now, instead of a bicycle, Faith cruised on her motorcycle. It was one she'd managed to fix up all on her own too. The bike's restoration was something she prided herself on, and if she could get her detailing and repair shop off the ground, she hoped to branch off to selling not only new models of motorcycles but restoring and selling some old models too. It was too ambitious, or so Kyle had sneered when she'd worked up the nerve to share her dream. With him gone and a new life in Roseley spread out in front of her like a smorgasbord of opportunities waiting to be sampled, she decided she'd had enough failure in the past to last a lifetime. Perhaps, she hoped, fate would throw her a bone and give her a little taste of success, and happiness, soon.

She'd swung around the back of Third Street, intending to take a shortcut to her shop on Main, when something caught her eye. Shattered glass made her swerve her motorcycle dramatically to avoid running over the shards. She'd just breathed a sigh of relief, believing she'd successfully dodged the array of glass, when her handlebars began to put up a fight.

"Are you serious," she groaned, muscling the handlebars to stay aligned. The resistance meant the front tire had been damaged and although she was only a couple of minutes from her shop, she couldn't drive as the crow flies. Without an ability to control the steering, she was momentarily stuck. Faith wobbled her bike to a stop without dropping it flat to the pavement like a hot potato.

"Well, isn't this dandy?" she said, cutting the engine and popping the kickstand. She glanced around the back lot. It was empty, not a soul in sight. Dusk was an hour away, still, the long shadows, growing longer by the minute, were creeping over every nook and cranny of the small town. Although it was a safe place, much safer than other places she'd lived, she didn't feel like abandoning her motorcycle while she hoofed it back to the shop.

The only things around were dumpsters, crates, wooden pallets and her. Squatting to inspect the damage, she could tell the tire's sidewall had been severely punctured and would need to be replaced.

Faith stood, irritated by the unexpected expense, and shuffled back toward the shattered glass to figure out what had caused the damage. The glass was strewn around the rear entrance to one of the shops. A window looked like it had been blown out of the glass door, which was opened a crack.

Faith scratched her head. As it was still daylight, she doubted it was one of those vandalism cases. Although, with the glass smashed and the door open, someone might be robbing the place. Without a getaway vehicle in sight, she found it unlikely. She also didn't understand how a simple break-in caused glass to shatter all over the pavement, leading her to pop a tire. Any good criminal would have given the window one good whack to break a hole big enough to reach in and unlock the door. This was not that.

Faith pushed the door open farther, prepared to find someone hurt or in need of help. As she didn't have her cell phone on her, an accessory she tried to leave at home as frequently as possible, she was prepared to assess the damage and run for help.

"Hello? Is anyone here?"

Silence greeted her as she flipped on a light and glanced around. A few things had been knocked to the ground and they looked expensive. Thankfully, Caroline had brought her up to speed on Roseley's local politics when she'd arrived, so she recognized the back of the shop as The Gypsy Caravan, owned by the famous Callahan brothers, Dash and Ledger.

Caroline had explained that when the newspaper had caught wind that the Callahan brothers were considering a shop in Roseley, a few locals had put together a modest protest. Miss Jenkins's shop had been the only antiques dealer in town for the better part of thirty years, and folks were loyal. They also didn't like that the two brothers had a reputation that preceded them. They had made a name for themselves on social media, traveling around the country to find antiques bargains and gaining a mass of followers. Most people in Roseley were split over the attention the brothers' fame would likely bring. On the one hand, more tourists meant more business for the rest of the establishments in Roseley. On the other hand, more tourists meant...more tourists. The protests had fizzled by summer, but the brothers were still a hot topic of conversation, especially because few had seen them, let alone met them.

Faith half expected to find one of the brothers lying helpless on the floor, clocked over the head with a priceless lamp, perhaps bleeding out on the Persian carpet. But once she'd stepped completely into the shop and glanced around, it was something else that made her stomach drop.

"What is this?" she cried, squatting to examine the damage to a vintage BMW motorcycle dumped to its side. The bimmer looked like it was from WWII. Covered in an aged paint, the hue coffee with cream, the BMW logo on the side fender made its value undeniable. So did the fact that it had an attached sidecar, its wheel sunny side up and rotating slowly on its axis. "Who did this to you?"

Faith stood and took a more serious look around the shop. Vases, jewelry, paintings and other antiques were strewn all over the floor, so whatever had happened in the shop had *just* happened. She decided she needed to get out of here before it happened to her next.

Hurrying to the door, she had no sooner made it outside, jogging toward her dumped bike, when someone screeched their tires to a halt.

"Hold it right there!" a man called.

Faith turned and found an oddly familiar face framed in the car window. She scrambled to place the fellow before he, no doubt, placed her. He was someone she used to know but how?

"I'm already on the phone with the cops so don't bother running."

"I wasn't planning on it."

"Who are you?" He stepped out of his car with his phone pressed to his ear. Faith didn't see how he was in a position to demand answers. As far as she was concerned, he was as much a suspect as she and the realization flooded her veins with authority.

"Who are *you*?" she said. There had been a time in her life when she would have fallen over herself to prove she was an innocent caught up in someone else's scandal. That time had passed.

The man blinked as if taken aback by her tone.

"Rick Murdock."

"Faith Fitzpatrick," she said, clenching her fists.

"What are you doing back here, Faith?"

"I was taking a shortcut to my motorcycle shop when I popped a tire." She jerked her head toward the glass strewn on the ground nearby. Rick eyed her and her bike before nodding.

"I called the guys who own this place. They'll be here soon so sit tight, okay?"

"What about the cops?"

"I'm sure Detective McTully is already on his way. He usually works break-ins."

Faith shifted on her feet. She didn't want to be standing around like a bad guy caught in the act when Detective McTully arrived. Given Rick's expression, she could tell he trusted her about as far as he could throw her. She couldn't stand to see the same expression on Tully's face.

"I have to get my bike to the shop before someone messes with it. It's getting dark."

"I'd stick around if I were you, Faith. I'm

sure Tully will want you to answer some questions."

"I'm sure he will," she muttered to herself, contemplating her options. "Look, Rick," she said. "I have to walk over to my shop and get my truck and trailer. I'll be back soon, obviously, because I can't leave my motorcycle overnight. Detective McTully knows who I am. He can follow up with me if he has questions."

"That's not a good idea," Rick called after her. "Leaving the scene of a crime like this… You're going to look guilty." She knew that was true, but she also knew the way things stood, she already looked guilty.

TULLY TURNED THE corner of High Street as the overhead lights flickered on. Even in the dim evening light, he could still spot the familiar hip swagger of Faith Fitzpatrick as she cut a diagonal line across the street in front of him. He rolled down his window.

"Jaywalking is up to forty dollars these days," he called. She turned, easing back across the street to meet him. It reminded him of their first encounter. He bit back a smile at how cute she had looked trying to keep her cool when she had scowled at him.

Now, as she stood at his truck window, she flashed a coy smile.

"Should I expect a ticket, Detective?"

"Depends. Do you have a good reason for jaywalking at dusk?"

"I popped a bike tire. I'm heading to my shop to get my trailer."

"Where's your bike?"

She hesitated. It was only a second too long, but he'd spotted it as clearly as if he'd had a map.

"You're going to find out in a minute anyway, and I don't want you to think I'm hiding anything." Tully's eyebrows flinched upward as she continue, "It's behind the shops on Third Street."

"Behind The Gypsy Caravan?"

"Nearby."

"How near?" There was that hesitation again. Tully rested a hand on the steering wheel at twelve o'clock and tipped his head toward the passenger seat. "Get in. I'll give you a lift."

"I'm capable of making it to my shop. The walk is only a few more minutes—"

"Get in, Ms. Fitzpatrick. You can tell me what happened on the way." She sighed before climbing up into the bed of the truck. "We're not going to your shop."

"Yeah, I figured."

"Who called in the break-in?"

"Rick Murdock."

"Rick's a good guy."

"If you say so."

"Why do you say that?"

"I'm sure he's a real gentleman if he doesn't suspect you of foul play. He wasn't happy when I left the scene."

"That's because you shouldn't have left." Faith shifted on her seat to better face him, drawing a breath of protest no doubt.

"I have to get my bike back to my shop before something happens to it. With thieves in this town breaking into stores and turning over vintage motorcycles, it's not safe—"

"Turning over motorcycles?" Tully's tone downshifted into detective mode as he glanced her way again. Her lips formed to speak but no words came out. "How involved are you, Ms. Fitzpatrick?"

"Okay," she began as Tully pulled behind the stores on Third. He took the drive painfully slow, scanning for anything out of the ordinary, aside from Rick's parked car up ahead. "Full disclosure before you talk to Rick."

"I'm listening."

"Someone broke into The Gypsy Caravan—"

"I know."

"There was glass all over the ground. That's how I popped my tire."

"Okay…"

"All the glass made me suspicious—"

"Suspicious?"

"Concerned. So, I went inside—"

"You what?" Tully threw his truck in Park with a force that made Faith jump. His emotional response had surprised her. Staying low-key was his calling card, but the thought that Faith had entered the shop alone and had possibly disturbed things before he had had the chance to investigate—

"I think I was the first person on the scene—"

"The scene? Do you work for law enforcement now?"

"Hey," Faith said, turning to face him squarely. "What if someone had been inside hurt and bleeding and in need of medical attention? Fortunately, there was no one, but this would be an entirely different conversation if someone in there *had* needed help. *That* was what was on my mind, Detective.

I couldn't just stand around with my hands on my hips waiting for you to roll up." She shrugged unapologetically, as if she bought her own explanation and considered the matter settled. "By the looks of it," she continued, "Rick is in the same place he was when I left a few minutes ago. *Someone* had to make sure the place was clear. That's what I was doing. You're welcome."

Tully couldn't help but stare. Few people knocked him off guard, but Faith Fitzpatrick had managed to make his jaw drop askew.

"And where does a tipped-over motorcycle come into it?" Rick hopped out of his car and waved them over as Charlie and Officer Dex Randall arrived in separate cars. Dex made his way to the back door, carefully avoiding the glass shards. "Never mind. I'm sure I'll find out soon enough."

"Tully," Rick said, nodding. Tully motioned toward Faith. Rick threw her a suspicious look before turning back to him. "We already met. She said she knows you." Tully couldn't tell the level of familiarity Rick meant with the statement.

"Wait here," he said to them both, while leading Charlie and Officer Randall through the back door. The store was packed with antiques, collections of items covering nearly every nook and cranny. Many items had been upended, but nothing looked damaged. He stopped in front of an old motorcycle, the sidecar tipped in the air, as a voice behind him made him turn.

"I think it's an R75 with the original sidecar. There aren't too many of these beauties kicking around anymore." Faith stood at his flank with Rick shaking his head from the doorway.

"I told you to wait outside."

Faith scowled at him. "Why? I've already been in here. I can't ruin anything."

"You've already been in here?" Dex hung a thumb in his gun belt, studying Faith.

"I was the first one here, I think."

"I thought Rick got here first."

"I called it in," Rick said, now sauntering into the shop to join them. "I found Faith coming out through the back door—"

"Oh, really?" Dex said. Tully had seen the look on Dex's face before. He was like a pit bull who'd picked up the scent of blood.

"I thought someone might be hurt," she said.

"Well, aren't you a regular Florence Nightingale." Dex's tone was pointed. Typical.

Faith squared off in front of him, her chest swelling.

"No one was hurt, Officer," she said. Her eyes darkened. "But I'm glad you managed to avoid the glass on the walkway instead of charging in here to look for victims."

"That's enough," Tully said, calmly moving between Faith and Dex before any other words could be exchanged. He gestured to Dex to take it easy, then he turned to Rick and Faith.

"I'll interview you one at a time. Rick, you're first." He moved toward the side of the shop as Faith made her way around the vintage BMW. "And *you*," he said, pointing a pen in her direction, "will wait outside until further notice."

Faith balked at his assertion until she noticed Charlie and Dex. They stood ready to escort her to the door.

"Is it necessary for me to even stick around? I have to get my bike back to the shop."

"I can take her statement," Charlie offered, glancing at Tully. "And then give her a ride home."

"That would be great," Faith said, beelining out the back door. Charlie shrugged at Tully before following Faith.

"How do you know her?" Rick asked.

"Yeah," said Dex, a scowl on his face. "I'm certainly curious."

Tully shook his head. Faith Fitzpatrick didn't know what was good for her, but because he was a detective on duty, investigating a crime where she was now a prime suspect, he couldn't let his growing interest in her cloud his judgment. He had a case to solve.

"She's new," Tully said, pulling his notepad out of his breast pocket. "Rick, tell me what you saw."

Rick nodded. "First, I saw Faith's motorcycle on the ground, then the broken glass, then Faith coming out the back door looking suspicious."

"Define *suspicious*."

"Running, looking around. She shouldn't have gone in there in the first place. I called Dash—"

"Do you know Dash Callahan?" As far as Tully understood it, no one in Roseley did.

"I met him when he and Ledger first bought the property. He came into The Copper Kettle and he and I got to talking. I told him I'd keep an eye on the store from time to time, until he moved here."

"That was nice of you."

"It's not a big deal. I just drive by occasionally. Tonight, I'm glad I did."

"Is Dash on his way?"

"He's not driving in from Traverse City until the morning."

Tully strode to the front of the store and examined the door locks. He circled around and kept his tone light.

"How's Gemma doing these days?"

"We're both exhausted. You try managing a restaurant and raising three boys."

"I'd imagine it would be tough, especially if Ricky Jr. is anything like you."

Rick met Tully's joke with a laugh.

"He's worse! He's already broken his arm swinging off the dock."

Dex chuckled. "That'll be expensive."

"It is, and the cast doesn't even slow him down."

Tully squatted by the back door and ran a finger over a sensor by the door frame. If the Callahans had a security system, it was a silent one. But had it been triggered by someone before Faith entered?

"Rick, what time did you get here?"

Rick shrugged and checked his phone.

“I called Dash at 8:10 p.m., so a minute or two before that.”

This was the first vandalism where he might piece together a decent timeline. He needed to talk to the Callahan brothers about their security system. Then he needed to talk to Faith.

CHAPTER SIX

FAITH STRETCHED AS morning light pooled in through the bedroom sheers. The warm smell of coffee perked her senses. She rolled over to find Caroline standing in the doorway.

"Well, if it isn't Roseley's favorite misfit."

"Says who?"

"Gemma Murdock and half the folks at The Copper Kettle."

Faith sat up in bed and motioned for the coffee. Caroline handed her an old coffee mug before crawling under the covers beside her.

Faith inhaled the rich aroma and wrapped her fingers around the familiar mug. Uncle Gus had had it in his kitchen cupboard for as long as she could remember. He preferred to use the same stained mug for the last thirty years, maybe longer. The feel of the mug, with the tiny chip on the handle, triggered happy memories of watching Uncle Gus on the back porch in the early morning, reading the newspaper and slowly whittling away at a single piece of buttered toast. He'd had time for his family and sometimes that included her.

"Is she any relation to Rick Murdock?"

"Wife of fourteen years, yes. They're married with three boys."

"What did she say?"

Caroline pulled the covers over her and faced her cousin. She thumped Faith on the head in a playful reprimand. "She said you were caught at the scene of the crime last night. True?"

Faith scowled. "I didn't know it was the scene of a crime when I walked in."

"But you *did* walk in and place yourself there right before the police arrived? That or you've taken up robbery since the last time I saw you. I certainly hope not, because the Callahan Brothers are not guys you want to mess with. They have a lot of clout."

"They had the most beautiful classic motorcycle, something I would love to get my hands on one of these days. I wonder how much they're asking for it."

"Would you be serious? Half of The Copper Kettle was talking about you. Believe me when I say it wasn't good."

"Did anyone refer to me by Talbert?"

"Not yet, but it's coming, cousin. Especially if you keep…"

"Keep what?" Faith sat up straighter in bed. "It's not my fault someone broke into The Gypsy Caravan. In fact, the break-in was the reason I had to stop in the first place. It threw my entire evening off. I had to leave my bike and then I ran into Detective McTully…" She thought of Detective McTully and how he had called out to her from his truck. If she hadn't known better, she might have entertained the thought he was flirting. Well, maybe he wasn't actively flirting, but his tone made for an interaction she wouldn't mind experiencing again. She wondered if he knew the effect he had on a woman, or more specifically, on her. His cool energy rolled off him like fog descending a mountain and it made her tingle with an anticipation to see him again. Though, under better circumstances when he wasn't interviewing her for a crime.

"Oh, no," Caroline muttered.

"What?"

"I remember that look."

Faith harrumphed. "I'm not making any look. I'm recalling the events of last night and trying to remember any details that could help Detective McTully solve his case."

"I wondered how long it would take before you worked his name into the conversation again."

"He's the detective on the case, isn't he?"

"He's the one person who made you pool on the ground like a melted Popsicle in high school. That's who he is."

"He didn't know I existed in high school."

"True." Caroline reclaimed the coffee mug and took a sip. "But he knows all about you now."

Faith's brow knit in a perfect bow. "Why do you say that? Was he at The Copper Kettle too?"

"No. But I overheard Gemma asking Charlie Stillwater about you. Rick seemed to think Tully was too lenient with you last night. He thought it was suspicious you were in The Gypsy Caravan when he arrived and even more alarming that Tully didn't find it suspicious enough."

"That's because I didn't do anything wrong."

"I know that, and you know that, but the people in this town don't. To them you're still new and mysterious."

"And guilty until proven innocent."

"Not exactly."

"Exactly." Faith scowled.

"I want you to be careful with your grand opening. You need to get off on the right foot. It's the only way you'll stick around town, and you know how much I love having you back. Trig does too."

Faith appreciated the sentiment, but it was the mention of her grand opening that had her rolling out of bed.

"That reminds me," she said. "I have so much to do today." She threw the covers over Caroline's head, making her cousin laugh. "What time is it? It feels so late."

"It's going on eight o'clock."

"Good heavens, Caroline. What time did you go to breakfast this morning?"

"You know I'm an early riser. Plus, all the good gossip happens before the tourists turn up."

"I'm glad you have your ear to the ground for me. I'll mind my Ps and Qs for the time being. Fair?"

Caroline nodded and made her way into the hallway. "I'll give you a hand this morning. It's going to be a scorcher today, so dress coolly."

TULLY CRUISED ALONG the lakeshore, diligently scanning his surroundings. He'd made a trip out to Heath Harrison's place and had a quick chat with both him and his son, Oliver. They'd been working on their pontoon boat when he'd pulled up and within seconds of reading Oliver's face, he knew the kid had no idea why Tully had stopped by. That was certainly a good thing.

When he'd made his way down Heath's dock that morning, the fifteen-year-old had greeted him like a long-lost uncle. Sometimes that happened when he helped redirect a kid to a better path, and after Oliver had gotten wrapped up with Cody Ward, stealing a speedboat and going for a joyride, Tully had made it a point to occasionally visit Oliver. He made a point to offer a word of encouragement when the moment deserved it, and Oliver seemed to bask in it. Though he visited Cody too, the teen was a harder sell.

"Looks like you've put this young man to work, Heath," Tully said. Heath, a man in his midthirties, wiped his brow and nodded proudly.

"If he wants to own a boat of his own someday, he needs to know how to fix an engine."

"Are you learning anything, son?"

Oliver nodded sheepishly as Heath stepped closer.

"What brings you by, Tully?"

Tully smiled at Oliver. "I wanted to check in on Oliver and see how his summer is treating him."

"A lot better than summers past, huh, kiddo?"

Oliver nodded again and wandered over. The fact that he came closer when he had a good enough excuse to avoid conversation or eye contact said a lot. Tully kept his tone friendly.

"Have you spent any time with Cody this summer?"

Oliver rolled his eyes. "Not really. He's been out in the woods a lot."

"Doing what?"

"I don't know. I think he's trying to build a fort or something. He told me he bought a monster bag of paintballs before school ended. Maybe he's shooting them off."

Heath turned to his son. "Oliver, go grab Detective McTully a drink out of the garage so he can take it for the road. It's going to be in the midnineties today." He waited until Oliver was halfway down the dock. "Is this about the break-in at The Gypsy Caravan last night?"

"Word travels fast."

"Oliver was home with me last night. Even

if he hadn't been, he's not getting messed up in any trouble again."

"I don't suspect Oliver, Heath. He's a good kid with a good head on his shoulders. I wanted your impression of Cody these days and the kids he hangs around with now."

"As far as I know, he's back at Karen and Moody's place for the summer. I haven't seen enough of him to help you."

"Have you seen Cheyanne?"

Cheyanne was Cody's biological mother. A dedicated single mom working two jobs as she went back to school, she relied heavily on her parents to help raise Cody.

"Word has it she's interviewing in Traverse City for a new job."

Tully had smiled as Oliver approached with a can of lemonade. He was glad to see the kid doing so well, but he hadn't gotten a lot of information. By the time he'd returned to his truck, he'd had a call from Dash and Ledger Callahan. The brothers had finished their inventory early that morning and had reported that nothing had been stolen.

It seemed strange to Tully that someone would have gone through the trouble to break into the antiques shop but not steal anything. Not only that, the brothers had tipped over the motorcycle themselves for repairs. Someone had shattered a window, tossed several antiques on the ground but hadn't stolen or damaged anything? It didn't make sense.

Unless, Tully thought as he drove back to town, it was a person who had intended to steal something but had been interrupted.

Tully pointed his truck in the direction of Faith Fitzpatrick's repair shop. He wanted a straight answer from Faith Fitzpatrick about the circumstances that had led her inside The Gypsy Caravan.

AS FAITH LOCKED the front door of her shop, she spotted Detective McTully. He stood nearby exuding an easy cool.

"Are you stalking me?" she said, surprised.

"Ms. Fitzpatrick, I need a minute of your time."

Tully stepped under the shade of her storefront awning and removed his sunglasses. His eyes were a warm chocolaty brown that could melt her in two seconds flat if she let her mind wander too much. He managed the softest, faintest smile, making a few fine lines at the corners of his eyes crinkle. There had always been something about him that could disarm even the most confrontational or guarded person, and Faith knew she was no exception.

"Is this about last night? I haven't eaten yet today so I'm grabbing an early lunch. Maybe when I get back—"

"I'll walk with you," he said. "Are you heading to The Sandwich Board?"

She hadn't intended to ever step one foot inside CeCe Takes's sandwich shop, but when Detective McTully began walking in that direction, she reluctantly followed.

"Do you have any leads from last night?" she asked.

"I need to better understand why you were riding through the back lot last night."

"I take that as a no." Faith glanced at the reflection of the two of them in the glass windows of each shop they passed. Caroline had warned her that the people in this town would begin to suspect her, especially if the vandalism continued without a culprit being caught. She only wished Detective McTully didn't suspect her.

"Ms. Fitzpatrick?" he prompted. "The back lot?"

"Do you ride, Detective McTully?"

"Ride?"

"A motorcycle?" If he did, it would make

his understanding of last night a lot easier. But he raised his brow impatiently, making her expedite her explanation. "I take back roads and shortcuts whenever I can. I enjoy the freedom of riding, and if I can do that without worrying too much about other motorists on the road, the better."

"Does the ride through the back lot have a pretty view?" His tone was pleasant, but it made Faith frown all the same.

"I know what you're getting at. I wasn't back there for the scenery. Dumpsters and wooden pallets aren't my thing, but it's a nice shortcut to avoid the traffic on Main. You must not ride, or you'd get that."

"I like my truck."

"You're missing out."

When they arrived at The Sandwich Board, Faith's mouth twisted in disappointment when she found it so crowded.

"I should have made a run to The Copper Kettle instead."

"Hi, Tully," a voice called over the murmur of conversation. Mara and a girl, no older than twelve, greeted them. She had pink, round cheeks and looked nothing like Mara. "Faith," Mara said, smiling when she noticed her. "It's good to see you again. This is my daughter, Lucy."

"Nice to meet you," Lucy said, drawing a proud smile from Tully.

"I'm Faith Fitzpatrick. I'm new in town."

"I know. I saw you painting your store window. Mom said you're going to advertise at our sports shop."

"Are you two eating here?" Mara said, glancing hopefully between Faith and Detective McTully. Faith shook her head without hesitation. This wasn't a social call, by any means. He was questioning her, albeit casually, because she was the suspect of a crime. As much as she wouldn't mind basking in his masculine energy for an entire lunch, she needed to get back to work. She had a lot to do before tomorrow.

Dolores Mitchell joined them.

"Thank you for offering to fix my mailbox, Faith," Dolores said. "But I ended up buying a new one."

Faith smiled. "You're an optimist."

"I choose to be, but if someone busts this one too, I might take you up on your offer to fix it."

"What are you saying, Faith?" It was CeCe.

"Does she have a reason not to be an optimist?"

Faith, along with the others, turned to find CeCe scowling from behind the counter.

"I only meant that she has a good attitude."

Dolores shook her sandwich bag at her friend. "CeCe, stop being such a...a—"

"A what?" CeCe said before turning to the register. Dolores rolled her eyes at the back of her friend's head. She motioned for Faith to step up to the counter where a short, retirement-aged man with smiling eyes winked at her.

"I'm Angelo, and I run this shop. What can I get you?"

"I'll take the number seven with no tomatoes, please."

"Number seven coming right up."

Faith remembered Angelo but he, along with everyone else in town, didn't remember her. She had always wondered how someone as friendly and jovial as Angelo could end up with...a CeCe. She knew opposites could attract but life was still strange sometimes.

Faith fished in her jeans pocket for a wad of cash and peeled off enough to cover her meal as CeCe busied herself at the register.

"You have a nice shop here, CeCe," Faith

managed, trying hard to be polite. Angelo winked at her but CeCe's smile turned brittle. The draft from CeCe's cold shoulder was enough to make anyone downshift into silent mode, but she refused to lower herself to CeCe's level.

Filling the silence, Angelo motioned to her sandwich. "Instead of tomatoes, how about a little diced cucumber or some avocado?"

"Avocado is extra," CeCe said. Faith let out a long, steady breath, biting back a snide quip. Perhaps if she ignored CeCe? What harm could come in not speaking to her? They could each mind their own business, without ever needing to socialize or interact. Some folks were just difficult people, Faith thought to herself. Kyle had certainly been a difficult person to be married to and heaven knew her father's personality was like a bulldozer aimed solely for greed. Her shop neighbor might be loud and pushy, but as long as she kept to herself—

"Oh, my goodness!" CeCe squawked, clutching her chest. Faith glanced behind her to find Detective McTully, Mara, Dolores and a host of other Roseley folks tuned in too. CeCe was not one to be ignored or talked over.

Faith slid her cash across the counter. "I

don't care if you ring me up for the avocado. It's not a big deal."

"Not that." She brought a hand to her cheek, overly dramatic. "It's been bothering me ever since you turned up in this town, Ms. Fitzpatrick."

Faith tipped her head, confused. "Pardon?"

"What are you talking about, CeCe?" Angelo said.

CeCe motioned for Detective McTully as Faith noticed how the people nearby quieted. "Detective, I'll bet you didn't realize we have a local celebrity in our presence."

Faith's heart slammed against the inside of her rib cage as her hand found the counter to stabilize herself. She watched the words roll off CeCe's bitter tongue in slow motion, knowing she was powerless to stop her. She wanted to spring over the counter and smack a hand over CeCe's mouth. Force her to swallow her own words rather than speak them to everyone in the shop. It would spell her demise. All she could do was stand motionless like a wax figure as museum patrons crowded and gawked.

"CeCe, what are you going on about now?" Dolores asked. Faith couldn't manage a word in her own defense. She knew exactly what

CeCe was about to lob at her next, and short of scooping up her sandwich and running out the front door, there was nothing she could do to stop it.

Faith beelined for the door. "You can keep the change." She wanted to walk out of the shop with her head held high, but most important, she wanted to walk out of the shop.

"Faith, are you okay?" Mara called, brushing her fingers along Faith's arm but not moving quickly enough to stop her. She'd held the slightest hope that Mara might become an ally. She'd even imagined them as friends, friendly acquaintances at the very least.

"Let her go, Mara," CeCe called. "Don't you know who that is?"

Faith made it past the crowd but hesitated before pushing out into the humid air. She turned to find Detective McTully staring at her as CeCe continued. The faces of everyone else in the crowd blurred except his. His handsome features with those kind, dark eyes stopped her. He still didn't recognize her, nor did he know her. She wanted to savor the last few moments before he did. She held his gaze, wanting to seal him into her memory as he stood—concerned, untainted by the knowledge of her past.

"That's not Faith Fitzpatrick. That's Faith *Talbert*, Ray Talbert's daughter." Any murmuring that had continued despite CeCe's squawking now ceased completely. "I never forget a face even if it takes me longer to place one these days."

Recognition seemed to fall over Detective McTully, but it was most likely due to her father's name, his infamy seared forever in this town's memory. He didn't remember her. The interaction they'd had in high school, when he'd been a graduating senior and she'd been a sophomore, wasn't memorable for him the way it had been for her.

Faith could still remember the day her little crush on John McTully had solidified into something more. It was funny how a tiny mistake, like forgetting a gym uniform, could end up changing how you see a classmate.

Not wanting to play volleyball in the dress she'd worn to school that day, Faith, a shy sophomore in high school, had skipped her physical education class and had hidden in an unoccupied art room. She'd quietly tucked herself into a nook in the dark room where a passing teacher wouldn't see her. After several minutes of silent sketching, a tangle of boys pushed into the room. It had been an unfair scuffle, roughhousing that escalated quickly as three upperclassmen targeted a single freshman. As Faith angled to get a better look from her hiding place, the freshman showed signs of deep distress. Clothes and hair disheveled, whimpering madly, his bloodied lip was a sign the tormenting could get a whole lot worse.

Chattering with fright herself, Faith considered her options. Even though she was no match for the three older boys, she knew she had to do something—and fast. If she popped up from the shadows, and raced for the door, the element of surprise might get her to the safety of the hallway before they could stop her. If she found a teacher, he or she would have to break up the fight.

The freshman shrieked again, propelling Faith to her feet and toward the door. Before she could reach it, it swung open. John McTully's athletic build filled the doorway for only a moment before he sprang onto the group, hauling the first of the three teenagers into a shelf of art supplies with a clamor. There had been a struggle, one of the boys cracking a fist to John's jaw before Faith flipped on the lights and screamed into the hallway for help. A few seconds of panic seemed to come over the bullies before they scrambled out the door, without even a glance over their shoulder at her. The freshman, though trying hard not to, cried as John helped him to his feet.

"I thought they were looking at you strange," John had told him, leading him out of the room. "Let's get you to the office."

He'd stopped then, noticing her standing there, staring.

"Were you in there too?" he'd asked, just realizing. "Are you okay?"

She'd momentarily gotten lost in his eyes, a fierce gaze that had shifted into true concern for her.

"They didn't know I was in there."

The freshman broke away from John, shuffling quickly to the office unaccompanied.

"I have to go with him, but don't worry about those guys," he'd told her. "They'll be mad at me, if they even noticed you at all."

It was not the first time in her life she'd felt unseen, but it was the first time she'd been grateful for it. The boys had been quickly suspended, and she'd believed John's assurance. She hadn't worried.

She'd wanted to smile at John in the halls after that, but nerves always seemed to get the best of her.A few weeks later, he'd graduated and soon left for college. She figured he'd forgotten all about her, though she'd never forgotten about him. The memory of him continued to resonate, the details of the encounter, even years later, still as ingrained in her mind as lines carved in oak.

Through the rest of high school, through her father's arrest, through the ridicule and loneliness that had followed, she'd daydreamed about John McTully. She'd never forgotten his courage or his kindness, and it would be a long time before she witnessed such traits in anyone else in her life. Not her father, who had loved only money and the unwavering pursuit of it. Not her mother, who had emotionally detached long before the scandal and then physically detached as Faith floundered into adulthood. Certainly not Kyle, whose kind gestures had felt transactional and self-serving most of the time. If it hadn't been for Uncle Gus and her cousins, she might have never believed good relationships of any kind were possible for her.

For her own protection, she had learned to put up a wall. Bonnie, a longtime friend at the last repair shop she'd worked at, had called it her edge. Bonnie said Faith always seemed to be white-knuckling her way through interactions with others, and Bonnie had been right. She was always waiting to be stung, and that constant frame of mind made her defensive. She didn't like it, but it worked for her.

It embarrassed her that her first encounter with John McTully since high school had been so contentious when he had been one of the only people in this town whom she still thought of fondly. Life experience had taught her to nip quickly and first, because the people she usually encountered tried for the same.

And that, Faith thought, was exactly what had happened to her at the hands of CeCe Takes. She'd fooled herself into believing she could be polite at no cost to herself. She'd been wrong.

As the whispers began in the sandwich shop, John McTully didn't waver. He'd kept a poker face amid CeCe's declaration, but at the mention of her maiden name his eyes had flinched. Whether it was pity or suspicion she found there, she couldn't tell, so she bolted rather than wait to find out.

Somehow the number of paces from The Sandwich Board to Heart Motorcycles had tripled since she'd last trekked it. If she thought she wasn't being watched, she would have taken her steps two at a time. When she reached her shop, she fumbled with the lock yet again, knowing full well that John McTully was behind her.

"Ms. Fitzpatrick," he called.

"What?" She pivoted and crossed her arms tightly over her chest as if he'd asked for the world. "I can't help you right now."

"I still need to talk to you."

She glanced at the heavens.

"Fine. I'm listening."

Tully glanced back at the people coming out of The Sandwich Board. They milled around on the sidewalk, staring at her like she was a newly discovered bacteria in a petri dish.

"Perhaps we should go inside," he said.

Faith reluctantly led him into her store, flipping on the overhead lights.

"Before you start," she said, surveying his demeanor, "I *am* Faith Talbert, Ray Talbert's daughter, but that doesn't mean I'm a criminal like him. I've spent the past several years trying to get on with my life. I don't appreciate being accused of someone else's crimes. I didn't vandalize any shop in this town, and I would never, *never* do such a thing so I will stop you right there before you go any further."

"I don't remember accusing you, Ms. Fitzpatrick."

"Didn't you?"

"No." He put a little distance between the two of them, rolling his shoulders. "I didn't."

"Now that CeCe Takes knows who I am, it won't be long before she forms a posse to prove my guilt."

"No one in this town is out to get you."

"I wouldn't be so sure of that." She paced the front of her shop, glancing a few times out the front window. "You weren't here when—" She paused, not wanting to relive the year after her father had been arrested. It had felt like the entire town had turned on her overnight. She hadn't blamed them at first. Her father had scammed many people out of a lot of money. She had understood their anger, but with time she thought they'd understand it hadn't been anything she'd done. She had been a child. It wasn't fair. It wasn't her fault.

Tully shifted on his feet, silently waiting for her to continue, but she didn't want to. She'd enjoyed the last couple of days when she had been a stranger to him. She'd rather be a stranger than what she'd soon become—a tagline on Roseley's page six.

"Give me the timeline of last night."

"I already gave it to Officer Stillwater."

"Give it to me."

She ran a hand through her hair and drew a breath. "I took the shortcut behind the shops on Third. My tire blew out after it ran over the shattered glass behind The Gypsy Caravan. When I saw the broken window, I worried there was someone hurt inside. I went in, looked around and bumped into Rick Murdock on my way out. *That's it.*"

"What time was that?"

Faith squeezed her eyes shut to remember. "I don't know exactly. I had dinner with Caroline around six thirty so…maybe eight?"

Tully nodded and looked out the front window. "CeCe Takes has a hard time letting things go…" he began.

"No kidding. But what I need to know is…" She drew a breath. "Who are you going to believe?"

"I follow the facts, Ms. Fitzpatrick."

"I wish more people did. Maybe then they'd let me have a place here. And it's Faith." He tipped his head, as if considering her words. "I've asked you before to call me Faith."

She figured he needed to stay professional where she was concerned. If he thought her guilty, she guessed, he'd continue calling her Ms. Fitzpatrick. Wasn't that what detectives were supposed to do? Keep their distance with suspects in a criminal investigation? Yes, she thought, stepping closer as a challenge of sorts. If he continued to call her Ms. Fitzpatrick, he would continue to see her as a suspect. It wasn't a solid conclusion, but she believed his next words would tell her everything she needed to know about where she stood with him.

His expression turned serious. The moments ticked silently between them as she waited for a response.

"There's a place for you here," he said softly. "Even if it doesn't feel like it right now. Back there at The Sandwich Board was a bad moment, but it won't be your only one. There will be good moments too."

Her throat clenched as she noted the sincerity in his voice. She wanted his words to be true, but it was easier to believe the bad stuff. When CeCe had spoken, a darkness had begun settling over her, and she wasn't sure if anything, not even the gentle timbre of John's sweet voice, could lift it.

"I'm not so sure about that," she said. "Not five minutes ago, you heard for yourself—"

"I heard. I saw too. There are good people in this town who will support you if…"

"If what?"

"If you let them."

He exited her shop and she realized he'd seen straight through her. That wasn't something most people could do.

CHAPTER SEVEN

TULLY EASED HIS boat up to the dock outside Little Lakeside Sports Shop and cut the engine. The trolling motor he'd bought several years ago had been worth its weight in gold if only to provide serene mornings like this. There was nothing better than fishing before the sun rose or the tourists hit the waves on their jet skis.

There were a handful of anglers he recognized. But each person preferred to stay in his or her own lane, as if to appreciate the silence as much as he did. Moments when the darkness slowly made way for the first whispers of dawn were his favorite part of the day, and the ideal time to reel in breakfast.

The lake smoothed before him like the blue-gray satin fabric his mother had wrapped around her shoulders to keep off the evening chill. Her perfume had lingered on the fabric a long time after she'd gone. As a boy, he had sometimes sought out her wrap that hung on the back of her closet door. He wouldn't disturb it, didn't dare remove it from the hook. He'd only bury his nose in it, recalling the familiar scent like the fuzzy images of a dream.

Once it had become clear to him, painfully and undeniably clear that she wasn't returning, he'd abandoned the slip of fabric just as he had tried to abandon memories of her. In a single night, he and his father and sister had found themselves on a new path, one that they had to trod without Evelyn. Their time for mourning her passed slowly, similar to her scent fading from that satin wrap.

Tully's boat pierced a line slowly through the still water. He crawled along at less than a couple of miles an hour, his fishing line trailing behind him, occasionally signaling a fish nibble.

He thought of his father and how he should be a dutiful son and drive out to check on him, but every morning as he sat in his boat, the silence working like a cool salve on his troubled heart, he'd find a good enough reason to postpone for another day.

His mind wandered to Faith Fitzpatrick and how humiliated she'd looked at The Sandwich Board. He could spot when a person was eager to hide, and from the moment he'd talked to Faith, he could tell she was on guard. CeCe's words, clearly intended to put Faith on the spot, helped him better understand why. He couldn't blame her for being defensive. CeCe was difficult to take when she adored you. If she didn't like you, he figured the fallout would put even the nicest person on edge.

His red fishing bobber jostled for a second before dancing in the boat's wake. He waited a moment longer before jerking the line and delighting in the resistance that he met. He snagged a bass, then two bluegills. He rested his hand on the steering wheel and gazed out over the lake that had been his home for most of his life. He couldn't imagine the ache if it no longer felt like a place where he belonged.

A common loon called from off in the distance, its warbly cry signaling a choir of birds that began singing as if on cue. The first rays of sunshine brought the first speedboats and a jostling of tourists eager to get the most out of their long holiday weekend.

Tully docked and made his way up the pier, his tackle box in hand, when he spotted Samantha stationed at his truck.

"Morning, sunshine!" she called. They were both early risers, something they valued for entirely different reasons. Tully loved the peace and quiet that came with early morning while Samantha had more energy than a classroom of schoolchildren loaded up on sugar. She couldn't sleep a wink past 5:00 a.m. before she was tearing into another day. "Did you catch me breakfast?" She grinned.

"I'll clean them if you fry them."

Samantha turned up her nose. "No way. I'm already dressed for the day."

Tully managed a chuckle when Samantha hopped into his truck without invitation.

"What are you doing here?" he asked.

"Already went for a jog, showered, recorded a new video for my vlog—"

"Hence the full hair and makeup."

"Naturally," Samantha said. "I have to renew my passport and run a few other errands, but I thought I'd visit my big brother first. How's work?"

He drove them the short jaunt back to his house. "Slow."

"What about that vandalism case? I hear the new girl is the prime suspect. Faith, right?"

"Where did you hear that?"

Samantha considered. "Gemma Murdock, Emily Peaches—"

"Emily Peaches?" Tully said. "I didn't know you were still running around with her."

"I bumped into her last night at The Farmers Market."

Tully nodded in understanding. The Farmers Market, open two evenings a week in the summer, was the place many folks in town went for homegrown produce, baked goods, floral arrangements and gossip. It made sense that news about Ray Talbert's daughter had likely been a hot topic of discussion.

"Emily asked about you."

"Uh-huh," Tully muttered. Women were always asking Samantha about him, and he had long suspected Samantha of playfully stringing them along. Samantha loved the drama of life and when there wasn't enough, she was good at kindling plenty of her own.

"I told her you weren't dating anyone at the moment..."

"Uh-huh."

"And she said *she* wasn't dating anyone at the moment..."

"Uh-huh."

"And I suggested you two not date anyone together."

"As in?"

"Oh, Tully, you're really impossible. Have

you talked to Emily recently? She's still sweet on you even after you let her down easy. You're missing the boat, you know."

"She's a lovely woman." It was true. Emily Peaches's name had always amused him, because she'd been blessed with the prettiest peaches-and-cream complexion he'd ever seen. He also admired the single dimple in her round left cheek that punctuated her smile like a happy exclamation point. She was kind, bright, someone he could imagine settling down with one day. But even though they'd gone out on a few dates and had had a very pleasant time, he'd never wanted to take their relationship further than that.

"She has a heart of gold too," Samantha said, going for the hard sell. Tully parked and they made their way to the porch steps. Tully got down to work cleaning the fish as Samantha leaned against a pillar and watched, silently, for a long time. "What else have you learned about Faith Talbert?"

"Faith *Fitzpatrick*," he said, shooting Samantha a direct look. He didn't want his little sister to fall into the trap other people in town might, confining Faith to a past she didn't deserve.

"Is she divorced or still married?"

Tully considered this. He hadn't seen or heard of a husband and quickly pushed his rising feelings of jealousy aside.

"I really don't know, Sam. It's not my place to ask questions like that."

"Not your place?" Samantha chortled. "Have you stopped being a detective since I last saw you?"

"You know what I mean." He tossed the first cleaned fish up on the porch steps dangerously close to Samantha's designer sandals. "Heat up my cast-iron skillet with a little butter, would you?"

"Are you doing the frying?"

"Don't I always?" he said, barely lifting his brow. Samantha headed into the house as Tully cleaned the last two fish in quiet.

He wondered what life had been like for Faith. He wondered what kind of courage she had had that enabled her to move back to Roseley only ten years after her father's scandal. He admired her. Liked her. But as she was a suspect in a crime he was investigating, he needed to keep those favorable feelings toward her in check. He followed the facts, and nothing could contort facts quicker than having feelings for a beautiful woman.

Tully's cell phone vibrated as he carried the

fish into the kitchen. He arranged them in the cast-iron pan already bubbling with hot butter. Thankfully, the savory aroma made him hungry for something other than a desire to see Faith again. Samantha's mention of her had sent his thoughts spiraling down a dangerous road, one where he lost his edge or discernment.

He washed his hands and checked his phone. A text message from the station changed his plans for the morning. There had been another incident of vandalism, this time at The Sandwich Board.

Tully knew he would need to visit CeCe and Angelo before revisiting the others involved in the earlier cases. That would make for a full morning, and as he finished cooking, he'd already decided to save the best visit, the one to Heart Motorcycles, for last.

TULLY HAD FINISHED his interview with Angelo, pleasantly surprised that CeCe hadn't been pacing beside him the entire time. He had expected CeCe to be bursting with accusations about Faith or to demand to know his next steps for solving the crime. Her absence was odd, but certainly appreciated.

Angelo offered Tully a cup of coffee and

explained that CeCe had run a bulk sandwich order to the fire station. Before leaving, she had given instructions for Tully to stay put at the shop until she returned. Since Tully didn't take orders from CeCe Takes, he had chuckled at the demand. Angelo had joined him, laughing the loudest. Angelo seemed to know as well as everyone else how over the top his wife could be.

Angelo had explained that the glass on the front door of The Sandwich Board had been shattered, but nothing inside had been disturbed. CeCe, he had chuckled, was angrier than a steamed bag of hornets nests about it.

"I don't know how many other ways there are to explain that our door was broken," Angelo had said with a wide grin. "But I'm sure CeCe will track you down to tell you in her own words."

He'd sent Tully on his way with a friendly wave and more questions than answers. Vandalism wasn't common in town before this spate of incidents, so Tully knew the crimes would continue until he found the reason behind them and the party responsible.

The Gypsy Caravan was Tully's next stop. Even though Dash and Ledger had reported nothing stolen and did not expect another formal visit, Tully added their store to his route that morning. He was glad he had because there had been something strange about their interview. Their answers had sounded well thought out and prepared, almost rehearsed. Once folks had had a day or two to think about events, they often later recalled a seemingly unimportant detail that proved to be helpful. Tully liked to give folks a bit of time before circling back and questioning them again. Frequently, folks didn't even realize Tully was interviewing them a second time. He was such a consistent fixture in town, stopping by shops and restaurants for short chats, people usually thought he was around only to say hello.

The Callahan brothers, however, had seemed quite irritated by Tully's visit, which left him perplexed. As they hadn't been around immediately following the break-in, he had expected them to be pleased to see him that morning. He had been wrong.

Dash Callahan had been helping a crew unpack two large stone equestrian statues from crates when Tully had strolled up to the front door. A pair of large men in work overalls had been moving the second crate on a dolly through the front doors.

"Mornin'," Tully had called, following the movers into the entryway. Dash Callahan had looked up from his clipboard and nodded as Ledger Callahan strolled out from the back of the shop. "Detective McTully."

"Good morning, Detective," Dash had said. He exchanged a glance with his brother and motioned for Ledger to continue working. Ledger surveyed Tully before claiming the clipboard from Dash and attending to the very large delivery.

"I'm sure I can help you with whatever you need. My brother has to get these crates unpacked as these gentlemen are on the clock."

Tully stared up at the equestrian statues that dwarfed him by a few inches. Though Ledger turned his attention to them as well, Tully knew he was all ears.

"What are you doing with these beauties?" he asked, trying for polite. He thought the regal-looking horses were some of the ugliest pieces of artwork he'd ever seen.

Dash groaned. "We were planning on placing these two outside the doors to act as a gateway into our shop. After recent events, we decided to bring them inside. We thought Roseley was safe enough to display antiques and artwork on the street but…" He shrugged in defeat. "I guess we were wrong."

"Roseley is safe," Tully said, surprised at the defensiveness that stabbed him in the gut.

"We'll see," Dash said. "The lack of crime certainly influenced our decision to set up shop here." Ledger harrumphed from behind his clipboard. "Hopefully," Dash said, clearing his throat. "This break-in is only a fluke."

"I'm only giving it to August," Ledger mumbled.

Tully trusted his intuition when interviewing folks, but even a detective novice would have picked up on the death stare Dash instantly shot his brother.

"August?" Tully casually maneuvered himself between the brothers, directing Ledger to focus on him instead of Dash. "To do what?"

His move was as calm and easy as an old man in the park coaxing pigeons to his outstretched hand. The Callahan brothers weren't suspects; they were victims of a crime. Yet something about the tension between the two of them gave Tully more questions than answers. He didn't want to leave until his detective hunch had been appeased.

"There are plenty of other towns that would serve our needs," Ledger said, now bold. He seemed like a man who wanted to talk, wanted to complain, and Tully was all too happy to let him. "All we have to do is hire movers and packers." He snapped his fingers. "We can be out of here in seventy-two hours."

"Unless?"

Ledger frowned. "I don't follow."

"That sounded like an ultimatum," Tully said, though he wasn't sure what Roseley would need to do to keep The Gypsy Caravan from turning tail so quickly.

"No ultimatum, Detective," Dash said. He stepped around Tully and jerked his head toward the back room. Ledger gave the huff of a willful child before shoving the clipboard back into his brother's hands and storming off. "My brother and I were not in agreement about opening the store in Roseley," Dash explained. "Being in business with family has its perks...and disadvantages, as you can see."

"How did you come to an agreement then?" Tully asked.

"We always agree to do what's in the best interest of our brand."

Tully nodded, certain he'd heard almost the same comment come from Samantha whenever she talked about her social media followers.

"And that meant Roseley?"

Dash shrugged. "Roseley made us a nice offer."

"Really? Which was what exactly?" He hadn't known Roseley had incentivized the Callahan brothers in any way. He wondered who from the town council had courted them.

"Surely you've heard of tax incentives, Detective."

Dash flipped through the sheets on his clipboard. "I really need to attend to this delivery so if there isn't anything else—"

"Have you noticed anything else out of sorts in your shop?" Tully asked, putting his curiosity about the incentives on hold—for now.

"No. We ran an inventory list immediately, as you know, and everything was in order."

"Was anything else damaged or misplaced?"

"No."

"Nothing?"

"We took our time and dedicated several hours to double-checking."

Tully paused. Perhaps it was the fact that Dash was distracted by the crates or maybe it was that a broken window was pretty insignificant to a pseudo-celebrity like Dash Callahan. Either way, Tully wanted a little bit more from him and if he could find a way to get him talking…"That bimmer of yours is a beauty." Tully motioned toward the motorcycle and sidecar, still tipped to its side. He wanted Dash to let his guard down, chitchat casually so he could get a better read on him. "I have to admit I admired it the other night."

"We thought we had a buyer lined up, but he fell through. There's more damage to the engine than we thought."

"Are you going to repair it or try to sell it as is?"

"Sell. It takes up too much space."

"Moving forward," Tully continued, "are you taking any extra precautions with security?"

"We're having a better security system installed later today. The one we have now is a silent alarm but the new one will sound as soon as someone fiddles with a door. It'll be loud enough to send them running for the hills."

"Any idea when the alarm was tripped the other night?"

"7:56," Dash said. Tully flicked an eyebrow prompting Dash to continue, "It's one of those notifications you get on your phone to let you know someone has passed over the door threshold. The new system will have video."

The rest of their conversation continued much the same, Tully asking questions and Dash having a clear, concise answer as if pulled from a queue.

Finally, Tully asked, "Do you have any idea who would want to break into your antiques shop?"

"Ledger and I don't know many people in town yet so we couldn't have crossed anyone intentionally. I know some folks weren't too happy about us moving in, but why would someone break in without stealing something? From what we've heard, our store hasn't been the only one targeted. The whole situation is a bit unnerving."

Tully thanked Dash and let himself out the front door, considering the man's answers. Most people included occasional pauses when they spoke, either to recall the truth or to think of a lie. Tully noted how Dash had had none. But once he reached Grandma's Basement and casually asked Miss Jenkins similar questions, he finally understood why. He'd been beaten to the punch, so to speak.

"Tully, dear," Miss Jenkins said. "I've already told Faith everything I know."

Tully followed Miss Jenkins to her cash register, where she plucked a peppermint stick from a giant glass canister. Her smile slipped into worry as she read his face.

"Did I do something wrong? I assumed she was helping you on your case. She certainly has a good head on her shoulders, don't you think? Her questions sounded so…I don't know…professional."

"What did she ask?"

Miss Jenkins thought for a moment. "She wanted to know where I was the other night. I explained that I was here closing up my shop. She asked how I'd heard about the break-in at The Gypsy Caravan, and I told her that CeCe Takes was the first to tell me."

"Did she ask if you're taking any further precautions to protect your shop?"

"It's funny. I wasn't planning on doing much differently until she suggested it. I suppose I've lived in this town for so long, it's hard to imagine anyone meaning me harm."

"Did she ask anything else?"

"Why, yes," Miss Jenkins said, patting her cheek softly as she recalled. "She asked if I had an idea about who broke into The Gypsy Caravan."

"She didn't ask about *your* shop?"

"My shop is small potatoes compared to the break-in at The Gypsy Caravan, Tully. At least that's what I figured. Anyway, I said I didn't know of anyone."

Tully nodded. He could only assume Faith had beaten him to the punch and interviewed every single person involved with the case, though he couldn't imagine how cordial Rick Murdock would have been with her, considering he suspected her as the vandal.

"Thanks, Miss Jenkins. I'll let you know if I uncover anything." Miss Jenkins waved him out the door and down the sidewalk. He had planned on saving Faith's shop for last, but he realized all too late that that had been a huge mistake.

CHAPTER EIGHT

FAITH FINISHED TIGHTENING a screw on a wall shelf when she heard the bells over her front door signal a new visitor.

"Detective McTully," she said, carefully coming down the ladder steps. She knew it was only a matter of time before he showed up demanding answers. Though she wished he was here for more social reasons, she didn't mind admiring his build any chance she got. She wiped her palms down the front of her camo cargo pants, as her hands had gone clammy. What was it about this man that made her heart race? "What can I help you with?"

"That's the problem, Ms. Fitzpatrick—"

"Faith."

He removed his sunglasses with an easy cool.

"I heard you've been interviewing people in town on my behalf."

"Interviewing, yes, but I never told anyone I was doing it on your behalf. That would be illegal." She smiled, playfully. "Plain wrong too."

"But you *have* been making the rounds, asking a lot of questions."

"Of course." Faith scooted her ladder to the other end of the wall shelf and climbed up to the fourth step. Without a word, Tully followed and held the bottom of the ladder to spot her. She wondered where his eyes, now level with her rear, had landed. When she looked, she found him ever respectful, staring at the floor. It made her smile to herself. "It's not that I don't have complete confidence in you or how you do your job—"

"Thanks."

"—but the people in this town think I'm responsible for all the things that have happened over the last few days. You should have seen the looks I got when I went into the hardware store last night. One old man nearly glared me out the door." She zipped the screw with her drill, making a resounding "Ha!" before backing her way down the ladder. Once she was on the last rung, she stopped to meet Tully eye to eye.

She couldn't ignore how he made her feel—nervous, excited, so easily thrown by the mention of his name or a quick glimpse of the man. She also couldn't ignore that she wasn't the kind of woman who ended up with the John McTullys of the world, no matter what the fairy tales said. He was Roseley's golden boy—good man, good friend and son, good at his job. The jury was still out on her. She was marriage challenged, aka divorced, her brand-new business was an unknown and she was, after all, the suspicious out-of-towner with a convict father. She knew she couldn't win Tully's heart, but she would certainly do her best to earn his respect.

"You're innocent until proven guilty, Ms. Fitzpatrick," he said slowly as if choosing his words very carefully. "If the people in this town aren't abiding by those rules—"

"Trust me. I'm used to it." She passed him the drill and when he took it, his hand brushed hers, sending tiny prickles up the nerves of her arm. His touch was electric, and she certainly wasn't used to *that*. Wondering if the sensation had left any impression on him, she paused and found him deeply focused. Was he sizing her up or searching for some indication of guilt? Was it too much to hope that he was feeling what she was feeling?

"No one should have to get used to that," he said.

"What about you, Detective?" His face flinched, waiting for more explanation. "Am I innocent until proven guilty in your book?"

He still hadn't called her by her first name, nor had he acknowledged whether he would anytime soon. It was as good a sign as any that he still considered her a suspect.

"I follow the facts."

"Good. So do I." She stepped off the ladder. "I could be a great help to you, you know."

Tully's eyes widened. "I work alone."

"Yeah, I wondered about that. What about Charlie?"

"Officer Stillwater."

"Right. Doesn't he help you solve crimes?"

"No."

"What about that other fellow… Dex, was it?"

"*Officer* Randall." Faith turned away, her face sour. Officer Randall was a jerk, plain and simple. She had spotted that from their first encounter at The Gypsy Caravan, and she had no desire for a replay.

"Don't you have a partner?"

"No."

"Well, maybe you need one. If these crimes continue, the list of possible suspects will grow. It could quickly unravel into a mess you can't handle all by yourself."

"I work alone," he said, punctuating each word gruffly. "This morning you interfered with a police investigation. Whether or not you're guilty of any wrongdoing—"

"*Not* guilty, thank you."

"—interfering with a police investigation will get you into trouble." She heard the warning in his tone. She knew her jesting would cross a line at some point, but she needed him to understand that this wasn't only her livelihood in jeopardy. It was her reputation, her entire happiness in this town.

"I wasn't interfering. I can talk to whomever I want. I'm a new resident, remember? I was getting to know my new neighbors. I doubt you bat an eye every time CeCe Takes goes running her mouth to folks about Faith Fitzpatrick and her convict father. Where does defamation fall in your personal code of ethics?" She could feel the heaviness of his stare. Those dark brown eyes could go from warm to thundering in under a second flat. But no matter how they transformed, she wanted them on her, studying her every movement.

She turned toward her tool cabinet and tossed the drill bit in the top drawer. Over the last few days she'd sensed his amusement bubbling just under the surface any time she'd encountered him. She'd found kindness, a dutifulness in the way he moved and spoke. She preferred all of that to his seriousness.

"I'm not trying to antagonize you, Detective, and I don't want to interfere with your investigation..."

"But you are. If you want to be absolved from any suspicion, you will stand back and not involve yourself with my case."

She glanced over her shoulder. His energy had shifted. He'd raised the stakes with a warning, ending their playful jesting of a moment ago.

"Oh, will I, Detective?"

"You will, Ms. Fitzpatrick."

"For not knowing me very well, you certainly seem to think I'll listen to you."

"You will."

"News flash—I don't listen to anyone."

He took a deep breath and released it. "Ms. Fitzpatrick, please listen to me."

"Detective, I never took you for being the overconfident type."

"It's in your best interest to listen. It's also in the best interest of my case. I know you'll do the right thing."

The right thing?

Faith faced him, the blood now surging through every vein in her body. She needed him to understand this next part more than she'd ever needed anyone to understand anything.

"What's in my best interest is getting my name cleared as quickly as possible. If it's not, there will be no place in this town for me—ever. I never wanted to leave Roseley. It was my home and the only place I have ever wanted to be. You've been a fixture in this town nearly your entire life, so I'd expect you to get that. I was run out of here, paying the price for someone else's crime and I won't—" Her jaw tightened. The nerves scaffolding her neck had gone taut, tensing more with each word, but she needed him to hear it. "A little vandalism, a few broken windows may not sound like big crimes to you, but they're enough for the people in this town to distrust me or boycott my shop or give me snide looks when I pass by. I lived through that once before, and it's a fate I wouldn't wish on anyone."

She glared now. She knew he was the one used to reading people, but this time it was her turn. "I could no sooner back off this case than you could, Detective. If anything, it'd be harder for me. It's your job, but it's my life."

It was a standoff, neither of them flinching. When she thought she couldn't stand the silence any longer, he blinked, then released a long, nearly inaudible sigh. It snapped her out of the fury that had consumed her quicker than a lit match set to a hay bale.

He gazed around her motorcycle shop as if taking in the contents for the first time. It was ready for the grand opening and, she hoped, ready to make some much-needed money.

"What did you find out?" he said. Faith brought her hands to her hips slowly as if moving them through water. She toyed with the belt of her low-slung pants.

"Pardon?"

"What did you learn this morning? I get a lot of information during second interviews, but I lost that edge when you got involved. I hope you got us something useful."

Us?

Emboldened, she explained, "The Callahan brothers certainly had all the right answers. Prepared ones." The corner of Tully's mouth ticked. He had apparently not enjoyed his interview with them either. "Miss Jenkins sent up a red flag."

"How so?"

"She said she wasn't planning on doing anything else to protect her store. Shouldn't she have at least invested in an extra door lock or something?"

"That's not surprising. She's pretty set in her ways, lived in this town for nearly forty-five years. She's overly trusting and always has been."

Faith shrugged. "I guess I can understand that. My uncle is the same."

"Right. Your uncle is Gus Waterson."

"If the lock broke on his front door, I'm sure he'd never fix it. I wish I trusted anyone as much as he trusts the people in this town."

Tully strolled across the shop, glancing in her direction at this confession. She hadn't meant too much by it, but the more she thought about it, she sadly realized it was true. She trusted Caroline and Trig but other than that...

"Are you riding in the parade?" He stopped at her motorcycle and flicked the sign she'd secured to the back.

"It's good publicity. I hope to return after the parade and officially open my shop. Having another person around here would come in handy, but I have to start somewhere."

"You're doing fine," he said. It was such a

simple sentence, but she was half tempted to believe him. It meant a lot.

"Thanks."

"Small businesses are our lifeblood around here," he continued. "I wish you a lot of success."

"I appreciate that."

"Just promise me one thing."

She raised an eyebrow. "Depends."

"Don't interview anyone else."

"But what if—"

"No one." Faith didn't make promises she couldn't keep, and she knew she couldn't keep that one, especially to someone she admired so much. Someone whose respect and trust she so deeply desired.

"You know I can't do that."

"Ms. Fitzpatrick—"

"Maybe we can come to a compromise."

"You're not in a position to bargain."

"Hear me out." She took a deep breath. "I won't interview people on my own or interfere in your investigation *if* I can tag along with you. I might see something you don't. I can pick up on subtleties you might miss."

"Doubtful and…no."

"I come from a riding background, Detective. The safest way to ride a motorcycle is with a partner riding at your side. It's another person to point out potholes in the road or spot a passing motorist cutting too close. I could tag along, be your extra set of eyes and ears. Maybe I could help you solve the case faster." He groaned and headed to the door.

"You ask too much, Ms. Fitzpatrick."

"It's *Faith*."

"You do pick up on subtleties." She caught his smirk before he slipped on sunglasses and made his way out of the shop. "Have a good day."

Faith moved to the window and watched him saunter to his truck. She wondered if he could sense her staring after him, but whether he did or not, he didn't look back to check.

CHAPTER NINE

FAITH AND CAROLINE arrived at Little Lakeside Sports Shop together, Faith happy to have her cousin by her side. Mara had been friendly after finding out she was Ray Talbert's daughter and though she had high hopes Mara would continue to be an ally, she didn't know who else would be in the store. She didn't need Caroline to go with her, but she appreciated the moral support all the same.

"Hi, Mara," Faith called as they entered. Mara waved from an aisle of fishing poles and hurried to greet them at the door. "I brought a few flyers for Heart Motorcycles."

"I hoped you would," Mara said, motioning them to join her near the register. She handed a tape dispenser to Faith. "You can post one in my front window there. I'll put the rest of them here at the counter."

"Are you getting a lot of business this week?" Caroline asked. Mara tipped her head back dramatically.

"Yes, thank heavens. The tourists have come out of the woodwork—" She lowered her voice to keep nearby customers from hearing. "And they're renting and *buying*."

"Hopefully they'll want me to detail their motorcycles."

"I'm sure you'll get a lot of business once word spreads about your shop." Faith hoped it was only the word about her shop spreading, but she knew that was wishful thinking. Everywhere she looked, she suspected someone was giving her the stink eye. Caroline warned her not to assume the worst in people, but Caroline hadn't gotten the brunt of Ray's blame, which should have been placed squarely on his shoulders and his shoulders alone.

"How are you doing?" Mara lowered her voice, her eyes pooled with empathy. Faith shrugged as if she hadn't given a second thought to her exploding notoriety. She could be honest with Caroline, but no one else in town was friend enough to know her heart—yet.

"Couldn't be better. I'm excited for the opening."

"Good for you," Mara said, breezing around her. "I love that Sportster you have."

"She's getting another motorcycle today," Caroline said. Faith didn't want to explain the circumstances surrounding Old Silver. She'd bought the bike off Bonnie, her former boss, after Bonnie's husband had died. Bonnie had a lot to sell, and when she learned Faith wanted her bike, she had dropped the asking price low enough to make it more of a gift. Faith had bought it after learning that Kyle had been cheating on her and didn't show signs of wanting to stop. Bonnie, worried that Kyle would try to sell the bike out from under Faith, suggested she store the motorcycle for her until Faith could figure out her next steps.

Now that she finally had a place of her own, and a place to not only store the motorcycle but also display it, she had asked Bonnie to ride Old Silver to Roseley for her.

"You own *two* motorcycles?" Mara asked.

"Sure. Why not? I love them."

"I guess I'm the same way with bicycles," Mara said. "Luckily, my shop lets me indulge my love of them."

The bell over the front door rang. Faith turned to find Detective McTully standing in the doorway with Samantha.

"Faith," Samantha said, side-glancing at her brother. "Caroline, what a lovely surprise."

"I had heard you were back in town, Sam," Caroline said. "I follow your blog faithfully."

"Really?" Samantha beamed, flipping her long locks. "Did you see my pictures from Cape Town?"

"Swimming with the sharks? *Yes.* Where are you off to next?"

Tully smiled lovingly and shook his head at Caroline's words.

"Don't encourage her," he said. "She's going to stick around town for a while, aren't you, sis?"

Samantha wrapped both arms around her brother's waist and broke into a wide grin. Faith couldn't help but swallow a murmur of yearning, wanting to be the one pressed against him, savoring his scent, his masculine build. When he gently wrapped an arm around his sister, his stance softened. Samantha patted him playfully on the chest.

"You miss me when I'm gone, don't you, big brother? I bring excitement into your life."

"Samantha, are you and Tully coming for dinner tonight?" Mara asked. "You're both invited."

Faith worked to find her most pleasant, polite face. It was the one she had learned to plaster on when others spoke of awkward personal things in front of her. Tully glanced at her before responding.

"Thanks for the invitation, Mara, but—"

"We'll join you," Samantha said. "I'll bring something too. I buy a mean summer dessert from the grocery store."

Faith's cell phone chimed with a text message. Bonnie had arrived and was parked outside the bike shop.

"Thanks for taking the flyers, Mara," she said. "I have to go. My bike arrived."

"Enjoy your new motorcycle."

"Motorcycle?" Samantha said, her eyelashes fluttering wildly. "Another Sportster?"

"Street Glide."

"I've seen those on the road. I've been interested in motorcycles for a while now, but I've never been home long enough to consider one. Haven't I been interested in motorcycles?" She playfully swatted Tully on the arm. "Mind if we wander down to your shop with you? I'd love to see it."

Tully's face was as neutral as a pool of standing water, and it drove her crazy. She'd wanted to talk to him again about helping with the case, or at the very least, she wanted to ask him about his leads. But more important, she wanted to see something in his expression that hinted at what he thought of her.

"Uh, of course," Faith said, leading them out of the shop after a wave to Mara. Samantha hurried to Faith's side, chatting while they strolled down the sidewalk. Faith didn't mind Samantha's exuberance to see her Street Glide, since she had a growing anticipation bubbling in her stomach too.

Bonnie nodded a hello as they approached. She was an unexpressive woman, hefty, brass and a little rough around the edges, so to speak. She was also a person who would step in front of a speeding train for the people she most cared about. She'd been Faith's employer at the mechanic shop, and over the last couple of years, Faith had come to think of Bonnie as something of a mentor.

"How'd it ride?" Faith asked as Samantha moved to straddle Old Silver. Bonnie tabled her response, addressing Samantha first. Her voice as stern as a principal overseeing detention.

"You'd better back your butterfingers off that bike, honey, if you know what's good for you."

Samantha froze before easing away from the motorcycle. Faith caught Detective Mc-

Tully's smirk, but it faded before Samantha could spot it.

"I'm...I'm so sorry, ma'am."

"You never touch another person's bike until they say so. It's not a puppy dog."

Samantha's eyes rounded. "I was only... Faith?"

Faith ran her hand over the handlebars and motioned for Samantha to go ahead. "It's fine," she said. "You can sit on it but climb on from the left side." She held the bike steady until Samantha could get her footing and swing a leg over. Once settled on the leather seat, Samantha smiled proudly. Her emotional-rebound rate seemed to be about ten seconds.

"John used to have a motorcycle in college, didn't you, John?"

"I rode a little."

Faith's face perked in surprise. He'd led her to believe that he had never ridden.

"Did you get your motorcycle license?"

"Of course he did," Samantha said with a chuckle. "He even took the extended class. He could probably teach it if he really wanted. John is nothing if not thorough."

Caroline gently pressed a nudge into the small of Faith's back as if she were passing her a note in study hall. Faith steeled herself against her cousin's teasing, refusing to acknowledge the newest development. As if she hadn't already found John McTully to be the epitome of attractiveness, he shared one of her passions as well.

"You should take this for a spin, big brother," Samantha suggested, climbing off the bike. "I'm sure you miss it."

"No," Tully said. "It's been a while since I rode."

"It's like riding a bike," Bonnie said. "That's where they get the expression, you know. Are there some deserted back roads you could practice on until you find your legs again?"

Caroline pressed more strongly into Faith's back. Finally, her cousin chimed in.

"I have to get back to the house. Faith, why don't you take Detective McTully out to see the sights?"

"But Bonnie just got here and might need me to—"

Bonnie wafted a hand as if batting away her excuse. "I don't mind, kiddo, and the engine is already warmed up for you. I need to get to the supermarket to pick up some snacks for my bus ride home. It'll be a long one."

"I'll take you," Samantha chirped. Faith assumed Samantha could make fast friends with nearly anyone, even someone who had scolded her not two minutes ago.

"Works for me," Bonnie said. "Faith, take care and I'll talk to you soon." She looked at Samantha. "Where to?"

"I'm parked down the street." And just like that, Bonnie, Samantha and Caroline scattered, leaving her alone with her detective.

"It's a beautiful bike," Tully said.

"Thanks. I wonder..."

"What?"

"Why didn't you tell me you used to ride?"

"I don't remember if I did."

"*You didn't.* In fact, you kind of led me to believe that you didn't like it."

"I don't think so."

"No?"

He strolled around to the other side of the motorcycle and she caught a glint of excitement in his expression.

"I rode in college but sold my motorcycle when I moved home."

"Why?"

"I have my reasons."

Faith squinted against his answer but decided to let it go—for now. She wanted to see him riding. She was curious to see if he could cut loose a little bit and tear it up on the road. Mostly she wanted to see if he would accept an invitation from one of his prime suspects.

"I can't picture you riding," she said. His head jerked, noticeably offended. "Nope," she continued. "I'd have to see it to believe it."

He threw a leg over the seat and gripped the handlebars. She'd seen the same expression on folks who had come into Bonnie's shop over the years. That desire to hit the open road and feel the wind smack you hard and cold in the face could be overwhelming sometimes. She could tell he was trying to work something out in his mind, but her instincts told her that she'd hooked him.

"I'll lock up," she said, jostling her keys before ducking into her shop. She didn't give him a chance to protest, to offer an excuse of why he shouldn't. She knew he'd decided to go for a ride with her from the moment the others had left.

WHEN TULLY FIRED up Old Silver, the loud thunder crack of the engine split his nerves like electricity skittering across his skin. The engine was hot from running all day, but there was still gas in the tank.

He waited for Faith and calmly told himself that a brisk ride would be fine. It wasn't like him to engage socially with suspects; in fact, he'd never done something like this before. But it seemed fine as long as he kept the ride short and sweet. A jaunt around the block would be harmless. His professionalism could stay safely intact for a few minutes.

He glanced behind him to gauge the size of the seat. With no backrest attached, Faith would hang on to him to keep from falling off. She'd have to slide her arms around his waist and press her curvy body to his. The thought sent another wave of electric nerves scattering over his skin.

As the minutes ticked by with no sight of her, he wondered if she'd had second thoughts. That possibility was sobering, but no sooner had he considered this than he heard her Sportster from down the street. She had gone through the back street and come around the block before pulling up next to him.

"Here," she said, leaning out to hand him a black helmet. When she did, the top hem of her tank top shifted, highlighting a delicate dip of palest skin not yet kissed by the summer sun. A deep hum escaped from his throat, masked by the rumble of their motorcycles. "Safety first."

He accepted the helmet and rapped his fingers against it.

"We're only going around the block." He appreciated being safe but a loop through side streets didn't pose much threat to his safety. Besides, the only person who could wear a helmet and do it justice was Faith. With her dark, messy locks sticking out from under her helmet, she looked every bit as gorgeous as she had when he'd first seen her at the gas station.

Her pretty mouth curled in a smile.

"That's what you think, Detective." Before he could reply, she sped to the stop sign and hung a right, glancing back in his direction as he hustled to secure his helmet. By the time he'd caught up with her, two stop signs later, her face was all smile, either pleased with him or pleased with herself.

She called over the idling motorcycles, "What's Tamarack like these days? Do they still maintain it or have the four-wheelers taken it over?"

The early founders had cleared Tamarack, a road leading straight through the heart of Roseley State Park, as efficiently as a pack of enthusiastic beavers. The thickly forested park had half a dozen trails perfect for day hikers, bicyclists or joggers, and Tamarack was the only way to get there.

"It's not bad."

"It's not too bumpy?" she said. "I'm relying on your judgment here."

He smiled carefully. "I'm surprised you trust anyone's judgment but your own. Aren't you the same woman who said she never listened to anyone?"

"I've been known to defer to others from time to time." He figured they were the same in that regard. Before he could say more, she turned onto the road that led to Tamarack, waiting until they'd hit the outskirts before cracking the throttle.

The road to Tamarack was hilly, but direct, with the residential neighborhoods shrinking behind them and the lush, vast tree line of the park ahead of them. Tully savored the wind in his face and the energy of the motorcycle speeding over the open road. He also didn't mind his view of Faith, sitting proudly on her Sportster.

He hadn't been on a motorcycle since he'd sold his. Hadn't thought it responsible to keep it when other things, other people, required his attention and focus. But as he loosened his grip on the handlebars and relaxed back on the seat, the ease of riding came back to him, his muscle memory hitting the cruise control. After all this time, he now regretted selling his motorcycle.

Tully pulled up beside Faith, the two of them sharing the lane as they approached the turnoff to Tamarack.

"How are you doing?" she called.

"I could get used to this!"

"That's the spirit!" She accelerated, widening the gap between them. He had no choice but to give chase, and he remembered his sister's words. He'd wanted to give chase from the first encounter with Faith, and now he had a legitimate reason for doing so.

There was something exciting about Faith, something about her that made him wonder if she'd always been a bit of a rule breaker. She had an unapologetic attitude about who she was and what she wanted. He had never thought of himself as being attracted to such an independent woman, but the more he got to know Faith, saw her spiritedness, the more he realized he'd been approaching his dating life all wrong. Sure, he'd gone out with nice women in the past, but he couldn't think of one of them to compare her to. They all blended together while Faith stood out. She kept him on his toes. As the road passed under their tires and Faith beamed at him, he began to consider she was one of a kind.

Tully scanned the landscape for four-wheelers as they directed their bikes onto Tamarack. He was pleased to spot none. At its wide mouth, Tamarack was paved with asphalt, but Tully knew that as they rode deeper into the woods, it would wind and narrow before finally transitioning to a dirt path.

Tully pulled ahead of Faith, as he knew Tamarack best, and signaled for her to slow down. He downshifted to a steady cruise as they escaped the blazing July sun and slipped into the wooded shade. The crackle of the engine felt invasive against the still backdrop of the woods, so when he pulled off onto the shoulder, at the foot of Falcon's Peak, Faith followed and didn't seem to mind.

They cut their engines and slid off their bikes, Faith taking off her helmet and shaking out her hair.

"Do you remember Falcon's Peak?" he asked, setting his helmet on the seat. "It's a pretty long hike, but there's a closer lookout we could see."

She nodded. "I know the one you're thinking of. I spent a lot of time up there after things with my dad blew up."

He understood. Nature was one of the few things he'd found that could help heal the broken bits, or at least provide a good resting place for a while.

"Are you up for a hike?" He glanced at her black leather boots and appreciated that she at least had the proper footwear.

She dug into her saddlebags, producing two water bottles, and tossed him one. Then she slipped off her jacket, folded it and tucked it into the saddlebag. Her saunter was confident, her gait wide for her frame, and her toned arms, most likely earned from working in a mechanic shop all day, swung carefully at her sides. She tipped her head toward the trail.

"Ready?" she asked. He wasn't sure. The idea of taking a moment to watch her crossed his mind. He wanted to run his hand over the bare skin of her sloping shoulder. He wanted to trace his fingers over her heart tattoo and linger there for an amount of time that wouldn't be deemed professional at all.

Instead he held out a hand for her to lead the way.

"After you."

They climbed for a while, their steps navigating the narrow trail that wound steeply up the mountain. Neither talked much, which was fine with him. He preferred to listen to the songbirds and his inner monologue that ran double-time, reminding him that he was a detective, and she was a suspect in a crime he was investigating. He wanted that monologue to talk some sense into him, reason with him about why thoughts of touching her were completely off the table.

Finally, when they'd reached the crest of the mountain, Faith released a labored sigh of exasperation.

"We made it," she called, jogging ahead to the steep ledge overlooking much of the town and lake. The ledge wasn't wide, five yards at best, and it was framed on either side by thick foliage in full summer bloom. Tully hesitated, looking for somewhere to funnel the inner turmoil that had only grown with each step up the mountain. Meanwhile, Faith crept closer to the edge and peered over.

"Careful," he said, his tone serious. She ignored him, dragging her boot to send small rock shards over the side.

"It hasn't changed."

"Did you expect it to?"

"So much else has changed over the last ten years that… Yeah, I guess I did."

Tully joined her on the ledge, lowering himself to sit on it. She followed and dangled her legs over the side.

"I can't quite see my shop from here, but the lake is spectacular."

It was true. The water ripples on Little Lake Roseley sparkled like white-hot firecrackers. Speedboats and jet skis skimmed the surface, leaving a wake in every direction.

"Do you live on the lake?" she asked.

"No, but I live pretty close. Mara and her husband, Peter, let me use their dock for my fishing boat."

"Ah. You're a fisherman."

"Among other things."

"Did you fish as a kid?"

"I used to wake up long before sunrise and fish until it was dark. Once in a while my dad would take me out on the boat."

"Is your dad still around?"

"He lives out that way." He gestured to the other side of Roseley State Park. They couldn't see it from where they sat, but Tully was all too familiar with the barren stretch of land between the park and the much larger Lake Roseley. There was nothing except fields of tall weeds and places where people illegally dumped their trash or committed other minor crimes. For as far back as Tully could remember, folks had coined the land "The Void" because there was nothing on it. Nothing, that is, aside from his father.

Faith squinted in the direction Tully had motioned. She winced back at him.

"On The Void? I didn't think anyone could."

"He squats there."

"Why?"

Tully had asked himself that question more times than he'd like to count. He believed his father to be of sound mind. When he talked to him, his dad had good judgment when it came to things that mattered. However, for the past few years his dad had preferred to stay in the little pop-up cabin he'd constructed. He said the quiet helped him think, helped him breathe. Maybe too, Tully often thought, it helped him forget.

"Does he live there year-round?"

"Mostly. When the temperature drops too low for his liking, he wanders home for a few days."

"So he has a real house?"

"Yes."

"Do you live in it?"

"No." Tully nearly huffed at the thought. He loved his father, but he had spent most of his childhood counting the days until he was old enough to move out. Eventually his dad might need to move in with him, but he wasn't about to rush that next stage of life—for either of them.

"Is he married?"

"Not…anymore." Tully leaned back on his hands and surveyed the landscape. He could feel Faith's eyes on him, could tell he had given something away by how he'd reacted. As much as he didn't talk about his dad with anyone, he absolutely refused to speak about his mother. Even he and Samantha had an unspoken rule to mention their mother only when it was absolutely necessary.

But there was a standard phrase he used whenever the topic of his mother came up.

"I lost my mom when I was a kid. It was sudden."

His words brought on a crashing silence, his throat suddenly going dry. It was uncharacteristic for him to feel anything at the mention of his mother because he rarely let himself think of her long enough to remember it all. But as Faith drew up a leg to better turn and study him, he found himself stumbling into unknown territory.

"I'm sorry," she whispered.

This was the part when he usually segued to another topic, but in the stillness, he couldn't think of anything else to say. Without realizing, he continued, "My dad tuned out after that."

"Tuned out? What do you mean?"

"He kind of stopped functioning, stopped parenting us."

She hummed a note, signaling her understanding. "I wondered why he would live out in the middle of nowhere like that."

"He's not mentally ill," Tully explained. He felt it important that she know that. He wanted to make clear that he would never abandon his father to his own devices if he was ill or unstable. "He just wants to be alone. My sister and I have tried to help him, tried to get him back on track, back into life. Anything we say falls on deaf ears. I maintain his house and keep it ready for him, for whenever he decides to come home. We keep waiting for that day, but the more that time goes by, the less likely I think that will ever happen."

"Do you visit him often?"

Tully sighed. “Not nearly enough. Talking to him can be difficult.”

“I understand. I don’t talk much to my mom either.” She said it as if he had been asking her to barter. As if she understood he had offered her something secret and vulnerable and might recoil unless she offered something up too. “After my dad got arrested,” she said, “he and my mom divorced. She skipped out on me to go live in Florida with an old high school flame who had seen her on the news. She didn’t take me with her. Nice, huh?”

He sat quietly, letting her finish. “I completed my last year of high school, living with my uncle and cousins. I didn’t want to be a bother, an extra responsibility to anyone, even if they were family.” She heaved a deep breath as if recalling something as pleasant as a toothache. “Being in the public eye was awful, so as soon as I graduated, I got out of here fast.”

“I know your uncle. I doubt he thought of you as a bother.”

“Well, after being a bother to my dad and mom, it wasn’t a narrative I had a hard time convincing myself of.”

“You graduated from Roseley High, right?”

She adjusted her shoulders. “Yes.”

"What class?"

"I was a couple years behind you." She pressed a palm to the ground between them and leaned her weight on it. It was as if she wanted to say something, something important. She held a look he had seen many times before, usually when interrogating a suspect. There was an energy that fell over someone when they had resolved to tell the truth. Confessing took a decision to let go of the lie, let go of the concocted story. To remember a lie, a person sometimes had to repeat it over again in one's mind. It kept the fabricated details fresh and at the ready. It kept the truth from seeping out. Right before a person confessed, eyes cleared as if a cool breeze of fresh air had awoken him or her from a hot, balmy dream. "It was a long time ago, I know, but…I…"

If she had something to tell him, something important to say, he wanted to help her. He wanted to guide it from her lips and release her from whatever it was that was holding her back.

He sat forward, out of interest, out of support, but when he did, her gaze deepened, sending a shock wave through every cell of his body. She'd read something more in his movement, saw something he'd been working to hide over the last few days. Perched above the forest, above the town and lake and all the people who would wag a finger and shake their head if they spotted the two of them together, they sat, drinking in the sight of each other. If she had something to confess, he might find himself trading a confession of his own. He'd have to confess that he longed to touch her—once.

The pitch of her breathing quickened. A soft breeze stirred around them, like some invisible entity circling and pulling them closer together. He needed to crane his neck, find a pocket of cool air somewhere above the clouds that could clear his senses and smack some sense into him. That was what he needed, but what he wanted…

He could feel his steadiness wavering, feel the inevitability of tumbling down a rabbit hole from which he could never climb back out again. There was a line he shouldn't cross with Faith, a code of professionalism he had never been tempted to bend until now. When he thought the moment couldn't go on any longer, she spoke.

"John," she whispered. His stare landed on the sweet parting of her mouth. He savored the sound of his name on her lips, wanting her to say it again. And for a split second, he thought she could read his mind, could run circles around his detective skills with some kind of telepathy, because as he wished, she said his name again.

This time he didn't hesitate. He took her chin in his hand, grazing that perfect bottom lip with his thumb. He lingered there, looking for her tell, a warning sign that he had wandered into something he shouldn't have. But when her eyes fell to his mouth, he leaned in and kissed her.

CHAPTER TEN

FAITH COULDN'T BELIEVE she was kissing John McTully. She'd fantasized about this moment since she'd first watched him defend the freshman. That one instance had stirred a longing in her heart to be near him, with him. To the other girls he'd been a handsome, popular, athletic upperclassman, and to her he'd been all that but more.

It had been an unfair fight that day in the art room, three against one, but the odds hadn't stopped John. He'd been admirable in a world where she didn't see many examples of that. His actions had captured her imagination instantly. In the few instances afterward when she spotted him, she'd wished to one day be cherished by him.

Meeting him again, after she'd accumulated a decade of mistakes and emotional scars, had her taking notice of him in a more meaningful way. Every encounter with him proved he'd matured into a good man, an honorable man, and it had not just reignited her attraction to him, it had her craving his presence like a weary traveler seeking shelter in a snowstorm. Strong, warm, safe—that was John McTully. But what could she be to him?

Her place on the high school totem pole had been low, if not nonexistent. She thought that that was the order of things and was willing to play her role until the day she'd watched John come to another's aid. Instantly, she had wished to be more—because of him, because she wanted him.

In the years since, she'd pushed so hard to be someone worth remembering. She'd made changes. The changes on the inside were harder to manipulate than the ones on the outside, and were still taking shape. Men were more aware of her, but she still didn't feel like they saw her, not in the way she wanted. But the way the man in front of her now looked at her felt different. She felt seen, safe and respected.

Faith touched her fingertips to the rough stubble along his cheek. Her lips melted against his, so warm and experienced. His kiss was everything she had imagined. He leaned closer, his cologne drifting over her, as he nipped delicately at her mouth. A smile curled at the corners of her mouth, one she couldn't help if she tried her darnedest, as she drew his tongue to hers, smoothly, sweetly.

She had spent the last few years learning to be strong, to be someone who others would think twice before messing with. She hadn't adhered to a survival-of-the-fittest approach to life before Ray's scandal, but she'd gotten a crash course in it soon after.

The summer before Ray ran the family name through the mud, she'd logged a lot of hours at Uncle Gus's house, hanging with him in the garage as he fixed up old motorbikes and four-wheelers. At first, she'd taken to the idea of spending time at Uncle Gus's house, toiling away in the garage with him. With Caroline turning her nose up at grease under her fingernails and Trig busy playing baseball, she'd discovered a job opening in Uncle Gus's garage as his dutiful apprentice.

As the year passed, Faith had begun to look forward to fixing up the motorbikes as much as she enjoyed the time with Uncle Gus. She was developing skills she hadn't thought she had before, tearing apart broken engines and rebuilding them to working order. She'd begun to see herself as someone else—capable, determined and, though she couldn't have put it into exact words back then, somewhat tougher.

Once her father was arrested and she was planning her next steps somewhere, anywhere, other than Roseley, she'd found that she liked her new skills and wanted to go somewhere where she could develop them. As if trying on an alter ego and zipping the collar tightly, she had decided to adopt the new persona that came with it. It fit just right.

In the years since leaving Roseley, she'd learned to take care of herself, to take pride in her work, to take responsibility for her actions when she made mistakes. And after she'd married Kyle, she'd learned that some mistakes took longer to heal than others.

At no time in the past ten years had she allowed herself to be weak, or at least, she couldn't be perceived as weak. She'd taken that accessory off the minute she'd decided to leave Roseley. She'd decided that she may not always be liked, and certainly not loved, but she would be respected.

Standing in John's presence twelve years ago, with his strong, confident energy, shifted something inside her. He didn't dominate or challenge or assert himself the way some men in her life had. He didn't chase money, like her father, or ignore her, like her mother. And not once in any of the conversations they'd had since she'd returned did he ever doubt her. In fact, there were a few times when he seemed to watch her with wonder. The satisfaction that gave her was intoxicating. It settled something in her soul, in the dark corners of her heart she fought so hard to hide from the rest of the world. She felt like a bull charging, like she needed to demand that the world take her for all she was. But he had begun to call her bluff. Instead of a matador who wanted to kill what she thought of as her enemy, he wanted to lead her back out the gate and assure her she didn't need to go into the arena in the first place.

He wrapped an arm around her waist and pulled her closer. Nothing about his kiss felt rushed or greedy. She felt moved by his tenderness. He was a man who could likely get anything he wanted without a second thought, but chose not to. He chose a restraint that had her leaning in more. He seemed different from the men of her past, the men who took without apology and scoffed when you didn't let them take enough. The thought that he could be this attractive and be good, truly good, honorable even, felt like more than she could wish for. It had her body tingling in all the places he touched and aching in all the places he hadn't yet.

She ran her fingers through his hair, drawing them down the back of his neck and pulling his face to hers. When she did, a groan rose in his throat. He delighted in her touch, in her kiss, in *her.* The revelation sent her heart thudding hard against her breastbone. So hard that she thought he would hear it beating.

She ran her hand up his chest, over the fabric of his shirt, feeling the tightness of his muscles, the quickness of his breath. She gasped for a breath she wasn't sure she'd taken since his mouth had first found hers.

Never in all her heart did she ever think she could draw a reaction from him. She'd never thought, in all her wildest dreams, that he would ever be interested in her, a woman who'd been shamed as a teenager and whispered about ever since. A woman who carried much more than her fair share of regrets and hurt and scandal. But here they were, together, kissing in a place where she'd cried salty tears as a teen, wishing all her sorrows away.

Suddenly, she felt him pull back. She blinked,

aware that somewhere along the way she'd gotten lost in the moment, in the sweetness of having a dream fulfilled. She'd lost an inhibition she now realized she needed to keep going.

He drew his hand from around her waist and held her face between his palms.

"Hey," she whispered, raising her hands to grip his biceps that hugged like bookends. Why did he have to be so strong? She squeezed her eyes shut, not wanting the dream to evaporate like his kisses on her skin. "I'm sorry. Did I do something wrong?"

He flicked his nose sweetly over hers before pressing his forehead to hers.

"No," he said, the word settling there between the two of them. He was lying. She knew she had done something wrong, had interrupted the momentum somehow. She could sense it. He had wanted to kiss her and had wanted to touch her, but she'd gunned it too fast, accelerated like it was a race when only a Sunday drive had been on the day's agenda.

"Are you seeing someone? Is that it?" she asked. Her cousins had mentioned women he'd dated, mentioned recent outings he'd had with Emily. It was too late to be asking the question, and as her heart now felt very unprotected, it was the wrong time to hear an answer that was anything other than no. But as perfect as he seemed, she knew there had to be something wrong, something that would prove this was too good to be true. A girlfriend she was unaware of was most plausible.

"No."

"No?" She wanted him to elaborate, to tell her why he held back. She brought her hands to cover his, which still cupped her cheeks. "Is it me, then?"

He leaned away slightly. The midday sun had lightened the hue of his dark brown eyes to umber. With each blink, they swelled with golden specks. She lost herself in them. His brow knit together as if he was forming a response that he really needed her to understand. He took another breath, but whether he did so out of resolve or frustration, she couldn't be sure.

When the corner of his mouth lifted, she knew he didn't want to elaborate, and she just hoped it was for a reason that didn't involve her.

His cell phone vibrated in his pocket, breaking their moment. When he answered it, pressing the phone to his ear and turning away from her, she smoothed her hair off her face and paused. His voice was low and serious.

He turned back, sliding the phone into his pocket.

"I have to take a ride out to The Void."

"Is it your dad? Is he okay?"

He frowned, and she could tell he didn't really know.

"Something's happened and I need to go help him—"

"Let's go," Faith said, scrambling to her feet.

"I'll return your bike to the shop when I get back," he began. "I don't know how long I'll be."

"Obviously. But I can ride out there with you. I don't have anything else to do today." It was a lie. She had a million things to do before the parade and her shop's grand opening, but she hoped he was too preoccupied with his dad to see through it. She'd be as free and eager as a schoolchild volunteering to run a teacher's errand if it meant a little more time with him.

"I don't expect you to do that. You probably have to get back to your store."

"Nope," she said, brushing off her hands as he stood. "I'll come and help you."

"Oh, you will, will you?"

"I'm happy to help. I want to."

"You don't even know my dad," he said, each word cautious.

"But I know you." Her reply was more chipper than she had intended, and his brow flinched as a result. Pretending she didn't notice, she picked up her water bottle, unscrewed the cap and took a few gulps. The water was lukewarm and did nothing to quench the thirst she still had to be in his arms.

"You don't know me that well," he continued, claiming his water bottle and following suit.

"You had your mouth on mine not a minute ago. I think we're at least *getting to know* each other, wouldn't you say?"

"Are we?" He nearly coughed, wiping his forearm over his mouth. She smiled, amused as he cleared his throat. "I appreciate the offer, but my dad is pretty hard to handle. It will be better if I show up alone."

"Yes, I suppose you think that would be better. Earlier you alluded to the fact that your dad can be a bit—" His brow flinched again, and she knew her word choice was important. "Prickly?" He nodded and took another drink. "Luckily for you, I have a history of handling prickly men. I'm somewhat of a pro." She hoped he understood that she was referring to her job working in the mechanic shop, dealing with huffy, scruffy guys and calling things like she saw them. And while that was true, 100 percent true, they weren't the only prickly men from her past. "Come on," she said, making her way back down the trail. "We'll be there and back before you can think of another excuse to refuse my help."

TULLY EASED THE Street Glide, the bike Faith had affectionately referred to as Old Silver, to a stop at the end of a narrow driveway. Nothing about the path, with its muddy, matted grass, suggested that anyone lived at the end of it, but he knew better. He had unfortunately walked this path more times than he could count over the last few years and each time his attempt to get his father home failed.

Faith pulled up behind him and cut the engine of her Sportster. He made sure to get off his motorcycle first so he could watch her reaction. He considered how he could get used to watching her expressions every day.

"We have to walk from here," he said, though it was no surprise. No one would drive a car up the path unless it was a truck with four-wheel drive. Riding a motorcycle was completely out of the question.

"How far is it?" she asked, matching her step with his.

"Not far." They moved silently, only the unrelenting buzzing of cicadas in their ears. They were out in the open, nothing but wild grass and tall weeds for at least a hundred yards. Without any shade, the July sun weighed heavily on them as if it was set to broil them alive. He figured Faith rode her motorcycle all summer and was therefore used to wearing jeans in this kind of heat. Still, he thought, as he caught her wiping perspiration off her face, trekking through The Void wasn't the kind of adventure he would have preferred after their first kiss.

Their kiss.

He still couldn't wrap his head around the fact that he'd kissed her, nor that he thought of it as their *first*. He implied, if only to himself, that he expected there to be more of them. That thought was in a dead heat against the opposing notion that there shouldn't be any more. He was investigating her. Maybe she wasn't a prime suspect, maybe he hadn't interviewed her officially at the station, but she wasn't free and clear from suspicion either.

He pushed his conflicted feelings for Faith out of his head, focusing only on the task at hand. After a minute, they rounded a bend. He pointed in the direction of his father's tumble-down shack. It had been assembled from a kit, the company promising that two men could build it in a weekend. From the looks of it, it was more likely two men could have assembled it in an afternoon. It peeked out from behind a nest of pine trees. His father said they kept the wind out, but Tully wondered if he hoped to also keep his demons out.

Faith's boot caught and snagged a piece of twine laid across the path. Tully groaned as the twine pulled a cluster of rusted tin cans off a nearby tree stump, their clanking sounding a fierce homemade alarm. She jumped, horrified at her mistake, but he held up a hand to show it was all right. For as many times as he visited, even he occasionally forgot and snagged the twine.

The clanking drew Duke, Walter's chocolate Labrador retriever, from somewhere deep in the nearby woods. He came leaping through the tall grass, cutting a straight line to Faith. Faith froze for a few seconds before Duke leaped up into her arms. Balancing on his hind legs, he planted a paw on both of her shoulders and slobbered wet kisses to her chin and neck. For a few moments, they danced awkwardly as Faith released a hearty squeal. Her laughter poured out of her as she collapsed to the ground with Duke. Kneeling over him, she tousled the dog's fur and scratched him hard behind the ears.

"You love that, don't you?" she said. "You need some lovin', don't you?"

"Some guard dog he is," Tully muttered. "He'll lick everyone to death." He'd surprised his dad with Duke the year before. Feeling slightly defeated by his dad's stubborn-to-the-core refusals to come home, he adopted Duke to keep his dad company. Tully felt a little better knowing Dad had Duke. He wasn't under any delusions that Duke would protect Walter, but the chocolate Lab had managed to work something of a miracle over the last year. He'd made his dad care about something, finally.

"You're such a good boy," Faith said, patting the dog on the neck as his tongue wagged in a happy pant. "I wish I had known about you. I'd have brought you treats. Yes, I would have," she whispered. "Lots and lots of treats."

"Tully? Is that you? Identify yourself!" The

old man's voice boomed from the shack. If the tin cans didn't scare trespassers away, the gravelly warning his father cried certainly would.

"It's me," Tully said, glancing at Faith, who hurried to her feet. He watched to see how she would take his dad, take all of it, take the oddity of this place when the only thing that carried any normalcy was Duke's slobbery grin.

Walter hustled as best he could, dragging his tattered, unhemmed overalls in the dirt at his heels. His salt-and-pepper hair was mussed. His gray shirt had most likely been white once but now carried enough stains to act as a modern timeline. Even from a distance, he could tell the orange handkerchief around his father's neck was soaked through with sweat.

Only he and Samantha ever came back here, and Samantha did rarely. Charlie had accompanied him a few times, mostly in the winter when he worried about what he would find in the shack and needed his friend to help carry groceries and supplies. Charlie was like the brother he'd never had, growing up alongside him from the time they were children. He had known his dad before the decline. He'd been a playmate before he and Samantha had lost their mother. But even Charlie had been banished to the truck. Besides Samantha and Charlie, he had never brought anyone else to this place, and he wasn't sure why he did now.

"Who's that with ya?" Walter stumbled over to them on shaky legs, propping himself up on some sitting logs, or so Walter had named them. He hoped his father's curiosity at seeing a new visitor would keep Walter preoccupied while he assessed the situation. Tully looked at her, trying to see her the way his dad might. She really was stunning.

"I'm Faith Fitzpatrick," she said, releasing her grip on Duke's collar. The dog went barreling over to Walter. His dad sat back in surprise when Faith stretched out a hand. Tully swallowed a surprise of his own when his father took it. If she wanted to convey she wasn't afraid of him, the message had come through loud and clear.

Walter frowned up into her face before finally nodding curtly.

"Walter McTully. That there is Duke."

"We met." She chuckled and turned her attention again to the dog, who was clearly waiting for her. "He's the perfect welcoming committee. He's beautiful."

"He's not bad," Walter said. Tully knew better. Walter loved Duke more than that dog loved bacon. His father turned his sights on him. "Did you get a motorcycle?"

"It's mine," Faith said, straightening. "I have a Sportster and a Street Glide." Walter shifted on his seat, squinting at Faith like she'd been outed as a double agent.

"You ride?"

"Sure do. I'm opening a motorcycle repair shop tomorrow."

"That right?"

"Yes." Faith looked pleased with herself, but Tully knew the feeling would be short-lived with his dad there.

Walter ran a hand down the length of his face, smoothing the patchy whiskers that added to his disheveled appearance.

"Now what on earth do you want to go and do a stupid thing like that for?"

"Excuse me?"

"That's about the dumbest thing I've ever heard, and I've been around a long time."

Tully stepped forward to quell his father's outburst, but Faith didn't seem to mind. She shoved her hands in the front pockets of her jeans and strolled around the clearing. His father, obviously bothered by how she infiltrated his space, muttered a series of unrecognizable words under his breath that Tully assumed were profane. Walter scrambled to his feet. He shifted his body to stay between Faith and his shack. They were doing some sort of dance, Tully thought, watching in amazement. If Walter had expected Faith to cower under his criticism, he was in for an awakening.

Faith studied the trees in the distance and then ambled around the sitting logs to stare at the shack, not ten paces away. She seemed careful not to wander too closely. Walter chattered to himself like a squirrel angry with intruders. He might not be hoarding an acorn stash, but the shack was all he had, and Faith apparently had experience peeking into trees.

"Do you ride, Walter?" she said, turning away to admire the impressive woodpile his father added to every day. Two feet high and at least six feet wide, each log was axed to the same length, making the woodpile seem less like a necessity and more like a work of art.

"Never."

"Dad, you used to ride a motorcycle," Tully offered, stepping into a shady spot and pushing his sunglasses on top of his head. Duke bounded over, happy to collect head scratches from all visitors. "You used to ride back before I was born."

Walter grumbled and waved a dismissive hand at him.

"You mean with your mother. Gah! Waste of time."

At the mention of his mother, Tully felt a muscle at the base of his neck tense. Faith seemed to sense his unease and patted a hand on the woodpile as distraction.

"Did you cut these yourself, Walter?"

His father shrugged. "Ain't nobody else out here going to do it."

"Will this last you the winter?"

"Nope. Needs to be shoulder high by the first snowfall."

"Are you allowed to cut down the trees around here—"

"Who is gonna stop me?" Walter bellowed. Faith tipped her head, studying him. The one thing Tully could be sure of was that Faith wasn't just putting up a good front. If he was a betting man, he'd say she truly wasn't afraid of his dad, while most people were.

"Dad, what did you need help with?" Tully asked. It was time to get on with things before Walter decided to test Faith's threshold for angry old men.

"Don't trouble yourself."

"It's no trouble."

"I can do it myself." Tully knew his father wouldn't have called him if he hadn't desperately needed the help.

"Faith, could you wait out here while I help my dad?" She patted the tops of her thighs, calling over Duke to keep her company.

Walter mumbled in concession. "I guess you're already here..."

Tully followed his dad through the pine trees, holding up a hand to keep from being hit in the face with branches. Inside, Tully found that the place was as he'd seen it weeks earlier. The wood-burning stove stood in the middle of the shack like the domineering eyesore it was. A tiny bed was pressed into a corner next to a generator. Some pots and pans, cans of food and tools were also stacked neatly along the wall. It wasn't much, the entire scene pulled from the pages of rural living. The only thing that was a clue to modern times was Walter's cell phone.

Tully had bought his father the smartphone years ago and was relieved to discover that The Void wasn't void of cell service. The monthly phone bill was something Tully happily paid since it gave him peace of mind. If his dad needed help, he could call. Whether or not he *would* call was another story, but he could at least give Walter the option.

Tully cringed when he noted the shack's ceiling, or lack thereof. The wooden planks, once nailed together with the precision of an engineer, had aged and rotted, buckling in like a slotted spoon.

The sight was a warning sign. He needed to get his dad home before winter.

Walter said, "I don't need your help fixing it, if that's what you're thinking. I need someone else to hold the load-bearing beam in place so I can reinforce it. Shouldn't take too long. Stand over there and push up, would ya?"

"What about these rotten boards? They won't keep—"

"I'm replacing those. It's only the beam I need for now."

Tully dragged over a step stool, climbed up and pushed the beam up as hard as he could.

"Hold 'er still now," Walter ordered, fumbling with his hammer and nails. Tully would have preferred the speed of a drill gun but said nothing as his father furiously worked. After a minute or two, his father told him to relax and take a breather while he moved to a new spot along the beam. Tully happily complied.

After what felt like an eternity, Walter declared the beam secure. He dropped his hammer in a bucket of tools, then wiped his hands down the front of his overalls. The fade marks on his upper thighs showed where he had made the same motion a thousand times before.

"That's it," Walter said, which Tully knew was the best thank-you he could expect. He led them back out to the clearing, where Faith waited at the sitting logs with Duke's head resting lazily in her lap.

"Samantha's home," Tully said, wanting to accomplish something other than mending ceilings. His sister's relationship with Walter was more strained than his, always had been. "She said she wanted to come out here one of these days to see you."

"What for?"

"She can bring you some magazines. Bacon for Duke."

Walter scowled and ran a hand through his hair. "That'll be fine."

"She just returned from Cape Town."

"Cape Town? Why the heck would she want to go there?" It was a common argument from Walter. He couldn't understand why anyone would want to do anything.

"Apparently she was swimming with sharks."

An insidious laugh crackled up from Walter's throat, bursting from a mouth he had pressed shut. Faith stood, sensing the visit was ending abruptly, and kissed Duke goodbye.

"Before that it was Sydney and before that it was Bali," Walter sneered.

"You know how she goes looking for adventure."

Walter made a tsk-tsk sound and crossed his arms tightly over his chest, surveying them both. "That's not what she's looking for and you know it."

Tully's body went rigid, knowing what the old man would say next. He'd spat it before, like a piece of phlegm into the wind. No caution, no concern for how it landed. No thought to how it stabbed Tully like a shiv to the gut every time.

"We'll see you later, Dad," he said, motioning for Faith to follow him. Walter trailed behind them, not one to be ignored.

"I said that's not what she's looking for, dammit!" Tully turned, keeping his breath slow and steady as he'd learned to do at a young age. "You know what she's looking for."

"Now, Dad—" he began but Walter would not be deterred.

"She's looking for your mother!" Walter's words dripped with a grotesqueness reserved for criminals locked away without a second thought. He nodded proudly as if he was the only one in the know, the only one who had pieced together the puzzle.

Faith's head snapped at the declaration. Tully couldn't bear to look at her.

"Text me if you need something, Dad," he said, walking back to the motorcycles.

"Goodbye, Walter," Faith called. He didn't know if his father answered her. He couldn't have heard another thing he'd said because of the ringing in his ears. All he knew was that he was thankful for the encounter to be over. He'd also be thankful if Faith never asked about the things Walter had said—ever.

CHAPTER ELEVEN

FAITH AND TULLY arrived at her shop. She had spent the ride back to town thinking about Walter. He was a surprising character, looking lost and acting as if the world was ready to come at him. She couldn't find a thing about the man that reminded her of Tully. Aside from the height, which Walter's rounded shoulders diminished, their temperament and attitude were opposites. For all the kindness and care Tully's words seemed to have, Walter's bit intentionally and frequently.

What puzzled her most was the mention of Tully's mother, who he had led her to believe had passed away when he was a child. Was she out there in the world missing or hiding? The bit about Samantha looking for her had Faith as curious as she was confused.

They backed the motorcycles into the angled parking spots in front of Heart Motorcycles when CeCe Takes poked her head out of her shop. They both pretended not to see her flagging them down. After they cut the engines, Faith took Tully's helmet and whispered under her breath, "As far as welcoming committees go, I prefer Duke." She had no desire to engage with CeCe just then. If anything, she needed to be alone to process the events of the afternoon. And as she sensed Tully's guard had gone up, a wall rising like a drawbridge to cover his heart, she wanted to leave him to his own thoughts as well.

"I doubt you want to stick around for this," he said, obviously bothered by the sight of CeCe beelining toward him.

"Maybe a moment longer." She stepped up onto the curb with him and he put his back to CeCe. She liked his unwavering focus. The fact that he positioned himself like a wall between her and CeCe didn't hurt either.

Safely hidden in the shadow of his tall frame, her skin prickled as she moved closer to him. She'd learned in grade school that static electricity was an imbalance of negative and positive charges that built up on a surface. In his presence, she felt the charges building on her, on him, between them. She touched his hand, wanting to complete the circuit, wanting to feel the shock that had made her jump but yearn for more. Whoever said things were cooler in the shade obviously hadn't stood in proximity to a man like John McTully. Enticingly close but never close enough.

"I have an idea to catch your vandal," she said, tugging at his fingers. He shuffled up to her easily and clasped her hand tighter. The effect she had on him made her smile.

"Is that so?"

"It's a great idea too. I started thinking about it on the ride back. One word..." He lifted his eyebrows, prompting her to continue. "Stakeout."

"I don't understand."

"You..." she said, "and I...go on a..."

"Yes?"

"Stakeout."

A soft chuckle rose from his throat, causing him to move his shoulders. He seemed to be dismissing her suggestion with ease.

"That sounds interesting but—"

"Yoo-hoo! Detective!" CeCe called, breaking the hold she had over him, or was it the hold he had over her?

"Your fan club is approaching," Faith said.

"She can wait a minute longer."

"Ah." Clutching the straps of both helmets in her other hand, Faith gently swung the protective gear, letting it graze his thigh and then hers and back again. He was looking at her like a man truly interested. He wanted to see her again. Wanted to see what she'd do or say next. If she'd sipped a glass of champagne too quickly, it wouldn't go to her head nearly as well as John's grin did.

"What are you doing later?" she asked.

He hesitated, glancing over his shoulder. "Not a stakeout."

"If we are going to catch this guy—"

"We?"

"I already told you I'm in this whether you like it or not. We should hide out on the street and watch for whoever is wreaking havoc. He's consistent, you've got to give him that. He'll turn up sooner or later, and when he does, we'll be waiting."

"Detective," CeCe said, finally reaching them.

"Good afternoon." Tully turned to face her.

"I was calling you from down the block. I thought you saw me."

"I was finishing a conversation."

Faith had to hand it to him. He was polite but firm and it only added to his charm.

"Hello, Mrs. Takes," Faith said. She felt like a crane operator fighting a dragline in high winds. She had to concentrate to lift the apples of her cheeks, millimeter by millimeter, in a polite smile. "I'll talk to you later, John." Faith hadn't wanted their motorcycle ride to end, but she was filled with a new hope that something even better might be developing between the two of them.

CeCe accompanied Tully down the block toward Little Lakeside Sports Shop. Since his sister had taken his truck and left him without a vehicle, he figured Mara's shop was the best place to catch a ride home, or even better, to Mara and Peter's house for that dinner Mara had mentioned.

On the other hand, he also wanted a little quiet to process what had happened on Falcon's Peak. When he'd agreed to ride the Street Glide, he hadn't anticipated that the events of the afternoon would lead to him savoring the delicious kiss of Faith Fitzpatrick. Sure, he'd thought about what it might be like to touch her. Everything from the way she looked to how she moved to how her verbal sparring pushed his buttons excited him. He found his thoughts drifting to her during the day, concocting reasons to stop by her shop and have another encounter. Never in his life had he thought of himself as a moth drawn to a flame. For a man who could set his watch by his daily routine, it surprised him that he would be so enthralled by Faith. She was unpredictable and he liked it. He knew she should be off-limits until the vandalism case was resolved. It was wise to back off until the initial attraction between them dulled a bit, and he could start thinking clearly again. But her presence was a solar storm flaring in front of him and it took more restraint than he feared he had to keep from flying into her orbit. He hoped he wouldn't get burned.

"Were you out riding with that woman?" CeCe asked, pecking her words like an angry hen.

"That woman?"

"You know who I mean."

"I don't." He did.

"Faith Talbert."

"I don't know a Faith Talbert."

CeCe scoffed. "Don't get smart with me, Detective. I've been around long enough to know when people are being cheeky. I've also been around long enough to sniff out a woman who is angling to get her hooks into a man. That's exactly what Faith *Fitzpatrick*—" she puckered her face "—is doing with you."

"Mrs. Takes—"

"*CeCe.* Good heavens. You know that."

"I appreciate your candor. I'll watch for… What did you call it? Angling?"

"Good man," CeCe said, patting him approvingly on the arm like a trainer rewarding a prized pup. "But that wasn't quite what I wanted to talk to you about. I asked Angelo to keep you at the shop this morning until I returned, but he said you got called away."

Tully kept his face blank to keep from agreeing with Angelo's lie, although he appreciated Angelo's spin.

As they reached the sports shop, he saw Mara watching them from behind the front window.

"Now," CeCe continued. "Word on the street is that Faith has been speaking to the shop owners who have had their stores vandalized. It's curious that she never showed up to speak to *me* about anything. I don't have to tell you what that means."

Tully knew it meant that Faith didn't care what CeCe had to say about the vandalism or life in general.

"No. What?"

"She's trying to intimidate the owners. She didn't come around my shop because she knows I'm a woman who can't be bullied. No one muscles me, Detective. No one."

"I'll keep that in mind."

"And keep this in mind too. I know how women like her think. I can tell what they're going to do before they do it."

"Okay..."

"She's vandalized several stores on this street—"

"Allegedly, according to you."

"But most likely," CeCe said, powering on. "She comes from a family who made their fortune swindling the people in this town—"

"Only her father did that and Faith wasn't even out of high school when he was caught."

CeCe leaned in. "Mark told me that he let Faith sign a *month-by-month* lease on her shop. He said it was better than nothing and wanted it occupied for the tourist season. If something happens to that shop, and she collects an insurance payment on it, she can skip town financially ahead of the game."

"It wouldn't really be worth it, Mrs. Takes. Think about what you're saying. It would mean that Faith is so deceitful that she moved here, pretended to open up a motorcycle shop and then lied about wanting a life here just to scam a few bucks."

"It could be more than a few bucks. At least it might have been if she didn't know I was onto her. Look at her shop. Aside from a painting on the front window and a tool chest and cleaning supplies in there, what else has she invested in the place? She's not going bankrupt fixing it up, if you know what I mean."

"Which means she wouldn't have anything of value to claim from insurance."

"No? Didn't I see you pull up on a new motorcycle? It wasn't yours, was it? I'm telling you, she's using these break-ins to set the stage."

Tully widened his gait, mulling CeCe's words over. Claim her motorcycles as stolen in order to collect? That was a giant hop, skip and leap from breaking a window or spray painting a few walls, and it wasn't Faith. That wasn't the Faith he'd seen that afternoon. A woman hell-bent on fooling him wouldn't have kissed with the conviction she had or leaned in to listen about the troubles with his dad the way she had. She wouldn't have insisted on coming to see his dad with him and waited so patiently as he helped his dad fix the shack. He had to believe she wasn't pulling the wool over his eyes but opening him up to a new possibility. The one where he entertained a relationship that lasted long enough for him to start caring for once.

Tully said, “I can tell you’ve given this a lot of thought.”

“More than that. I’ll even do you one better. She’s set the stage not only with the break-ins but with—pardon me for saying so—but with you, Detective.”

“Angling…hooks in me…got it.”

CeCe huffed. “She’s vandalized a few shops, played up pretty to you, and what’s coming next is so obvious.”

“Is it?”

“Mark my words. The next shop she’ll target will be her own.”

“Excuse me?”

“It’s smart, isn’t it? She’ll throw suspicion off her by playing one of the victims. It’s like in those hostage negotiations when one of the kidnappers pretends to be a hostage, then flees from the building with his hands in the air. She’ll be laughing all along to the next poor, unsuspecting town before anyone even realizes they’ve been hoodwinked.”

Mara pushed open the door and smiled brightly.

“There you are, Tully. I was about to send

out a search party. I'm getting ready to take off and can give you a lift to the house..."

"I'll let you go," CeCe said. She twinkled her fingers at Mara in a friendly wave before cocking a finger at Tully. "Think about what I've said. The logic is sound."

"Thank you, Mrs. Takes."

CeCe scurried back to The Sandwich Board, pausing to peek into Faith's store before continuing.

"What was that all about?" Mara asked.

"I wish I knew." The problem was he did know. Faith had said she felt like some people in this town were looking at her like she was a criminal, and CeCe was a prime example. She really wouldn't be able to get a fresh start in Roseley if everyone else looked to the past to determine the future. Her future. He wished there was something more he could do about that.

FAITH AND BONNIE drove to Uncle Gus's house, a grocery bag of Bonnie's snacks in tow. She wanted to have more time with her friend, but Bonnie was eager to grab dinner and have a quick chat before making her bus. Bonnie was nothing if not efficient. She'd sleep on the bus all night and be ready to celebrate the holiday back home.

Bonnie had helped Faith finish up last-minute details at the shop before Caroline had called, luring them back to the house with a home-cooked meal. Faith had been so busy, her mind and body moving in double time, it wasn't until Caroline mentioned food that she realized she was starving. There had still been things to do when she'd locked up the shop, things she should have done instead of flitting off for a motorcycle ride with Tully, but she didn't care. The time spent with him had been well worth it.

Bonnie shouted over the roar the wind made through the truck's open windows as Faith steered them to Uncle Gus's house, but she only half listened. In fifteen hours, she'd be riding in the Fourth of July parade, opening her shop for business and, if fate was kind, seeing Tully again.

When they got onto Uncle Gus's street, Trig pulled out of the driveway. He gave a wave to acknowledge them before heading in the opposite direction.

"Is that your cousin Trig?" Bonnie asked. She had always been good at listening to Faith's stories and descriptions of her family, recalling details months later. Bonnie had never met either of the cousins, but she knew of them.

"That's him."

"I thought he lived in Detroit."

"He scheduled his vacation so he could come support me."

"Your uncle has a full house, then."

"And I know he prefers that. After he and my aunt Helen divorced, he never quite figured out how to take care of the place himself. I know he appreciates Caroline doing it while he's gone, but I'm itching to move out."

"Let's hope paying customers stampede your shop tomorrow."

"From your lips to buyers' ears." Faith parked and led Bonnie into the house. Bonnie slung the bag of snacks up on the kitchen counter.

"Where's your Uncle Gus now?"

"Fishing." Bonnie checked her watch as Caroline sauntered in from the backyard carrying a plate of barbecue chicken and roasted corn on the cob.

"When will he be back?"

Caroline answered, "September. He can't stand the tourists this time of year. He'll stop home for a few days to check in on us, then he'll be off to his other favorite camp in Canada for hunting season."

"My dad was like that," Bonnie said. "My brothers too. We all liked our space. My husband, Paul, on the other hand, could carry on a conversation with an exhaust pipe as long as it puttered away with nonverbal encouragement of sorts. I guess that's how the two of us stayed happily married for so long. Well… more or less happy, God rest his soul." Bonnie's eyes misted before she sniffed. "You must be Caroline. I've heard a lot of good things about you."

"I've heard wonderful things about you as well. Faith says you helped her get through her…" She winced an apology.

"Divorce," Bonnie said. "No use tiptoeing around it. *Divorce* is a happy word, huh, Faith? It was the bolt cutter setting you free from that rusty bucket of chains."

Faith pulled out dinner plates as Caroline poured them each a glass of sweet tea. Her friend certainly had a way with words.

"You shouldn't have gotten married in the first place," Bonnie continued. "Luckily, it didn't take you long to realize it. Kyle was as respectable as a bottom feeder in a cesspool, and I was happy to help you wade a path out of the deep end."

"Hear, hear!" Caroline said, passing them

each a glass. The women clanked a toast and each took a sip of her tea.

"He's been calling all week," Faith said. "Texting too."

Bonnie harrumphed. "He knows you're on to bigger and better things. It aggravates him like a jagged pebble in his shoe."

"What does he want?" Caroline asked.

"I don't answer the phone so I couldn't tell you."

"He wants to insert himself into your success!"

Caroline raised her brows at Bonnie's declaration, then broke into a laugh.

"Tell us what you really think, Bonnie."

"Bonnie has been psychoanalyzing Kyle and me for a long time," Faith explained. "She says it's no wonder I married him, considering the upbringing I had."

"But that season of life is over, Faith," Bonnie said, like a motivational speaker inspiring a crowd. "You had some insecurities when I first met you—"

"That's putting it mildly, Bon."

"And Kyle exacerbated those. But no longer."

"Yeah, I'd say his cheating and making no effort to quit is a good example." Faith managed a laugh, though it was anything but funny. When she'd first suspected Kyle was seeing other women, a sickening feeling had filled her gut, like barbed wire twisting. Whenever she thought about Kyle's indiscretions, that wire tensed and twisted again. She figured that the only way to expel it was to remove Kyle from her life for good.

"That was a big one, but there were little daily examples too," Bonnie said. "Like horseflies stinging you every time you left the house."

Faith had appreciated Bonnie's support over the years since she hadn't had a lot of places to turn to for help. When she looked back at who she'd been, she couldn't blame herself for making a mistake in love. If she'd hadn't had Bonnie to speak some loving truth into her…

"Here's to not seeing him again," Bonnie declared, taking another swig of her drink.

"Speaking of seeing someone again…" Caroline began and leaned against the counter like it was a locker and she was ready for cliquey gossip.

She nodded at Faith, and Faith smirked at her from over her glass, secretly bursting to share her news. She whispered excitedly to Bonnie, "I met someone." The thrill in her voice made Bonnie shimmy her shoulders in a tease.

"Is it that fella you were ogling before?"

"I wasn't ogling anyone."

"Honey, your eyeballs would have leaped from their sockets if they weren't fastened in. I could have given myself whiplash from watching you stare at him, then look away whenever he glanced in your direction. Back and forth, back and forth."

Faith and Caroline laughed, making Bonnie nod knowingly.

"Please tell me what's wrong with him because a man as handsome as that should not go walking around in public without a permit."

"He's a police detective." Faith beamed.

"He serves and protects too? Heaven help you."

Faith chuckled, appreciating it for the escape it was. It wasn't often she felt this excited about something.

"He's honorable and kind and—" Faith threw her head back, forcing the last word out with a cry "—good."

"She had the biggest crush on him in high school," Caroline supplied. "As you can see, her feelings have only magnified."

Bonnie harrumphed. "Can you blame her? You can't fix a man who ain't good. Believe me. I've seen a lot of friends try and fail.

Good will keep you warm during the cold times. And, Faith, you deserve some good."

Faith ran a fingertip around the rim of her glass, a thoughtful whimsy overcoming her. As Bonnie and Caroline fixed their plates and scraped back chairs from the kitchen table, she thought of all that had transpired this week and all of the hopeful things that beckoned from the horizon. She had wanted to be a business owner by the time she'd completed technical school and now she was taking a calculated risk to make that dream happen. And after the afternoon she'd shared with John—

"Earth to Faith," Bonnie said, before turning to Caroline. "She's daydreaming about Detective Be Good."

Faith fixed herself a plate and joined them at the table. Preparing to open her shop played a close second to what had transpired with John that afternoon. Finding success as a small-business owner would fill a part of her identity she'd always known she'd needed and craved. If John McTully wanted to be a part of her life, her romantic life, her forever life, she hoped the hole in her heart could begin to heal too.

CHAPTER TWELVE

TULLY ROSE WITH the sun, but his mind had been awake much earlier. He'd stayed late at Mara and Peter's house and let the others do most of the talking. Samantha loved carrying most conversations, and as she had returned from Cape Town, she had plenty of stories to hold her audience captive. They'd grilled and eaten and listened to stories of Samantha's adventures in Africa until the nightshade of ink chased the sun below the horizon.

Tully had dropped his sister at her apartment after solidifying plans to meet the next morning. Then he'd taken the long way back to his house, watching fireworks some locals fired off from their backyards. He had cruised slowly around Lakeshore Drive, determining that the fireworks were coming from the Garners' lakefront property at lot 99.

Mr. and Mrs. Garner had had five children of their own while fostering several others over the years. As kids, he and Charlie and

Samantha had sought out the Garners' yard for long games of hide-and-go-seek. As teenagers, the Garner kids had thrown the best parties when Mr. and Mrs. Garner were out of town. A couple of the Garner kids had married and had children of their own, growing the clan to lake-wide fame. If the rest of the bunch finally settled down and started having children, Little Lake Roseley might not be big enough for all of them.

Tully had loved the days spent at the Garners' house. Mrs. Garner would put out a spread of food so the children could graze, darting to snag a hot dog or handful of grapes before returning to play. By late evening, when all the children were filthy and stinking of sweat, fish and bug spray, Mr. Garner would pull out the garden hose and call everyone in for a shower. Tully and Charlie had raced alongside the Garner children like two more puppies in the rambunctious litter. They'd taken their turns, squirming and laughing as Mr. Garner hosed them down, before waving good-night and riding their bikes home.

Tully had arrived home, smiling at the few childhood memories he enjoyed revisiting. Sleepy but unable to sleep, he lay on his bed, staring at the ceiling and recalling every detail of his motorcycle ride with Faith. It was unlike him to put emotion ahead of duty. The people in town thought of him as responsible, reliable and level-headed, and it was because he was—until, perhaps, now.

His first stumble had been agreeing to go on a motorcycle ride with Faith in the first place. If anyone had spotted the two of them out of town together, tongues would start wagging faster than Duke's did over bacon strips. Tully would have had a hard time justifying his actions to anyone, but he had the hardest time justifying it to himself. Faith was an unofficial suspect, sure, but practicing caution where she was concerned would have been wise.

His second stumble had been into her kiss, though the positioning had been a lot smoother than that. He didn't mind replaying it all in the hours since it had happened, but his lack of caution would make things convoluted when they shouldn't be. She'd think he was interested in her and wanted her—and didn't he?

Didn't her lips taste sweeter than warm honey collected in August, tasted and savored before it could be melted from the honeycomb? It had been impulsive of him. CeCe had warned that Faith was angling for him when all he had felt on Falcon's Peak was a desire to angle for her.

Then he'd taken her along to check on his dad. He'd never wanted to get married, still didn't, but even in the few instances where the thought of marriage, still very vague and distant, crossed his mind, he knew he wouldn't take his bride to see his father. Probably wouldn't introduce them unless Walter agreed to go home and live among the people who cared for him and where he belonged.

But he'd allowed Faith to persuade him. If he was honest, she hadn't had to try very hard either. He'd deferred his better judgment given her promise she would help him, as if anybody could where his father was concerned. He'd agreed and, for the life of him, he couldn't quite understand why.

He recalled how assertively she'd led them back to the motorcycles, how she'd fired up the engine and had taken off in the direction of The Void. She hadn't strong-armed him into it, because no one could strong-arm him to do anything he didn't want. He was used to stepping forward and being a leader. He'd assumed that role ever since Samantha was a little girl. He had been her only consolation when his dad zoned out and his mother—

Tully cringed recalling his father's words. *She's looking for your mother.*

Something deep inside him began to ache after he recalled what his father had said. The only relief he'd finally found was when he fell asleep. It had been a fitful sleep, topped off with a phone call from the police station the next morning. He learned that the vandal had struck again. This time, just as CeCe Takes had predicted, the target had been Heart Motorcycles.

FAITH SAT ON the curb outside her shop, elbows on knees, head slumped on fists. Caroline swept the broken glass shattered across the sidewalk, but Faith was too distraught to work. She needed some time before picking herself up by her bootstraps and getting on with the cleanup. She didn't want to appear to be wallowing in her own misery, but she knew that was exactly what she was doing. She gave herself permission to sit and wallow her heart out for one minute more. Then that would be the end of it.

"It's okay, Faith," Caroline said, continuing the pep talk she'd begun as soon as she'd arrived and saw the damage. "Trig said he knows someone who might be able to repair the window tomorrow."

Faith thought it was unlikely. She wouldn't be able to get anyone to repair it until after the holiday weekend and that was only after the insurance adjuster visited. She'd have to meet her deductible first and that would set her back—money she didn't really have yet...

"Good morning," a cheerful voice said, making Faith climb to her feet. Dolores Mitchell stood with a basket of muffins in hand. "Betty and I had planned on bringing these over this morning to wish you luck. Now I see they're to cheer you up."

"Betty?"

"Betty Jenkins."

"Ah, yes. Grandma's Basement," Faith said. "We've met but I haven't heard anyone refer to her by her first name yet."

"She chooses to be formal, a throwback to earlier generations where young whippersnappers referred to their elders as Mr. and Mrs."

"I'm hardly a whippersnapper."

"Compared to Betty and me, you sure are, but you know I prefer Dolores, right? Anyway, is there anything I can do for you? Betty said she'd be down in a little bit to check on you. Her air-conditioning unit went out and today will be so darn hot. Today is usually one of the most profitable days of the year… Well." She caught herself and fumbled to correct as Faith's face fell. "For most of us… Sorry, dear."

Dolores quickly offered a basket of muffins. Faith accepted it as a ceremonial way of letting her off the hook for her faux pas.

"I think we'll hit a heat record today," Caroline said, leaning on her broom. "Ten o'clock isn't early enough in the morning for this parade."

"Don't I know it. I hope they have plenty of water and Popsicles on hand for the children walking in it. Anyhoo, I have to get back, but call me if you need something, Faith. Anything at all. Okay?"

Faith watched Dolores walk back to her store, where she'd get a slew of customers later. She, on the other hand, would only be able to secure the front of her shop with flattened cardboard boxes and duct tape. If anyone wanted to get inside and steal her tools tonight, it would be as easy as picking up lint with masking tape.

She shuffled through the front door and placed the muffin basket on the counter. She couldn't eat. She surveyed her shop, determining what she would need to store at the house until the window was fixed. After repacking a few boxes she had unpacked only a few days earlier, she heard Caroline chatting with someone on the street. She peered through the open front window, the jagged glass shards around the edges framing her view. It was Rick Murdock. He had a passenger in his front seat, a man she didn't recognize.

"Sorry to hear about your misfortune, Faith," Rick said as she joined them. "How are you holding up?"

His words carried the message she'd expect to hear from a concerned neighbor, but his delivery was anything but sympathetic.

"I'll get through it," she said, straightening. She hadn't liked the way Rick had looked at her at The Gypsy Caravan. He'd glared in her direction more than a handful of times the night someone broke the window there. Now she imagined that he knew she was Ray Talbert's daughter and his disposition had only darkened.

"Do you have any idea who would do this?" The man in Rick's passenger seat leaned forward to get a better view of her. She waited for him or Rick to make an introduction, but they didn't. They weren't here to get better acquainted, she thought. They were here to send some sort of message.

She took a step closer to the car, standing shoulder to shoulder with Caroline.

"If I knew that, I wouldn't still be standing here, would I?"

Rick turned and muttered something to his passenger. Faith couldn't be certain, but she thought she caught the words *ain't she a treat*.

"Hey, Heath, how's Oliver these days?" Caroline asked, her tone the sharpest Faith had ever heard from her sweet cousin. The passenger, Heath, shifted in his seat.

"Great. Thanks for asking."

"Staying out of trouble, I hope."

It was Rick who snapped, defensively.

"Oliver's a good boy. He's been working hard all summer, even helping Gemma and me at the restaurant."

"I'm glad to hear it," Caroline said, wrapping an arm around her cousin's waist. "That's what I love about our town, Heath. Everyone rallied around your family after Oliver got involved in something he shouldn't have a couple summers back. That's because it was the right thing to do. Everyone deserves a clean slate like that, don't you think?"

Faith had to force herself not to stare in amazement at Caroline. She hadn't expected her cousin to grow so fierce in the years since she'd been gone, but kindhearted Caroline had just put someone in their place all for her.

"Yes, everyone certainly does, Caroline," Heath said. His demeanor had toughened in respect, the way some people did when they met a decorated hero.

"They'll catch the responsible party," Faith said. "I have no doubt about that." Though at the rate things were going, she wouldn't hold her breath waiting.

Once the two men had driven away, Caroline explained, "That was Heath Harrison. He and his wife divorced a while back, and he's been carrying most of the responsibility of raising their son, Oliver."

"I take it he's friends with Rick?"

"They're pretty close. Oliver got into some trouble a while back, and Heath came down on his son like a coal mine collapse. I think he felt a lot of embarrassment over the idea Oliver could behave so irresponsibly and wanted to make sure Oliver never did anything like that again. I think he's a good kid who got caught up with the wrong company."

"Do you think Oliver could have done something like this?"

"I really don't."

"But the way you talked to Heath made it seem like—"

"Heath is a good guy. So is Rick, Faith. Unfortunately, I think they've had their opinions of you tainted by outside parties."

"Yeah, and I know who did the tainting."

"Not just CeCe. You've been the subject of gossipy fodder since you arrived. Heath needed to be set straight and I think the message was received."

Faith hugged Caroline.

"Look at you defending me."

"To hell and back." She peeked over Faith's shoulder as a truck pulled up to the curb and parked. "Here comes your Detective Be Good," she whispered.

Tully climbed out of his truck at a pace faster than Faith had ever seen him move. He was at her side in a blink. Dressed in long, casual shorts and a T-shirt that showcased his fine upper body, he looked more like Detective Looks Good.

"Do you like what I've done with the

place?" she asked, wafting a hand toward the broken glass.

His stare was firm. "What time did you call it in to the station?"

"Five o'clock this morning."

"Were you here that early?"

"I did have a lot to do before the parade, but it looks like my morning freed up."

"Can you still open your shop today?"

"I'll do my best, but this was not the first impression I wanted to make for my grand opening." Nothing about her arrival in Roseley had gone how she'd hoped. As she'd never get a second chance to make a good first impression, she and her shop were now batting zero for two.

"Are you on the clock, Detective?" Caroline asked. He shook his head.

"Just on call. I wanted to see if you were okay. I'm sure an officer will be here shortly to take your statement."

"Officer Randall already stopped by." What Faith refrained from saying was that he had been as cold and short with her as he'd been during their encounter at The Gypsy Caravan. She didn't want to complain about him. He and Tully were still colleagues.

"Are you going to ride in the parade?"

"Absolutely. My Sportster is already decorated."

"Do you need help with something?" He moseyed to inspect the window as Caroline winked at her and disappeared into the shop. If she could ask for anything from him right now, it would be a hug. She wanted the kind of hug you could lose yourself in, and he looked like he could give good ones.

But they were not at the hug stage. He had kissed her for a few brief moments, but by the way he had pulled away, she knew a hug was outside the bounds of intimacy he was comfortable with. For now.

"There is something," she said. He turned; curiosity peaked on his brow. "People in this town not only think I'm capable of vandalizing these shops, but they think I vandalized my own."

"People? You mean CeCe?"

"I'm sure CeCe is down at her sandwich shop rallying against me right now—"

"Don't assume. It doesn't suit you."

She choked out a laugh but there was no humor. "I don't need to assume. I only need to pay attention to how she's been acting the last few days. And no, I'm not even talking about CeCe. A few guys came by before you got here and weren't all that sympathetic."

"Who?"

"It doesn't matter who. What matters is what I'm going to do next to clear my name. I'm going on a stakeout to catch this guy and put an end to these break-ins once and for all. If you really want to help me, you'll come too."

He laughed as if she'd said she was off to photograph the Loch Ness Monster.

"You're not serious? Yesterday I thought you were only—"

"What? Kidding? *Flirting?*"

"The thought crossed my mind." His voice teased, but she would not be distracted.

"John," she said, moving so that the tips of their shoes nearly touched. "I'm not proud of a lot of things I've done in my past, but it's the unfair blame that hurts me the most. I've wanted to move back here for years, but I was too scared of people not receiving me. Now that I've finally had the courage to show my face again—" She could feel the tears welling, hot and salty. She had to get through this, deliver her message as quickly as she could before her voice cracked and her face contorted in an ugly cry. "Without clearing my name, I won't stay. I won't subject myself to the daily ridicule. I don't want to give up on my dream of making this place my home, but I refuse to live like that. I don't know how many more fights I have in me before I pack it up and leave for good. Do you understand?"

From his towering stance to the unreadable look of his eyes, she couldn't tell if she'd moved his opinion about the stakeout in the right direction or not. As the seconds ticked by, expanding the distance between them just like The Void, quiet and vast, she figured she might have had better luck moving a mountain at its base.

"Faith?" Caroline called from the back of the shop. "Do these boxes go back to the house?"

She clenched her fists, all the fury she felt at her situation collecting at the fingertips digging into her palms. Fury at CeCe, at her father, at the sales she'd miss this morning because someone shattered her front window.

"I'm going on that stakeout tonight whether you support it or not. I'm going to camp out on the roof of my shop because it's something I can do to control my life. To fix this. I want you to join me because—" Her voice hitched, making her turn toward the shop. "If you show up, you show up."

She left him standing on the sidewalk. Her throat clenched, logic suppressing the next words her heart wanted to cry out. *Please, John. Please show up for me.*

CHAPTER THIRTEEN

TULLY HAD ATTENDED the parade, as he did every summer, but even the beating sun and melodious voices couldn't distract him from thoughts of Faith. He returned smiles of passersby, of people in this town he had known his entire life. He downshifted into an emotional autopilot when faced with a crowd, presenting a professional decorum and an open attitude at all times. He thought of Faith and what sort of face she had to put on to show the world. She hadn't received the welcoming people in Roseley usually extended to new neighbors. It weighed on him.

The heart of Roseley was good; the people in it were good. They had their share of bad apples, but as he spotted Moody Ward, the grandfather of troubled teen Cody Ward, he reminded himself that even troubled cases could go in the right direction with encouragement.

Cody had had a rough start. His father had

skipped out on him and Cheyanne when Cody had been only three. Cheyanne had done her best by Cody, working two jobs outside Roseley to support him. The last few years his grandparents, Karen and Moody, did their best to provide a loving and disciplined home for Cody so Cheyanne could return to school to get an accounting degree. Unfortunately, they had become grandparents at an age when they should have been coasting into retirement and Cody's teenage years had been particularly taxing. Moody, who'd retired as city manager but still stayed involved in local politics, carried the wear and tear of it all in his weathered face, more years on it than the calendar had ever recorded.

"Moody," Tully said, extending a hand. Moody adjusted the brim on his straw hat, which looked like it had seen as many summers as he had. He grasped Tully's hand in a firm shake, then spoke.

"I heard about the break-in at the new motorcycle shop. Was anything stolen?"

"I don't know."

"Why not?" Moody's tone was equal parts surprise and disapproval. Tully dipped hands into his front pockets and flinched a look that read *want to try again?* Moody wiped a

thumb over the rough stubble of his chin. "I mean Karen heard about it this morning. I'm curious about your leads. We can't let something like that continue."

"Agreed."

"I was worried the Callahan brothers would change their minds about their store."

"Worried?"

Moody clicked his tongue, a sad hum reverberating behind his teeth.

"They could do a lot of good for this town, for businesses and such."

"They mentioned tax incentives they received."

"Yes. The town council didn't want to possibly lose out on their business, so they'd agreed to pretty much everything."

"What's everything?"

"Well..." Moody turned and faced him. "The town had to agree to some unusual terms, like deeming Roseley imprecise."

"Imprecise?"

"It's an unusual word, ain't it? I'm sure it was conjured up by their lawyers, a catchall for everything and anything. The basic gist is that they can back out of the store if Roseley isn't as great as we presented it. The town has to buy their lot and store. Anyway, I stopped by to talk to them yesterday and fortunately, they sounded like they wanted to stick around in spite of the break-ins."

"I didn't realize you were so friendly with them."

"Oh, you know how I am," Moody said. "I still keep my ear to the ground on all matters in this town."

"You and me both."

"Sure. Roseley has been my home my entire life, same as you. It still needs tending, and I'm happy to help as long as I'm still kicking."

Moody managed a curt nod before Tully continued, "And how is Cheyanne doing these days? I haven't seen her around in a while."

Moody's posture slumped as if the thought of his daughter's troubles weighed just as heavy on his shoulders as the reality weighed on hers.

"Karen and I are worried about her. The long hours she works ain't healthy for anybody. Then you add night school on top of that, it's a wonder she can stay awake long enough to give Cody five minutes of attention. No fault of her own, mind you, but a shame all the same. Their connection should be stronger. Well…" He let a pause hang in the air. "You, more than anybody, know how hard that can be."

Tully stared ahead to avoid Moody's pity. Occasionally, when his past sprung up without warning, he had to sturdy himself like a boat weathering a squall. Folks didn't usually make comments about his mother in front of him. He assumed that if her name came up in his absence, it was in passing, included in conversation as a cautionary tale. He could no sooner get defensive with Moody than he could get defensive with a puppy dog nipping at his ankle. The intention meant everything, especially when he knew Moody's mind was more on Cheyanne and Cody than on him and his own mother.

"Is Cody walking in the parade?"

Moody harrumphed. "He agreed to walk with the soccer team—"

"Soccer team?"

"Karen and I bribed him to try out. We hoped sports would help funnel some of his—" Tully waited patiently, letting the grandfather grapple for his own word *"—energy."*

"Teamwork and discipline would be good for him."

"If he doesn't get kicked off first. For a

while there, he was sneaking out of the house at night, hanging out with his buddies."

"When was this?"

"A while back," Moody said, running a hand down the length of his face. "Beginning of the summer."

"Were you able to remedy that problem?"

"Yes, thankfully. The coach helped with it too. He enforces a strict curfew and expects the boys to stick to it."

Tully listened, wondering if Cody was invested in the soccer team enough to abide by the coach's rules. He sure hoped he was.

"He's a good boy, Detective," Moody continued. "Karen tries so hard to love on him, protect him—"

"As do you."

Moody huffed a laugh. "I do my best."

Tully had parted ways with Moody, appreciative of all the man had disclosed. He'd looked up to Moody since he'd been a boy, considering him a pillar of the community. He'd like the Callahans to become pillars too, but he couldn't rule out what Ledger had said regarding the new location. The excitement, at least on Ledger's part, had not been mutual. And what about his frustration when Tully'd first met him. Was his anger directed at his brother, at the town or meant for someone else entirely?

None of his questions were evidence of anything amiss or out of the ordinary. Still, he'd puzzled over them for a spell as Samantha met up with him at the start of the parade route. He'd already watched Cody bunt a soccer ball continuously on his head as he walked with his team. The children standing along the street had cheered for him. Tully wondered how much positive affirmation a kid like Cody would need to make up for the deficit of not having a stable parent in his life. But the children didn't know any of that and cheered him as if he were a rock star.

The Roseley Fourth of July parade had a reputation for bringing out that kind of excitement in folks. It also had a reputation for offering lots of free swag so clever children attended the parade with a grocery bag at the ready. Dolores Mitchell and her grandnieces passed out packets of tea from The Cutest Little Tea Shop. The Lollipop Candy Store threw handfuls of suckers, scattering them like marbles on the playground blacktop. Patches and Pleats, the local fabric store, passed out refrigerator magnets in the shape of large buttons with their logo in the center.

The Midnight Pumpkin, the pottery shop and art studio, handed out coupons to paint a pottery piece for free. Perk's Pizza passed out mini slices of cheese pizza, the greasy slices soaking through thin paper plates. The Sandwich Board, mini wrapped sub sandwiches; The Spice Trader, tiny packets of grill seasonings; Little Lakeside Sports, lanyards. And dozens of clubs and organizations passed out water bottles, cans of soda, flags, patriotic glow sticks, Popsicles and *lots* of candy.

At the parade's conclusion, children had already begun comparing their hauls as moms and dads dipped sticky fingers into the bags, claiming prizes as a parent tax.

Tully joined Charlie near the police station's table, where Lucy was helping officers pass out free bicycle helmets for kids ten and younger.

"I saw Faith riding in the parade this morning," Charlie said. "It's a shame what happened to her shop, today of all days."

"I know." He'd seen Faith pass by, but she hadn't seen him as the crowd had been several people deep.

"I heard a few people talking about her when she rode by."

Tully growled, *"What they'd say?"*

Charlie crossed his arms, but his tone was amused. "Whoa. Easy. They said they'd check out her shop."

"Oh."

"I hope they do. She needs to get to know people in this town, maybe win them over one at a time."

"She shouldn't have to do that."

"No, she shouldn't, but that's the reality of it."

Tully looked out over the crowd, sandaled feet shuffling in all directions. Red and blue helium balloons bobbed a foot above the crowd as little children stomped in melted pools of Popsicles. A local band, The Hometown Jamboree, cranked the volume on their amps. The jaunty music of their star fiddler set a festive mood. Against the dense heat, the aroma from the nearby hot dog cart took him back to childhood dinners where he and Samantha were left again to their own devices. It made a place in his heart tug, looking for escape.

Lucy bounded over and asked her uncle if he would buy her a tall cup of homemade lemonade. Her fair cheeks, smartly hidden under a white sun cap, had ripened to tomatoes. Charlie reached for his wallet, but Tully waved him off. He needed an excuse to walk, to get away from the smell of hot dogs and all the memories that had been triggered over the past few days.

"Lead the way, Ms. Lucy," he said. "I could go for some lemonade myself."

They had no sooner slugged back their lemonades, Lucy scooping her straw at the sugary sludge at the bottom of her cup, when Tully felt a tug at his elbow. Miss Jenkins held up her lemonade, ceremonially tapping her plastic cup to his.

"I hope you're both staying cool today," she said, peeking at Tully from under a wide-brimmed hat. By the look of it, she was wilting more quickly than a daisy under a heat lamp. Tully handed Lucy money for another round as Miss Jenkins waved a fabric fan in front of her face. As she favored dresses from the 1950s, the shin-length skirt of her patriotic dress swished as she swayed. The tiny white and silver stars on it glittered in the sun.

Growing up, Tully had usually focused more on her scent of pressed powder, somewhat like what his mother had worn. Then again, he thought, shaking the ice at the bottom of his cup, perhaps he had only wanted the scent to be similar. Maybe he had only wanted something else to hold on to back then.

"Did you catch the entire parade?" he asked. The apples of her dewy cheeks rounded.

"My air-conditioning went out last night, so it doesn't matter if I come to the parade or stay at the shop. I melt either way." She fanned herself harder.

"Do you have someone coming to look at it?"

"Yes, but not until tomorrow."

Tully's protective instinct shifted into gear. "Would you like me to stop by this afternoon? I don't know much about air-conditioning units, but I can take a crack at it."

"You've always been so good to me, Tully, but, no. The fella from the company is coming out in the morning. With the holiday I'm so thankful he even answered the phone. I can make do until then."

"It's a bad time to have it go out. If the maintenance man can't make it out tomorrow, give me a call."

"Thank you, dear," she said, waving to Dolores, who darted through the crowd toward them. "That reminds me. I meant to stop down to Faith's store earlier. Dolores said she was in good spirits."

"She's hanging in there."

"Do you have any leads on a suspect?"

"I'm circling."

Miss Jenkins patted him affectionately on the arm. "Of course you are."

"Speaking of which, have you installed new locks on your shop?"

"I've meant to. I'll get around to it once I get this air-conditioning problem resolved. If it's not a maintenance issue with the shop, it's one with the house."

Dolores arrived as Lucy returned with the lemonades. Tully handed his to Dolores, who was likely much too hot to refuse.

"Bless you," she said, taking several gulps. She turned to Miss Jenkins and lowered her voice. "I thought I'd find you over here. I overheard Dash Callahan asking around about your antiques shop."

Miss Jenkins's face crinkled instantly. "What did he want to know?"

"How long you've been in business, and if you were looking to get out anytime soon."

"Geeeet out?" Miss Jenkins's voice warbled more syllables than the rules of language allowed.

Tully had figured that Dash and his sister would eventually find one another, each a homing beacon to the other's desire for adventure and attention. So, it was no surprise when he spotted Samantha laughing loudly with the antiques dealer. Ledger, however, was no where in sight.

"I'm sure he meant to say *retire*," Dolores said, comforting her friend. Miss Jenkins drew a handkerchief from her dress pocket and patted her forehead. "I think he's on his way over here though. Would you like to hit the road?"

Miss Jenkins nodded. "Thanks for the lemonade, Tully," she said before hurrying off through the crowd, her loyal friend at her side.

TRIG HELPED FAITH hang a giant blue tarp over her broken window. She'd taken anything of value out of the shop and stored it in Uncle Gus's garage.

"Just when I think I'm finished unpacking..."

Trig leaned against the door frame.

"This is a minor setback, you know."

"How do you figure?"

"You'll get the window replaced, throw a little paint on it and only be a couple of days behind. In the big scheme of things, a few days of waiting isn't bad. It might feel like the end of the world now, but this will pass."

"You sound like Caroline."

"We're both glad you're here, Faith. Don't let this spook you into..."

"What? Quitting?"

"Leaving."

Trig prized perseverance at nearly all costs as the next big sports story waited for no journalist.

"I appreciate you coming home to Roseley to support me, Trig. I know you usually don't like to take time off work."

"Who said I haven't been working?" His smirk teased but Faith knew Trig's working vacation was still a loving gesture. She appreciated his presence more than she could convey.

"It's funny how things worked out this week, huh?" he said. "The three of us under the same roof? We could have some killer parties like the ones I wanted to throw back in the day. I could have rivaled Garners' parties if Dad had trusted me long enough to get out of town for the weekend."

She thought about what she would have been like at a high school party: meek, timid, self-conscious. Faith chuckled. "From what

I've heard, no one could have rivaled the Garners." She knew she wasn't one to talk as she'd never attended one of the Garners' famous parties, but she'd overheard enough conversations from her classmates to have a clear picture.

Her cell phone vibrated in her back pocket. Reaching for it, she discovered Kyle's cell number on her caller ID.

"Is it him again?" Trig asked. "He's been calling you all morning. Let me answer it."

Trig waggled his eyebrows comically, bringing a giggle to her chest. She shook her head. If she and Kyle hadn't been able to solve their problems while married, they certainly wouldn't be able to solve things now. Trig's involvement, though possibly amusing to watch, would only fuel Kyle's persistence. She shoved the vibrating cell phone in her back pocket as Caroline arrived.

"I passed out a handful of your business cards," she said.

"Where?"

"The Nutmeg Café. A group of motorcyclists were having dinner out front. I asked if anyone was interested in a new detailing shop in town, and they all said they were—"

Faith's phone vibrated again in her pocket. She pulled it out and frowned.

"I don't recognize the number."

"Answer it," Caroline said. "It's probably one of those bikers."

Faith pressed the phone to her ear. "Hello? I mean, Heart Motorcycles. This is Faith."

A woman's voice on the other end of the line wanted to get a quote. She had arthritis and wanted to hire Faith to detail her trike. Faith soon hung up, buzzing with excitement. She had scored her first client who might even become a recurring customer.

"Starting a business is a slow-moving train," Trig said. "But referrals and word of mouth will help. It'll pick up."

Booking her first customer was exciting, but Faith wouldn't feel like she belonged until she was cleared of all suspicion too. She watched the sun sink behind the stores. She felt certain that tonight she would spot the person responsible for the vandalism. Even if she couldn't snap a photograph quickly enough or prove who it was, she would know. More than anything, she wanted to *know*.

Her phone vibrated again. It was Kyle.

"Excuse me while I take this," Faith said,

ducking into her shop to speak in private. "What on earth do you want, Kyle?"

The voice on the other end of the line crackled with laughter. "Is that any way to speak to your husband?"

"Ex-husband. It was official ages ago."

"Against my wishes."

"What do you *want*, I said."

He cleared his voice. "I heard you were opening your shop today, and I called to wish you congratulations."

Faith shuffled across her shop and back again trying to decipher Kyle's tone.

"How did you hear that?"

"About your opening? Was it a trade secret or something?"

"No, but—"

"But you didn't think we could still be friends, is that it? Faith, I only wanted to see how your opening went."

She paused, running a hand through her hair. She didn't want to lie, but she also didn't want him to know anything about her life.

"It went fine."

"Did you get a lot of new clients?"

"I've had several bites."

"Good for you."

"Thanks."

She was waiting for the other shoe to drop because where Kyle was concerned, there had always been another one.

"What did you end up naming your shop?" She brought fingertips to the dainty gold heart charm resting on her clavicle. "Let me guess," he continued. *"Heart Motorcycles."* His delivery made her store name sound like a punch line. His voice was a hundred miles away yet still so mocking in her ear.

When she'd first told him she wanted to open a shop one day and name it Heart Motorcycles, he'd said no biker would ever take their motorcycle to a shop called that. He'd said she couldn't run a business by herself. He'd said a lot of things she'd not soon forget. But she'd try.

Faith ended the call, cutting off Kyle's laughter. It brought an abrupt silence to the empty space.

"Faith," Trig called, poking his head through the doorway. "We're going back to the house. Caroline wants to have a few people over to watch the fireworks so I'm picking up drinks on the way. Are you still staying here tonight?"

"That's the plan."

"Are you sure you want to do that? Caroline wants to introduce you to a few people."

"I have to, Trig. I don't expect you to understand—"

"Nah, but I do," he said. "I'd be the same way."

After he left, she glanced at her phone, vibrating in her hand. This time it was a text message from Tully.

I'll be there in an hour.

She smiled to herself. "It looks like my plans for tonight just got upgraded."

CHAPTER FOURTEEN

Tully carried a soft cooler of drinks and snacks up the fire escape to the roof of Heart Motorcycles. There he found that Faith had already scoped out their best vantage point of the street and had set up two camping chairs. She'd already thought of binoculars and blankets, though the humidity of the day would take a long time to dissipate, if it even did.

Dusk had already been tucked to sleep. Against the backdrop of the clear night sky, a million stars, like glitter scattered over a black canvas, blanketed the town. It was a good night for fireworks and for sitting quietly.

Faith smiled up at him from her chair as he settled into the seat beside her.

"When we talked earlier today, I wasn't sure you'd show," she said.

"Neither was I." He'd thought the idea of a stakeout had been ludicrous when she first mentioned it, but the events of the day had shifted his perspective enough to give the stakeout a shot.

He eased back into his chair. “I don’t have any new leads, and I want this finished. Maybe this stakeout idea of yours is just wild enough to work.”

“Oh, it’ll work.”

“Is that so?”

“It has to. I want this finished too, you know.”

He had been thinking about her over the past few days, and about how different their experiences in town had been. Everyone had always rooted for him and for his success as if he’d been their son too. Everyone had known Faith just as long but by no fault of her own, they had looked at her like a stray cat who’d wandered in from the gutter. It made him understand why she sometimes scratched back at people. She’d been wounded first, deeply.

“I get why you want to help me,” he said. “You need to know your shop is safe. You need to know that you won’t be accused of any future crimes.”

“Yes, that’s the start of it, but that’s not all of it.”

He turned. “You also want CeCe’s respect.”

Faith cracked a smile. “I won’t hold my breath for CeCe’s respect. I’d settle for her keeping her thoughts to herself. She trades gossip about me like a kid trading baseball cards."

"I think you're brave for coming back and starting over. You knew you'd have to face people like CeCe, but you chose to return anyway. That takes guts." She stared at him as if uncertain what to say next. She fumbled over a few inaudible words, and he felt he had to help her. "You can just say thanks."

"You have no idea what that means coming from a person like you." She readjusted in her seat. "I grew up feeling like I had no guts, no backbone. After the scandal with my dad broke, I had no choice but to toughen up. Eat or be eaten, right? Not a day goes by where I don't wonder who I would be today if my dad had never been caught. What kind of path would I have found—for better or worse?"

"Would you be here?"

"Who knows. I probably would have never moved away, and you would have never heard of me." Her eyes danced, the rising moon reflecting in them. There was something supernatural about the tint as they stared back at him, as if she could foretell his future but was biding her time before letting him in on it.

"The moon," he said, grappling for a distraction from Faith, from the ache coming over his body once again. It was an ache to draw her close and touch her and kiss her, like he'd done at Falcon's Peak. "You can see it now."

It was true. The globe had risen above the tree line, looking close enough to touch. It cast an eerie glow over the street, lengthening shadows of streetlamps, cars and passersby.

"I brought flashlights, but I don't think we'll need them," she said.

"You weren't planning on chasing anyone on foot were you?" His tone was joking, but he wasn't sure she wasn't.

"No. I'll leave that up to the police."

"Good answer."

"What do you think your dad is doing on a night like tonight?"

He groaned. "Huh, let's see. He's probably in his shack sharing beef jerky with Duke."

"That doesn't sound too bad. Duke is a sweetheart. I'm packing bacon for him next time."

Tully studied her, surprised that she thought there would be a next visit with Walter and Duke. If she realized she'd misspoken, presuming more than she should have, she didn't show it. Her face was as relaxed as Duke's when he was ten minutes into a good belly rub.

"I know you couldn't get a good sense of it when we were there, but my dad adores that dog. He relaxes more when I'm the only one visiting. I get to see him with Duke, see how affectionate and doting he can really be."

"Bonnie always says that everyone needs someone or something to love in order to be happy."

Tully chuckled. "Is that all?"

"Well, no. She actually says that everyone needs someone to love, something to look forward to and something to give them purpose every day."

"What about you? Do you think your motorcycle shop will give you purpose?"

"I think so. I've wanted it for a long time, even when other people told me I couldn't do it on my own."

Tully scowled. "Who would tell you a thing like that?"

"No one worth mentioning. I stupidly believed they were right too. But Bonnie helped me find the courage to follow my heart."

"Is that why you named your store Heart Motorcycles?"

"Pretty close. How about you? Does being

a detective give you a strong enough sense of purpose?"

"It sure does."

Her face eased into a pleased smile. "Really? What do you love about it?"

He reached into the cooler as he considered her question. He retrieved two bottles of water and handed her one.

"I don't think anyone has asked me that before."

"Never? I hope you've asked yourself that question."

He wasn't sure if he ever had. He'd known since the time he'd been a child that he wanted to be a police officer. Somewhere along the way that path had led to detective work.

"I like learning about people's behavior, analyzing evidence, discerning the truth from the lies. I have strong instincts as far as that goes, so I've learned to hone my skills. It helps me to excel at my job but it's not why I love it." He took a sip of water, contemplating. "I know what it's like to be vulnerable, to need someone to look after you. People in this town have been doing that for me since I was a kid, and I don't know how I might have ended up without them." He thought of Miss Jenkins, of the Garners, of Charlie's family. He'd heard folks say that it took a village to raise a child, and as far as his experience proved, that had been right.

"Do you feel like you need to give back to the people of Roseley, then?"

"I do. The people here sometimes feel like an extension of my family." When Faith didn't respond, he'd wondered if he'd lost her. Although she had returned to live here, he imagined her feelings about the town didn't run nearly as deep as his. He searched to explain it.

"When I was in the police academy, my field training officer described himself as sometimes being a sheep dog. Not all the people in my class identified with the job specifically in the same way, but his illustration resonated with me. Sheep dogs dutifully protect the flock—that's how I try to serve this town. Diligently, fairly. So when you ask if that brings me great purpose, I can wholeheartedly say it does."

"Dutiful, protective—that's you, all right."

"Do you think so?"

Faith nodded slowly, stare unflinching. "I know so." After a few beats she shifted in her chair, voice growing softer. "Can you tell when someone is trying to hide something from you?"

Sometimes. Right then he knew what she was really asking. She wanted to know if he could read her feelings for him. He knew that was what it was, because he'd already been asking himself the same thing. He'd been reading her since the day she'd rolled into town and had thrown his world off-kilter.

"Yes."

"Always?" She was baiting him. It had him leaning closer to double down on his confidence.

"Why don't you put me to the test?"

The corner of her mouth flinched. "Who says I'm not already?"

"Okay," he said. "Your body tells more of the story than you even realize."

"I'm listening."

When he leaned more heavily on the armrest of his chair, he saw her breath catch. She was working to keep her control, her confidence.

"Are you still married?" he asked, studying her. There was that mouth flinch again.

"What makes you ask if—"

"Your new last name is an obvious reason. You're also a woman seeking out family and stability. Perhaps you're coming off a broken relationship. Maybe you have a desire to start over or prove something to yourself. Maybe you want to prove yourself to someone in your past. Your dad? An ex-husband?"

Her jaw tightened, the jaw muscles flinching a warning sign for him to tread more carefully.

"Which is it?" she said. "My dad or ex-husband?"

He took her hand and turned it over in his. The skin up her forearm broke out in goose bumps under the heat of his touch. He enjoyed the story her body told him now. "I noticed the other day that you don't have a mark on your ring finger. Either you were never married—" he rubbed his calloused thumb down the delicate length of her finger "—or the marriage didn't last long enough to leave a lasting impression."

She squeezed her eyes shut as if recalling a memory.

"Unfortunately, any time a marriage ends, it leaves an impression."

"How long were you married?"

"The divorce paperwork was finalized before we made it to eighteen months."

"I'm sorry."

"I'm not. I learned a lot from my failed marriage to Kyle. Bonnie helped me understand why I married him in the first place. She and her late husband, Paul, really steered me to turn my life around for the better."

"I think I like your friend Bonnie more and more."

"Her friendship is one of the best things that ever happened to me after I moved away."

"So this Kyle guy..." At the mention of his name, she quickly claimed her hand back to the safety of her lap. Tully had tripped up, a rookie move. "Is he out of the picture?" She bit her lower lip before nodding. It wasn't exactly the kind of answer he'd been hoping for. "People are usually lying when they bite their lower lip like that." She released her lip quickly. "Is he still around?"

"Maybe you really do know your stuff." She laughed, uncomfortably. "He still calls, but I don't usually answer. He'll eventually tire of being ignored. At least I hope so." She took a drink of water, studying him for a moment. "What about you?"

He shook his head. "Single."

"Has there ever been anyone serious?"

"Define *serious*."

"Have you ever been engaged?"

"Never. I don't see myself getting married."

She tipped her head, perplexed. "Anything to do with your dad?"

Tully shook his head again, more violently than he had intended. With it, a calm recognition, a knowing, came over her face. Perhaps, he thought, she could read his tells too.

"Anything to do with your mom?" She said it softly, like she was gently easing off a bandage that had been covering a wound for a long time. He sucked a breath.

"I don't talk about my mom," he muttered.

"I know." Her voice lulled. "When you mentioned her the other day, you made it seem like she had died."

"She may as well have. It's how I've thought of her for a very long time."

"Do you think of her a lot?"

"Sometimes."

She didn't speak for a while, letting his answer hang longer in the air than he'd intended. Finally, she continued.

"When I graduated high school, my mom moved to Florida to escape all the public scrutiny caused by my dad. She calls from time to time. Sometimes she invites me down to Florida for a visit, but I never go."

"Why not?"

"A relationship works both ways. She hasn't been back to Michigan to see me since I was seventeen, and for ages before that she wasn't emotionally present in my life anyway. I got used to surviving without her."

"I'm sorry you had to do that." He pursed his lips, the words failing to convey all he felt. "You should *never* have had to go through that. Mothers should be more."

"Something tells me you know what I went through," she said. This time her hand found his arm, encouraging him to share something he'd sworn not to relive. He'd normally slip away, redirect, change his line of questioning. But in her he sensed a kindred spirit of sorts, someone who knew how to touch and hold and whisper to make that deep well of pain settle down again. Someone who had yearned for a little settling of her own. "Something tells me, John, that you know better than most people."

He wasn't the detective to her nor the golden son of Roseley—dutiful, constant, faultless, or so he felt he had to be most days. She saw him as something else, something like her. A person who could lay his past demons on the table in front of her without worrying she couldn't handle them. Something told him she wouldn't disappear into uncontrollable pity, because she had had her own hurts, her own demons that could nearly match his own. Her touch was soft and comforting, but her will was strong enough to handle it, handle his past.

He tugged at the collar of his T-shirt, pulling it down to expose a scar over his collarbone. It was low enough on his chest that he never had to reveal it, never had to worry that it would peek out of his shirt and elicit questions. Aside from Samantha and his father, only Charlie as a boy had ever asked about it. Even through high school when he'd changed in locker rooms with teammates or had spent summers cutting lawns or swimming shirtless, no one mentioned it. He wondered if it was because everyone already knew. If it was an open secret following him since childhood.

He refused to look at it in the mirror and sometimes he could almost forget about it, at least, for a while. "I got this scar the last night I ever saw my mother."

Faith reached without hesitation to press her thumb over it. He stiffened, surprised at her boldness. Not since he'd been stitched up in the hospital had anyone ever touched the scar, but her hands made quick work on it now. Her eyes followed the path of her fingers. The jagged line from the crook of his neck ran down along his collarbone before disappearing beneath the folds of his shirt.

"Oh," she sighed, pressing her hand firmly against the scar. For a second, he thought she might cry. But when she finally lifted her eyes, he saw the fury blazing in them. In law enforcement, he'd seen that same look over the years. He'd had it himself every time he'd met with a survivor or faced evil. Though he could tell that she had jumped to the wrong conclusion about the scar, finding her both concerned and outraged stirred something in him. Until now he'd never felt like he needed to explain. If the secrets of his childhood had been lying dormant, hibernating for all these years, Faith Fitzpatrick made him ready to wake up. He dropped his hand, letting the fabric cover the exposed skin. She settled back in her chair, letting him begin.

"I want you to think of the most glamorous woman you can," he began. "Picture her. Whatever room she enters, she fills it from ceiling to floorboards with her presence. That," he said, "was Evelyn McTully. That was my mother."

He paused, remembering the good bits.

There had been good bits, he was sure of that. He knew he hadn't imagined her love or playfulness; otherwise, the pain of losing her wouldn't cut so deeply.

"She was always the life of the party and craved attention like oxygen. She thought she was too big for Roseley or for most cities, I think. I doubt she wanted to get married, at least not in the sense that most people think of marriage. She liked the *idea* of getting married, of having children. She liked the idea of a lot of things."

"How did she fall for your dad?"

"Ah, the age-old question." Considering his parents had seemed to come from two different planets, Tully had asked himself that very thing. "It was a case of opposites attracting, but I overheard her yelling at him one time. She said he'd promised to take her out of Roseley and move them to Paris. I have a hard time believing that, because, well, you met my dad."

"Maybe he was a lot different when he was younger?"

"I figure he was enamored with her, and Evelyn could certainly dominate a conversation. She most likely thought my dad's lack of interjection meant his acquiescence."

"Although, who knows," Faith said. "Maybe he wanted something different in Paris with her."

"Possible but not probable. At any rate, he changed his mind when she got pregnant. He wanted roots for Samantha and me. He bought my mother a house he couldn't afford and tried to make her happy. I'm sure, outside of moving to Paris, he would have promised her the world if it would have made her settle. She wanted something else." He stopped, remembering how he would have promised his mother anything too back then if it would have made her stay.

"I was only eight when she left so I remember a bit more than my sister, but as hard as I try I can't recall the days leading up to that last night with her. I don't remember my parents having any big fights before that night, at least none bigger than usual. I don't remember her hinting at it or packing suitcases or kissing us goodbye. I was supposed to be in bed sleeping, but something woke me up that night. It was probably the front door opening and slamming, but to this day I'm not sure. So much of the night is seared into my memory and other bits are foggy or missing completely.

"Samantha was sleeping in the bedroom next door, so I crept to the landing above the stairs to listen by myself. Their voices were muffled, occasionally an angry word or two would rise above the fray, giving me more questions than answers."

He clenched his fists and released them again. Recalling it all, putting it into words for the first time, had him grasping for some semblance of control. He was used to knowing each word before he spoke it, but this was foreign. It was like trying to describe his impression of an abstract painting. He knew it could be done, but it would be far from eloquent.

"I overheard her telling my dad that she had another family and was leaving us for them..."

"She had another *family*?"

"That's what she said, but I've wondered over the years if it had been a lie. My dad thought she was pregnant with someone else's baby, but I don't know for sure. I only rely on facts, and I don't have any evidence there were other children. Another man, yes, but not another family." He'd allowed himself to picture other children before, but the thought of half brothers or sisters having 100 percent of his mother while he and Samantha lived with her absence made him think dark and twisted thoughts. It wasn't who he was, and it wasn't what he would tolerate in himself.

"How do you know there was another man?"

His voice scraped his throat gravelly as he continued, "I saw him in the car. He was a shadow, like a bass hiding under a dock, but even at eight years old I knew she wasn't just leaving—she was leaving with him. He was waiting in the dark to claim her and take her away from us. How another man could do that, I'll never understand."

Faith nodded. He read acknowledgment in her face that told him she'd asked herself the same kind of question, wondered to herself how people could do the things they did. After a few moments, she spoke, cutting to the worst of it. "John, tell me about the scar."

The scar.

He had been young enough to believe that some things were worth fighting for, the themes of movies and a boy's adventure novels. He had been old enough to comprehend that his mother was walking out on all of them and he felt old enough to do something about it. He wanted to make her realize that he needed her. If he could get to her, grab her and hold her, he could make her see that he loved her. He thought she'd come to her senses. He thought she'd stay.

"I was on the landing, straining to listen, when I heard her say she was leaving. Her heels clicked on the linoleum floor, carrying her closer to the front door and farther away from me. I panicked. From the landing window, I saw her cutting a line through the front yard to his car parked on the street. She hadn't taken the path down the walkway. She'd been in such a hurry to escape us, she'd cut a straight line through the dew-stained grass. She left a visible path, like a bread crumb trail for me to follow and get her back." His throat clenched. He remembered the tail exhaust swirling as the man in shadow loaded his mother's suitcase in the trunk. He'd slammed it and flicked his cigarette butt into the street, the orange glow darkening as his mother climbed into the passenger seat.

The next part played like a high-speed chase scene in a TV show. It had all happened so fast, made his heart pound even now.

"In a frenzy, I raced down the stairs. From the hallway, I could see the front door open and my father standing on the front stoop, watching her leave. He was just standing there, motionless, arms crossed over his chest like his disapproval would be enough to dissuade her. My voice was stuck in my throat. I couldn't scream out to him to stop her, nor could I scream for her to come back. I raced to stop her myself. I knew that if I could get to her and grab her…if she could just see me…"

He held a fist to his lips, some part of him wanting to cover his mouth to keep the next words from spilling out. But he'd come this far. For once in his life, he was telling his story and he had to get it all out. Some part of him needed to purge the last part, the worst part.

"I sprinted through the threshold not realizing the glass storm door had closed and latched shut."

He remembered his mother insisting his father install the storm door only a few weeks earlier. She said she wanted to leave the front door open in the summer so she could see the people on the street. She said she was suffocating in the house. She said the storm door was more inviting, that neighbors would come to the house more. She said the long pane of glass would keep the bugs out and let the sunshine in. In the end, it had only kept him from getting to her.

Faith gasped. "You shattered the glass?"

"I cut myself up pretty badly. Most of the cuts healed quickly, but the worst of it was a slice here. A large jagged piece pierced my upper chest." He touched the scar on his collarbone again, remembering how the bleeding gash hadn't been enough to make his mother come back. The taillights of the car had disappeared around the block by the time his father caught him in his arms and laid him on the ground, attending to his wounds like a trauma surgeon in a war zone. He knew she hadn't seen or heard any of it, but at the time he'd still believed she would return. He thought some sort of maternal telepathy would pull her back to him at his time of need.

His father had rushed to call an ambulance, leaving him on the front stoop. Lying there on the cold cement, he'd craned his neck to watch for her even though the pain was tearing through his entire body. He'd been so sure she'd realize her mistake and return, sprinting from the car before the man in shadow even brought it to a complete stop. He'd been wrong.

Below them on the street, a few stragglers

milled past, making him shift his attention to watch them. They were most likely making their way home or to the shore to watch the fireworks. In the far distance, the faint music of a band playing at The Bayshore Bar rose above the silence. The restaurant deck would most likely be crowded with folks dancing and drinking, kicking off the beginning of their holiday weekend. He was on a rooftop too, but he felt like he was sitting at the bottom of a dark cavern, staring far up above him at a world carrying on without him. His mother was somewhere up there among the joyful faces while he struggled.

"Did your dad do a good job of taking care of you?"

Tully shifted his gaze back to her. His dad had done the best he could. He knew his dad loved him and wanted to protect him, shield him from his mother's abandonment, but he had never quite been the same after that. None of them had.

"He left Samantha and me to our own devices a lot more than he should have. We fared okay." Okay, fine... That was all he could ask for. He'd pushed all his chips to the center of the table, doing everything in his power to make his mother stay with him, and in the end, it hadn't been good enough. It drove home a point his father had lived by and instilled in him too: there wasn't much in the world to get that worked up over. In the end, what really mattered enough to get worked up over? He was okay. He and Samantha were okay.

She touched his chin, her graceful fingers grazing the stubble. He parted his bottom lip when her thumb traced along it, electrifying every nerve.

He'd told another person about his mother, finally. He'd recounted the order of events, and now she would carry that knowledge about him forever. There was no use trying to erase it or change it. He'd tethered some part of her, permanently, to himself by sharing his experience.

It crashed over him—the relief. The sweet relief of unburdening his secret, his pain. And if he were honest with himself, his shame. There was a shame in his mother not wanting him, finding him deficient enough that she could leave him like an abandoned box of kittens on the side of the road.

"You shouldn't have had to fair okay, John. Neither you nor Samantha. You deserved better than okay. You deserve better now. You're worth so much more and—" Her voice caught as her eyes moistened. "I need you to know that you deserve the world." She brought her face closer to his, stroking his cheek and murmuring, "The whole world."

The crack of the first firework sounded over the lake, a burst of red light illuminating the contours of her face, the swanlike slope of her neck. Purple light crackled to blue, then green, then red again, each color reflecting against the porcelain skin he now had to touch or he'd go mad.

Taking her hand from his chin, he pulled her to her feet and to his lap. She slipped her body into his arms and pressed a hand to his chest. His heart thudded hard under it. He knew the moment she felt it when she released a sigh as whimsical as dandelion seeds floating on a breeze. He imagined a future where he could be satisfied with that sigh every day for the rest of his life, satisfied with letting it carry him right along on the breeze that was Faith.

She ran her fingers around the scoop of his collar and pulled the fabric down, revealing the scar. His skin chilled at being exposed, at the possibility that he'd find pity behind her stormy eyes. Instead her expression cleared, a boldness taking hold of her. She dipped her mouth to the scar, skimming kisses there. He let his head fall back to his shoulders as her lips lingered over his skin for a moment and then a moment more.

A carnival of colors exploded overhead, one after another. All over town, people congregated together to make the most of the shared experience. Tully leaned forward and guided Faith's face toward his. He couldn't remember a shared experience in all his life that felt as sweet as holding her in his arms.

He ran his hands around the apples of her cheeks, peering into a face he couldn't believe he hadn't known until now. A week ago, she'd been a stranger, but here she felt like something so much more, so important like his heart had known her longer or maybe forever.

When she moved, cozying her body into his embrace, he wrapped his arms snuggly around her. The thunder of fireworks had faded to background music against Faith's murmuring in his ear. He kissed along her throat, pecking kisses in tune to the vibrations she hummed for him along the way. His thoughts, at first hurried, now slowed. The world could come crashing down around them, but all his focus was on this woman in his arms whom he never wanted to let go. He didn't know what the next day would bring or what the facts of the vandalism case would present, and he didn't care. His present, this moment where they were safely hidden from the rest of the world, was solely for her. If he could hold her right here until the sun rose, he'd consider himself the luckiest man on earth.

Her kisses tasted like sweet nectar on his tongue, satisfying a craving he hadn't realized he'd had and for so, so long. But it was all of her that satisfied something for him. He drew back and her eyes fluttered open. He wanted to see what it was that had bewitched him.

She pressed her forehead to his, the way he'd done when they'd been on Falcon's Peak. She held him there. When he'd first done it to her, it was because he'd known he'd overstepped by kissing her and needed to pause. He hadn't wanted to hurt her then or lead her to believe that his decision to stop had anything to do with not wanting her. She'd been the best thing to happen to him and still was here.

He'd tied a weight to his painful memories and had tossed them overboard. Before Faith, he might have thought talking about those memories was like dragging a muddy river, dredging up things that should stay sunk. But with Faith, through her gentle pressing, talking about the past had felt more like a cathartic release.

"Hey," he said.

"Hey, yourself. Are you okay?"

"More than okay."

Her mouth curled. "More than okay is good for now. I'll take it." Then she kissed him again. Together, in the secluded spot, overlooking the town, she seemed to be losing herself to the music they were making together, and the melody was carrying him right along with it.

CHAPTER FIFTEEN

FAITH AWAKENED SLOWLY. She was curled in her oversize camping chair. Her head rested on a rolled blanket she had brought to the stake-out. Another blanket was tucked around her and gathered up to her neck. She wanted to stretch. But something had woken her and until she knew what it was, she wouldn't move.

It was still dark, but not silent. The song-birds had awakened, crooning to each other over the buildings and treetops. She'd risen before the sun numerous times over the years and had usually groaned at their songs as if they gloated about having something happy to sing about. But this morning, for the first time since she could remember, she delighted in their tunes. Perhaps, she thought, it was because this morning she had something of her own to be happy about.

She recalled the evening's progression and how her stakeout had turned into a make-out session. Pulling the blanket slowly over her mouth, she smiled at the memory of it all. She had kissed men before. Heck, she'd been married. But everything about kissing John had felt like she'd been roused from a hazy dream. It was as if she'd been walking around the house with the shade drawn, thinking it was raining outside, and then suddenly someone opened the windows and let in the sunshine.

She had savored his kiss the day they had hiked up to the lookout. She'd figured his feelings for her weren't as strong as hers were for him, considering her feelings had been simmering for over a dozen years. But on the roof, his second kiss had told her more than his words could have ever conveyed. He had confided in her about his mother and trusted her enough to tell her the ugliest details. She could tell by the break in his voice that he had never told another woman about the night his mother left. It was a secret you didn't reveal until you were sure your confidant was someone who could be trusted, someone special. Someone, she hoped, who could stand the test of time with you.

Once the fireworks had faded and the night air had finally begun to cool, he had drawn back and she had traced the crinkle lines around his eyes. He'd smoothed her hair off her face and guided her head to rest against the crook of his neck. She'd never felt more at peace.

When Tully had pulled a blanket over the two of them and held her close, she'd told herself that returning to Roseley had been the best decision she'd ever made. Dreamily watching for shooting stars, she'd nearly believed that he could be her home. They could be each other's home together.

"GOOD MORNING," TULLY SAID, the early chill making his voice gruff. Faith poked her head out from under her blanket before sitting straighter at the sight of him. Arms crossed over his chest and legs extended and crossed at the ankles, he had no blanket while she monopolized two.

"Are you cold?" she said, yanking the rolled blanket from under her head and holding it, apologetically, out for him. He shook his head and reached for a thermos.

"Nah, the air is still warm, don't you think?" He poured a cup of steaming liquid and handed it to her.

She smiled and happily accepted it. "Did you have this in the soft cooler all night?"

"I wasn't sure if you drank coffee, so I improvised. Besides, I always like hot chocolate on a stakeout."

"Tell me about your stakeouts. Have you been on many?"

"Only a couple when I first made detective."

"Were they dangerous?"

"Stakeouts are rarely dangerous. They're mostly for gathering information or learning someone's routine."

"What were your stakeouts for?"

He crossed his arms again. "I don't usually talk about past cases."

She swallowed an audible "oh," disappointed that his candor from the night before hadn't extended to the morning. Though the sun was still far from breaking above the horizon, she could easily see his features as her eyes had adjusted to the dark. The streetlamps below gave off a steady glow. She thought the connection they had had the night before wouldn't dull with the dawn, but as he stayed tight-lipped about his work, she wondered if she wished for too much.

Faith wrapped her chilled fingers around the warm cup and took a sip, savoring the chocolaty sweetness on her tongue. Tully tipped his head, noticeably pleased she liked it, before he craned an ear toward the direction of the lake.

"Sounds like we're not the only ones awake this early."

It sounded like a canopy of songbirds were swaying above their heads, each elbowing for lead diva in an opera only they knew.

"I think I heard the first one sing," she said. "I'm pretty sure it woke me up."

"I've been awake for a while, and you're probably right. You didn't stir until they began singing."

She wondered what he'd been doing, sitting there awake. Had he been watching the street for criminals or watching her sleep?

"Do you usually wake up so early?" she asked.

"Yes."

"*Gokotta*, then?" Tully raised an inquisitive brow. She chuckled at stumping him. "It's a Swedish word. It's the act of waking up early in the morning and going outside to listen to the first birds sing. Uncle Gus says he practices it every day."

"I'm awake early enough to hear the first birds sing but only because that's when trout and largemouth bass start biting."

"Well, the next time you wake up to hear the birds sing, you'll know the word for it." She took another sip and smiled at him over the rim of her cup. He returned a smile of his own. "I don't know what time I nodded off last night. Did you hear or see anything?" She was referring to the vandal and hoped he hadn't heard her talking in her sleep, piecing together dreams that had been about him.

"Nothing. I stayed awake for a long time—"

"And tucked me in, I see."

He shrugged as if to convey it was no big deal.

"Listen, I have to get into the station early this morning."

"If they broke into another shop and we missed it, would you have gotten a call last night?"

"Not necessarily. I haven't been getting called until the morning when someone sees and reports it. I'll drive around and check the storefronts when I leave. Can I give you a lift home?"

She shook her head. "I have a lot of work to catch up on too. I might as well get up and get moving."

"Keep your shop door locked, remember, until the rest of the world wakes up."

"Right." She drank the last of her hot chocolate, tolerating the heat as best as she could. "And I know how to take care of myself, remember? I was the one who invited *you* along to *my* stakeout."

He kissed her gently on the forehead without another word before leaving. She stayed perched at the edge of her chair, listening for the sound of his truck engine powering on before she hugged herself and let out a happy squeal. Things around here were finally looking up.

TULLY HAD SPENT the morning getting caught up on some cases that had been opened the day before. The Fourth of July celebration brought good fun, but it also brought problems too. A couple of fellas had drunk too much beer and had gotten into an altercation late in the evening. Neighbors had filed noise complaints about the Garners, who fired fireworks long into the night. There were also the typical parking and speeding violations, but no vandalism.

Officer Allison White collapsed onto her desk chair, coming off the third shift.

"Talk about a great way to start a forest fire," she said. "I had to break up a group setting off firecrackers in The Void. That grass is as dry as straw. I don't know what they were thinking."

Tully immediately thought of his father and what he'd do if a fire broke out and he had to find his own escape. It was another reason to get his dad home once and for all, but as Walter was a grown man, what could he do to persuade him?

"Was it anyone we know?"

"Nah. Seemed to be a group of out-of-towners letting off too much steam. They were getting a little out of hand when I got there. I confiscated the firecrackers and sent them on their way." Allison pulled a few peppermint sticks out of her breast pocket and handed them to Tully. "From your fan club."

Tully took the candy and dropped it into a cup of pencils on his desk.

"Did you drive past Miss Jenkins's place this morning?"

"Yep. The walking club was there. Something about Miss Jenkins having to wait for a repairman."

"That's right," he said. He'd forgotten about the air-conditioning problem. He hadn't thought of much else the night before with Faith Fitzpatrick's kisses distracting him. "I told her I'd come take a look at it today if she needed help. I can swing by later when I check out the rest of the stores..." He crossed the office to check the call notes from the morning just as Charlie arrived. "No vandalism cases were logged last night. Did you respond to anything this morning?"

"Nope."

Tully scratched his chin. "Maybe the vandal was a tourist and is heading home today."

"Could be," Officer White said. "I saw a lot of unfamiliar faces at the fireworks. Caught a couple of guys slashing car tires too."

"What? Where was this?"

"Outside The Bayshore Bar. Too much booze plus a scuffle in the parking lot ended with two guys, midthirties, slashing their supposed friend's car tires."

"Did you arrest them?"

"After backup arrived, the friend showed up and said he wouldn't press charges. Couldn't do anything but wait with them until they called for a ride."

"Who'd they call?"

"A woman came to pick them up. I don't know what her relationship was to them—girlfriend, wife, friend—but she didn't look happy at having been called for chauffeur duty."

Tully drummed his fingers on the desk, contemplating. Two men in their midthirties slashing a friend's tires after a drunken argument wasn't quite the profile of someone vandalizing a series of stores.

"Hey, what happened to you last night?" Charlie asked. Tully frowned and sipped his coffee. "Did you watch the fireworks from home?"

"Something like that."

"Something *like* that?"

"I had plans last night."

"Plans?"

Tully scowled at his friend, aware of what he was doing. One technique to get more information from a tight-lipped suspect was to repeat the last thing they said as pleasantly as possible. Most people got uncomfortable with it and kept talking and divulging more information as a result.

"I know what you're doing."

"What I'm doing?" Charlie smiled mischievously.

"You're trying to get more information about my night with Faith."

"You spent the night with *Faith*?" His

friend sat back on the edge of his desk. Even Officer White perked up at the new development. The technique really did work. Tully slammed his cup on his desk, surprising even himself.

"Look, it wasn't like that."

"No?" Charlie said. "What was it like?"

"She wanted to watch for the guy responsible for all these break-ins. I came along for support."

"Hmm… What kind of support? I know Allie's curious."

Allison waggled her brows as Tully's eyes narrowed. He gathered his keys, ready to escape Charlie's line of questioning.

"It's not a big deal. We sat on her roof and watched the fireworks and talked."

Dex arrived, looking noticeably more irritable than he usually did first thing in the morning.

"Did I miss anything from last night?" he said. When he didn't get an immediate answer, he glanced between the three of them as if reading the situation. "What's going on?"

Tully shot Charlie a *don't you dare say anything* look, but that left Officer Allison to her own devices.

"Well," she began, "Tully and his lady

friend had a date to the fireworks last night. It sounds like they were on some kind of stakeout."

"Lady friend?" Dex said in a harrumph. "Not Faith Talbert?"

"Faith *Fitzpatrick*." Tully eyed the doorway, but Dex had caught a blood scent and nothing could distract him now.

"You're not serious, are you? Tell me you went out last night with anyone but her."

"Take it easy, Dex," Charlie said.

"He's the one who should be taking it easy. She's been playing him like a fiddle ever since she arrived." Dex pantomimed the fiddler from The Hometown Jamboree band, even stomping his foot for embellishment.

"She's innocent until proven guilty," Tully said. "Or have you forgotten the presumption of innocence?"

"Me? Have you forgotten how to be a detective? Motorcycle rides and dates to watch the fireworks? Oh, yeah. I heard all about that. Remind me again how you can be impartial with a woman who has been turning your head all week. I saw the way you were looking at her at The Gypsy Caravan when you should have been questioning what she was doing there in the first place. She nearly stomped all over the crime scene, and you let her. She's been going around town questioning folks like she's running your case. Did you know she talked to Ledger Callahan about the break-in? Wanted to know where he was when it happened, like the guy has to prove something to her. She actually questioned the guy about his whereabouts as he was trying to get his store door fixed."

Tully hadn't known exactly how Faith's interview with the Callahans had gone down and now wondered if Ledger's defensiveness with him had been a direct result of Faith being too bold.

Dex continued, "Rick Murdock swung by her place yesterday and found the whole situation fishy."

"So Rick Murdock is your new lead investigator, is he?" Tully said. "That's rich."

"He brought up good points. The worst vandalism on the block happens to be at the store of the number one suspect?"

Tully recalled CeCe's prediction that Faith's shop would be vandalized next.

"She's not the number one suspect," Charlie said.

"She should be. Tully says he was with her all last night?" He turned to Allison. "Did anyone call in a vandalism case today?" Allison shook her head, giving Dex more momentum. "*That's* rather convenient, wouldn't you say? Did our serial vandal decide to take the night off or what?"

Charlie sauntered in front of Dex as if trying to break his glare. "Hey, anything could have made him go quiet for a night. There were more people out on the street last night because of the fireworks. He didn't want to be seen."

Dex held up his hands in mock surrender. "If you say so, Charlie. I'm merely following the facts, like our detective usually does."

Tully struggled to hold his composure. He'd never been accused of not doing his job well. He was excellent at being a detective. It was probably the one thing in his life he was proudest of. So to have one of his colleagues, a colleague whom he had shared a mutual respect with for years, suddenly question his integrity…

"Do you think I've compromised myself, Dex?"

Dex snorted. "We all know you have. Even the people in this town have been talking about it. CeCe Takes came to *me* yesterday instead of you, because she thinks your judgment is impaired. I gotta tell you something, Tully. I never thought I'd see the day when anyone in Roseley accused you of being soft. You're known for your wit and your unflinching… I don't know." Dex flapped a hand at the air. "I always thought of you as doing the right thing. Now I'm not so sure."

Tully couldn't muster a response, a rebuttal, anything. He felt like he'd been socked in the gut—hard. It might not have been a two-punch knockout, but it was all he could do to stay standing on his feet.

Charlie stood next to him. "If you're questioning Tully's integrity because he—"

"*I'm* not the only one questioning it," Dex said. "*Get it?* I'm relaying what other people are saying. In fact, they've been saying it for days now. Tully's been too distracted to notice."

There was a long silence between the four of them, but it wasn't a standoff. For Tully, it felt more like an intervention, a wake-up call. If there was one thing he valued, it was the fact that folks respected his judgment. If that was called into question or if they started to lose faith in him, where would that leave him? His job was everything. He was the job.

Before Tully could respond, there was a

buzz at the entrance door signaling a visitor. When it opened, it was the last person Tully had expected to see at the police station, and the one person he needed to stay as far away from as possible now.

CHAPTER SIXTEEN

FAITH CAUGHT THE surprise in Tully's expression as she walked across the room to meet him. The silence between, not only the two of them, but also the other police officers gawking nearby, expanded like a balloon. The hair on the back of her neck prickled as she became aware she'd stumbled into a conversation, possibly about her.

It had been a tumultuous morning to say the least. After the blissful time she'd spent talking and cuddling with Tully last night, she'd spent the early morning hours occasionally pinching herself as she worked in her shop. He'd warned her to lock her door, not that it made much difference considering an intruder needed only to rip off the tarp to step into her store, but she'd heeded his advice. Instead of keeping an intruder at bay, it had been CeCe Takes who had attempted to open her front door.

Once Faith had reluctantly stepped out onto

the sidewalk, CeCe was all too happy to inform her that after doing a little surveillance of her own the night before, watching the street from behind her darkened windows, she hadn't spotted anything all that suspicious. Faith had been pleased with the news, suggesting that the vandal had moved on, perhaps because he had been an out-of-towner gone home after the Fourth of July festivities. CeCe hadn't agreed.

"To an untrained eye, I suppose it looks like the worst has passed."

Faith wasn't about to tell CeCe that she and Tully had been conducting their own surveillance of the street and that Tully's *trained* eye hadn't spotted anything. Maybe it was only the newest development between her and Tully coloring her outlook, but Faith really hoped the vandalism was over for good.

"You didn't spot anything suspicious?" Faith had asked. She was more curious about the fact that CeCe was so eager to share news with her.

"It depends on how you define *suspicious*."

"Things that don't belong," she said. "Things that seem out of the ordinary or could lead to a crime. Take your pick, Mrs. Takes."

CeCe's face had smoothed into a pleasant expression.

"As a matter of fact, I did see something out of the ordinary."

"Oh?"

"I saw a truck that looked familiar but was parked on the street where it isn't usually."

"Uh-huh." Faith had remained as stoic as possible, suddenly fully aware of the truck in question. "Why don't you hurry down to the police station and tell them all about it, Mrs. Takes. I can't help you with something like that."

"Nor can I help you, Ms. Talbert—"

"Fitzpatrick."

CeCe grinned. "But there seems to be someone in town who is all too eager to help you, isn't there?"

Faith closed the door to her shop and pretended to work until CeCe had left the area. She knew CeCe had spotted Tully's truck, either during the night or early in the morning. She might even know that it had stayed parked on the street near her shop all night long. She could sputter an explanation that they had been conducting a stakeout of their own, but CeCe wouldn't care anything about that. She would tie Tully's presence to no vandalism on the street *and* the lack of vandalism to her guilt.

Faith had hurried to the police station to tell Tully what had happened, but once she'd arrived she suspected the damage had already been done.

"Hey," she said, as casually as she could manage. She hoped he would give her a sign that he was happy to see her or that he'd been thinking of her. He didn't.

"Ms. Fitzpatrick," he nodded. "Nice to see you again." His words had never sounded so cold before, nor had his expression felt so distant. He'd addressed her by her last name—the opposite of what her heart longed for.

Officer Stillwater managed a warm smile, giving her some small hope that all was not lost. But at Tully's downcast expression, deepening by the second, her jaw tightened. He worked a muscle in his jaw, highlighting something he needed to say but couldn't.

Officer Randall snorted and brushed by her, exiting through the door she'd just entered. She looked to Tully.

"What are you doing here?" he finally said as the door slammed. Officers Stillwater and White redirected their attention to paperwork on their desks, though she knew they were still listening.

"Can we go somewhere and talk?" she said. Tully shook his head.

"I have a lot of work to do. Is it anything to do with the vandalism case?"

A lump formed at the back of her throat.

"I heard there weren't new acts of vandalism last night." He shuffled paperwork on his desk but said nothing, so she continued, "CeCe is drawing her own conclusions..." He'd been so attentive the past few days and now it seemed he wanted to look at anything but her.

"I'll keep an eye on that."

"What does that mean?"

"It means, thanks for letting me know."

"Thanks for letting you know?" Faith took a step nearer, ducking her head to try to get in his line of sight. "Did you hear what I said?"

"Yes, Ms. Fitzpatrick, I'm aware of how the situation—"

"*Ms. Fitzpatrick?* The *situation*?" She laughed but it was only to keep from yelling...or crying. "Are we back to this? I'm Ms. Fitzpatrick to you again, new resident, shop owner, suspect number one? Is that it? Did the last few days mean nothing to you?" She lowered her voice. "Did last night mean nothing?"

He carefully laid down the papers he'd gathered and faced her fully.

"Last night was a lapse in judgment."

"What part exactly? The part where you bared your soul to me or the part where you kissed me like no man ever has before? Because I gotta tell you, John, I'm having a little trouble keeping up with this one-eighty you're pulling." Hot tears burned, but she wouldn't give them the satisfaction of their falling. Her only defense was to jump into the lion's cage and wildly wield a weapon. Why cry when you could fight? "Look at me, dammit."

He did and his poker face was steadier than any she could imagine would be at a world championship game.

"I wanted to help you last night," he said. "But I realize now that that was a mistake. I have my job to do, a case to solve, and you have your shop to open."

"Are you saying that those things can't coexist in a world where you and I spend time together romantically?"

"To be clear—"

"Oh, please be clear. You felt something

for me last night, but I'm not worth the risk to your…what? Work? Ego?"

"You're a great woman but—"

"Don't let me down easy, John. I'm not the kind of woman who needs that." It wasn't true. She might be trying to steel herself against the fact that he was dumping her before they'd even really started dating, but inside she felt as fragile as porcelain. She pressed her lips together to keep her bottom one from shaking. She had already pictured a life where they could help each other and be exactly what the other needed. If she'd wanted to try love with anyone ever again, it had been with John McTully.

Instead, he was standing in front of her and saying he wanted to try for his job. "What a waste," she said, swallowing the lump filling her throat. "I thought we made a pretty good team."

He brought his hands to his waist in a superhero pose, but he was anything but a hero to her now. He looked like a coward.

"That's the problem, Ms. Fitzpatrick. I work alone."

It was then that she realized the other officers had left the room. Even they couldn't stand to watch what was quickly becoming the worst humiliation of her life. She'd run from this kind of rejection for her entire adult life, but the moment she'd let her guard down and entertained the possibility that Tully was different, that he would never treat her how the others did, she'd been gutted to the core.

She'd known how foolish it had been to want him. It had been a pipe dream, wishful thinking at its most delusional core, to think that someone like him could fall for someone like her. He was Roseley royalty, and she'd been run out of town. He was admired by all, and she could count every friend and loved one she had on a single hand. He was honorable and good and desired, and she had married a man who hadn't cared about her from the day they'd married.

If the ground would open up and swallow her whole, she'd be eternally grateful and not just because she wanted to escape the embarrassment. He needed to stay on his disciplined, familiar track and couldn't indulge in a relationship with her. She felt like a walking, cautionary tale to all young women who dreamed of something more, of something good, but overreached. He'd been the sun she'd flown too close to and he'd scorched her in an instant.

"It's *Faith*," she snapped. "Faith who *listened* to you and *cared* about you and—" She couldn't choke out the last words as it would hurt too much to admit her feelings and leave them unrequited in the open air. "Who still cares deeply about you. I counted on a lot of people in this town treating me like I was unworthy, but I never expected it from you. I'd give you everything if you asked, but all you're doing is pushing me away, pushing us away."

She turned on her heels and marched out of the police station. She'd no sooner made it to her car when she heard a voice behind her. She spun, thinking Tully had realized his mistake and followed her, hurrying to swing her up into his arms. Unfortunately, it was Officer Randall's chuckle that met her ears.

"You can fool some of the people all of the time and all of the people some of the time, but you can't fool all of the people all of the time."

Faith glared at him. He thought he was some purveyor of truth and justice when all he looked like to her was an arrogant jerk who couldn't see past his own prejudices.

"Should I cross-stitch that on a pillow?"

"You'd better get your house in order, because Lady Justice is going to come calling for you."

"I can't wait until she shows up, Officer. Because on that day, I'll be awaiting your apology in writing and in person."

He smiled. "So bold. I recall your dad acting the same when he was arrested. The apple never falls too far from the tree." And with that he climbed into his squad car and pulled away, leaving Faith dumbstruck. She'd overheard the same words from her high school guidance counselor years before. He hadn't known she was standing near the doorway, in earshot of his conversation with the principal.

Keep an eye on the Talbert girl, the counselor had said. *The apple never falls far from the tree.* At the time she'd nearly dissolved into a puddle of tears. How could she be so misunderstood when she'd done nothing wrong in the first place?

She may not be that frail young woman anymore, but his words made her doubt that returning to town was wise. After overhearing her guidance counselor, she'd begun making plans to move somewhere far away. And now, as her heart shattered into a thousand pieces, making it hard to breathe, she realized it was probably time to leave Roseley again.

Tully pushed Faith's parting words from his mind as he drove along the lakeshore. The afternoon sun shimmered on the waves like gold. The lake was always good for distracting him and helping him think and today he needed it. He wanted to come up with a reasonable explanation for why there had been no crime committed the night before. CeCe's suspicions about it didn't sound quite as ridiculous in the morning light. She'd referred to the idea that it was a premeditated plan on Faith's part, some sort of long con, but to what profitable end, Tully couldn't say. Dex's words rang in his ears as he drove, and he wondered how many other people thought he was playing the fool.

When Charlie called, Tully decided to answer it just to interrupt his ruminating.

"Have you talked to Faith yet?" Charlie said. "Have you fixed what happened this morning?"

"What's to be fixed? It isn't going anywhere."

"No?"

"No."

Charlie huffed, "How long have we been best friends?"

"Forever."

"Something like that. I think I know you pretty well, wouldn't you say?"

"Better than most, but cut to the chase, Charlie. I'm pulling up to Moody Ward's house."

"Forget the case for a second. You need to work on your life."

"Excuse me?" Tully threw his truck in Park.

"You're letting Dex cloud your judgment, which is something you never let anyone do."

"You're the second person to question my judgment today. That's the problem." But it wasn't Dex's influence that had him worried. It was Faith's. He hadn't been in his typical detective mode over the last few days, and it was letting the town down. He needed logic.

Charlie continued, "The facts of the case don't point exclusively to her."

"I know," Tully said. "I know that she's an easy scapegoat." Unfortunately, the facts didn't eliminate her as a suspect either. "I have to go. I'll talk to you later."

He stepped out of his truck as Cheyanne, Moody's daughter, crossed from the house to the shed and spotted him. She waved as he approached.

"Cheyanne, good to see you again."

"Detective McTully, I wasn't expecting you."

At her greeting, Cody popped out from behind the shed with a fishing pole and tackle box. Tully offered a relaxed wave.

"I saw you in the parade," he said to Cody, who shifted uncomfortably on his feet. "Word has it you're starting with the soccer team this fall."

Cody looked at his mom.

"As long as he can keep his grades up," she said.

"I'm sure he can do it," Tully said. "Have practices kept you busy this summer?"

The teen shrugged. "It's been mostly conditioning and drills."

"He falls into bed every night."

"I'm glad to hear that. Take advantage of your energy while you're young. I'll be sure to catch your games."

"Seriously?" Cody scoffed as if Tully was pulling his leg.

"Seriously. I caught a few home games last year. It looks like Roseley High is putting together a good team again. I wouldn't be surprised if you had a record-breaking season. Are the games still on Saturday nights?"

"They are," Cheyanne said, smiling at Cody. "Cody, now you'll have four people at your games."

Cody flinched like he didn't care one way or the other, but Tully knew he'd hit a nerve—a good one.

"Are you catching anything?" He motioned to the fishing poles.

"He snagged several perch yesterday," Cheyanne said. "We fried them up last night for dinner. Even Grandma ate two helpings."

"Perch is some of my favorite. What kind of lures are you using?"

Cody held up his fishing pole for Tully to examine.

"That'll get 'em. That one's top rate."

"Grandpa bought it for me."

"He wants you out of the woods and on the lake."

"Yeah, yeah."

"Go catch us dinner." Cheyanne chuckled. Cody waved her comment away, noticeably awkward from her encouragement, but Tully had already turned his attention to Cheyanne.

"Speaking of your dad, is he around?" Tully wanted to talk to Moody more. Aside from CeCe Takes, Moody was most knowledgable about Roseley's inner workings, and Tully was fresh out of leads—decent ones. At the parade he'd sensed that Moody might have a few more things to say about The Gypsy Caravan.

"He's out with my mom for the day. They won't be back till tonight for a little celebratory dinner."

"Oh?"

Cheyanne beamed with pride. "I graduated from my accounting program."

"Congratulations."

"And just got a new job."

"That's right. I heard about your interview in Traverse City."

"That was where the interview was, but it was for a job in town. The Gypsy Caravan hired me to keep their books."

"How did you manage that?"

"They asked my dad to recommend someone local, so he put in a good word for me. I've been in talks with them for a while but had to keep it quiet. We've all been crossing our fingers for the last week, hoping I'd get it. It means better pay, better hours and, most importantly, more time with Cody."

It all made sense, Moody's worry the Callahan brothers would leave Roseley. Their store was not just good for the town, it was good for his daughter and grandson.

"That's wonderful, Cheyanne. No one deserves it more than you."

"Thanks." She glanced at the dock where

Cody was impatiently waiting for her. "What did you need to talk to my dad for? Should I have him call you?"

"Nope," Tully said. "Just driving by and thought I'd stop to chat."

By the time he made it back to his truck, Cody and his mom had already cast their lines. His instincts had been right. Moody had left out a nugget of important information when they'd talked at the parade. But as he caught a glance at Cody and Cheyanne in his rearview mirror, happily fishing together, he was pleased to see it was for a good reason.

TULLY HAD MADE it to Grandma's Basement in time to find CeCe and Dolores paying a visit. He was glad to feel a blanket of cool air greet him at the door.

"Detective McTully," Miss Jenkins said, a warm smile spreading over her face. "What are you doing here?"

"I wanted to see how the repair company treated you. It feels like they did a good job."

CeCe held up two hands to draw his attention to the rest of the shop.

"The fella got it working about a half hour ago. We're having a celebratory drink." Miss Jenkins motioned for him to sit down at what looked like a midafternoon tea. Dolores poured him a lemonade.

"Have you gotten any business today?"

Miss Jenkins frowned. "Unfortunately, not much. People have been strolling the walk looking for places to get cool and up until a little bit ago, I didn't have much to offer in the way of an oasis. Hopefully, it picks up. I'm half tempted to put a sign in the window advertising that I have air-conditioning."

CeCe wrapped both hands around her glass, pausing for dramatic effect.

"I spoke with Gemma Murdock at The Copper Kettle, and she overheard Caroline and Trig Waterson talking at lunch. Apparently, Faith announced to them this morning that she's packing it in and leaving town for good."

Tully could no sooner stop CeCe from spreading gossip than he could wrangle a locust storm, and where Faith was concerned, both were just as damaging.

"I know you're sweet on her, Detective," CeCe said, "but Faith has behaved in the way I warned you about."

"Hardly. She's probably leaving town because people have judged her too harshly. I judged her and the only crime she's ever committed was being born the daughter of Ray Talbert. I wouldn't wish that life sentence on anyone." He kept his words steady, unthreatening as he took another sip of lemonade. Miss Jenkins's face fell, noticeably distraught at his words.

"She seems like a sweet girl," Miss Jenkins said. "I'm so sorry for what happened to her shop. And the part you said about her father… It's right, isn't it? It's a lousy hand to have been dealt, and from such an impressionable age."

"She might not be able to change who her father is," CeCe said, "but she can certainly keep a rein on her *attitude*."

"What attitude?" Dolores said. "She's never shown an attitude to me."

CeCe rolled her eyes. "She's doled out plenty to me."

"You're not the easiest person to know, CeCe," Dolores said. "You're a stinker." She poured her friend another cup of tea as if to soften the blow.

"What's *that* supposed to mean?"

"It means you're a difficult person with a capital *D*. I was lucky to land on your good side when we first met twenty-seven years ago, otherwise you and I probably would have found ourselves in an ongoing feud."

CeCe scrunched up her face, noticeably offended, but Miss Jenkins was quick to pat her hand, redirecting her the way a preschool teacher redirected a student throwing a tantrum.

"It's true, honey. Sometimes you don't bring out the best in people. You can be a little harsh."

"*Harsh?* I'm not harsh. I'm honest. I'm *protective.*"

"You're also a wee bit—" Miss Jenkins hesitated and glanced at Dolores, who nodded "—divisive."

"What on earth are you saying, Betty?"

"If you think someone isn't with you, you think they're against you, but that's not how life works. For one reason or another, you pitted Faith against you as soon as she arrived. I don't know why, but your attitude toward her has been…"

"What?" CeCe softened, leaning away from the table as if a bomb was set to explode from Betty's mouth.

Miss Jenkins's face darkened, her words low and serious. "Oh, so *foul.*"

"Betty." CeCe's face stretched in horror. Miss Jenkins winced to convey it was unfortunately true.

"But," she said, squeezing her hand, "we still love you, dear. Don't we, Dolores?" Dolores patted CeCe's other hand.

Tully lowered his eyes to give the trio as much privacy as their close proximity would allow. Miss Jenkins was as sweet as a bunny rabbit, but she had just landed a punch that had CeCe seeing stars. It wasn't easy to hear the truth from a friend, but if CeCe could be sure of anything, it was that there was nothing mean in her friends' honesty. It was compassionate and firm, like words from a good coach.

He thought of his earlier conversation with Charlie, but pushed it away for the time being. He needed to focus on the case. Well, he needed to focus on the case once the shock wore off. For once, CeCe Takes didn't have a word to say.

He watched the women and realized that not everyone agreed with CeCe's opinion. Dex had made it seem like everyone was doubting his judgment and suspected Faith, but that hadn't been true. There were people who had seen in Faith what he had seen all along. He wondered if that meant his detective skills weren't going awry after all.

"How long have you known this about me?" CeCe asked. Dolores snorted.

"For as long as we've known you."

"Why didn't you say something sooner?"

"We tried to talk to you all week," Miss Jenkins said. "You turned your nose up at every kind word we spoke about Faith or every kind thing we did for her."

"I was trying to protect you. You're too nice."

"I'm not," Dolores said. "Betty, you might be a little too nice, but it's why we like you."

"That's true," CeCe admitted. "I don't want you to be like me, Betty. Have you been upset with me all week?"

Betty sadly nodded. "I haven't been able to sleep and it had nothing to do with my air conditioner being out. The other night it was so darn hot, and all I could do was fan myself and go round and round about poor Faith and how she's trying hard to—"

"It was so hot?" Dolores said. "Did your air-conditioning go out at your house too?"

"What?" Miss Jenkins said, sitting back from the table.

"You said you were up at night thinking about it and it was hot. Have you been sleeping here in your store?"

"N-no. I meant that I couldn't sleep because I was thinking about Faith."

Tully sat motionless, waiting. It was a funny thing how people could be drawn to give up the truth when they thought no one was digging for it. By the flush of Miss Jenkins's cheeks and the sweat percolating on her brow, he sensed that the truth was about to come bubbling out.

"Why would you spend the night at your shop?" Dolores asked. "Were you worried someone was going to break in?"

"No, I..." Miss Jenkins wavered on her chair. "I wasn't in my shop. It was too hot."

CeCe frowned and studied Betty. "But you said you couldn't sleep because it was so hot. You slept here the night before? The night the air-conditioning went out? The night..."

Miss Jenkins's eyes now widened in the same horror CeCe's had only a moment ago, but where her friend had taken offense, Miss Jenkins seemed to be struggling to not break down crying. She looked from one person to another as her fingers fiddled over a napkin, folding and unfolding it again.

Tully studied each movement as his heart sank. She'd been such an important part of his childhood, of his healing after his mother had walked out on him. He hated to leave her squirming on her seat like a worm wriggling to free itself from a hook, but the truth needed to come out, completely, finally.

"Miss Jenkins," he said. Her head swiveled to him. "Are you the one responsible for all the vandalism?" She sucked in her lips, pressing them together as a last holdout. "Miss Jenkins?"

"I… I…"

"We'll still love you, Betty," CeCe said, now taking her friend's hand in a moment of solidarity. "You can tell us the truth. You owe us that."

Miss Jenkins dropped her head, tears streaking her freshly powdered cheeks.

"I never wanted to bother anyone. I want you to believe that. I just wanted to spook the Callahan brothers."

"Your competition?" Dolores said, confused. She had good reason to be. Miss Jenkins didn't have an adversarial bone in her body, making friends with everyone and striving for peace at all costs if it came down to it.

"It's not about that," Miss Jenkins tearfully explained. "I've had this business for almost my entire life, and I've always made do, even if just barely. When the Callahan brothers announced they were moving in, I knew everyone would go to their shop, especially the tourists who were starstruck by the Callahans themselves. They've been on television, for heaven's sake. I didn't want to break anything or damage anything in their shop. I only wanted to scare them. They'd said before that they had been considering other towns, and I thought if I made them see Roseley as a more dangerous place, they'd take their store somewhere else. I'm so sorry."

"But you broke my window," CeCe said. "And Faith's and even your own."

"I couldn't just vandalize the only other antiques store in town or everyone would suspect me." She covered her face with her hands. "Instead you suspected that poor girl. I didn't mean for any of that to happen to her. I broke her window hoping it would make her look innocent, but it made you press her harder."

Tully pulled his chair closer to Miss Jenkins. When he began rubbing her back, she leaned into him and sobbed.

"Honey," CeCe said. "We had no idea you were so worried about losing your shop. We would have helped you. That's why you've got us."

Miss Jenkins wiped her eyes.

"Can you ever forgive me?" she asked. "Do you think Faith ever could?"

"She's a tough cookie," Dolores said. "But she's a good one too. We'll help you explain it to her."

"Does this mean I'm arrested?"

Tully nodded again. "As a sworn officer of the law, I have no choice but to take you to the police station, but as your friend, I think I can tell you it'll be okay."

"I won't press charges!" CeCe sputtered. "And I'll come to the station with you, Betty. Dolores will too. We won't let anything happen to you."

Miss Jenkins managed a sorrowful smile. CeCe might be a hard old bird, he thought, but her protective instinct was a quality Miss Jenkins could use right about now.

As he escorted Miss Jenkins to his truck and settled her into the front seat, her friends assuring her that they would be right behind her, Tully knew Miss Jenkins would be fine in the end. He doubted anyone, like CeCe said, would press charges against Miss Jenkins, aside from maybe the Callahan brothers, and even the damage she'd done at their store hadn't been terrible.

He wanted to offer Miss Jenkins a few

words of comfort on the ride to the station, but the relief she felt was obvious as she babbled like a brook. Amid her chatting, his mind wandered like a man lost in the desert. At times like this, he usually felt pleased to have wrapped up a case, marking another tally on the mental scorecard he kept of his professional successes. Instead, he struggled not to succumb to a melancholy that had washed over him. There was only one person he really wanted to see, one person he really wanted to tell about the case: *Faith*.

Unfortunately, he thought, he hadn't left himself in a position where he could casually drop by her store to talk. He'd hurt her, deeply, and he felt at a loss as to how to fix that.

CHAPTER SEVENTEEN

CAROLINE RESTED ON the corner of Faith's bed and watched her.

"I don't understand why you need to leave," she said as Faith clicked away on her laptop.

"Can you picture a scenario where people aren't whispering about me as soon as I walk past them?"

"Who cares what they say? You have Trig and me and Dad—that is, when he finds his way back to us. We love you, and in time, the rest of the people in town will start to love you too."

"I'm glad that you're happy here and have friends," Faith said. "But your experience hasn't been my experience."

"Yet."

Faith pretended not to hear Caroline. Instead she clicked away on the laptop. She needed to figure out where to go next.

"I'd rather get out of here before I lose too much of my investment."

"You're not going to get the shop window replaced?"

"Based on the terms of my lease, I have to get it fixed, but then I'm outta here."

"Where will you go?"

"Wherever I can find a job."

"But your shop…your dream…"

Faith touched the heart charm dangling around her neck. At the thought of losing her shop, the delicate gold necklace grew as heavy as a lead weight.

"I'll start over somewhere else, I suppose."

"You suppose?" Caroline's words offered a challenge.

"I did it once, and I can do it again." She tried to deliver the sentiment with conviction, but she wasn't so sure she'd have the will to start again. Or…if she wanted to start again anywhere other than Roseley.

She couldn't deny that the thought of moving back to Roseley had charmed her a long time ago, but maybe she should try finding happiness somewhere else. If she could forget the one person she'd never stopped loving…

"You've changed a lot over the last ten years and a lot of those changes have been good," Caroline said. "But running away like this—"

"I'm not running away. I've been subjecting myself to rejection and ridicule ever since I got here, and I don't want to do it anymore."

"You're leaving on an air of self-preservation? Is that what you're calling it?"

"I gave it a shot, Caroline. I swung and I struck out. I've wanted to be a different person ever since my dad… No…" She covered her face with her hands before ripping them away with a pressure that had been building all week. "I always wanted to be a different person, even before what happened with my dad. I've never felt good enough to get the things other people had, but coming back here showed me how I was fooling myself. My fate was determined for me a long time ago—"

"You are a different person, a better person. It wasn't easy getting here but you got here. You're standing on your own two feet and looking your detractors in the face. At least that's what it seemed like to me."

Faith frowned. She didn't want to let other people get to her but they did. They still did, and she didn't know if she'd ever get past that. Wasn't it better to go somewhere else, where no one knew her history?

Caroline stared. "I don't think you'll be able to live with yourself if you leave."

"Why do you say that?"

"Because you want this so badly. You belong, Faith." Faith's cell phone rang. Caroline reached for it and glanced at the caller ID. "He's calling you again. What does he want?"

Faith reached for the phone. Kyle's calls had become more persistent over the last day, as if he could sense that her emotions had bottomed out.

"Caroline, do you mind giving me a minute?" But her cousin was already out the door. She answered the phone. "What do you want, Kyle?"

"Whoa. Hey, sweetheart. Is everything okay?" He was abnormally careful, concerned even.

"Just peachy."

"It sounds like things aren't going so well."

"I've been better."

"I'll bet I can cheer you up."

"Try me."

He chuckled. "Do you remember that weekend we went up to Traverse City for the National Cherry Festival?"

Faith paced her bedroom, recalling the weekend they'd shared. It had felt like a daydream, the two of them role-playing a happy couple, young and in love. It had been there that Kyle had tucked a baby pink cherry blossom sprig in her hair. Then he had proposed. Well, he'd sort of proposed. He'd proposed the idea of moving in together and had casually dropped the idea of getting married the way a person casually said they were in the mood for Italian for dinner.

"What about it?"

"It's this weekend."

"So?"

"So, I was thinking—" Faith bit her lip; Kyle was always thinking big ideas when he was in the mood for convincing her of something that was in *his* best interest "—we could drive up there for old times' sake. You, me and a few days to cut loose."

Faith sank to the corner of her bed.

"Why would I want to do something like that?"

"You've been working so hard, and I'll bet you could use a break. And more importantly than that—" he paused, letting the silence grow in anticipation "—we belong together, sweetheart. I know I messed up and it was completely smart of you to leave and teach me a lesson—"

"I wasn't teaching you a lesson. I divorced you. You cheated on me."

"I was a cad."

"Obviously."

"I was a terrible husband." Faith nodded in agreement as if he could see her through the phone. "I didn't know how to be a good husband even though I wanted to be. I want to be one now. I made the biggest mistake of my life losing you, Faith. And I haven't been able to stop thinking about you. I want you back, baby." The soft timbre of his voice was getting to her.

"But it's too late."

She wanted to tell him that life had never been better since she'd left him, but she couldn't. Instead, she pressed the phone to her ear and waited for him to say more sweet things because she desperately needed to hear them.

"Nah, it's the second chance we need. Don't you think?"

"I don't… I'm not sure…"

"Come home to me, baby. This place isn't right without you."

She thought of her little house with Kyle. Every move she'd made after they'd married had been her attempt to make the house a home and their life together a good one. She'd given her all. Her all. Maybe she could give her all again. If he was ready to change and she was ready to forgive, maybe they could make things work.

"I suppose I could use the garage for a while…"

"What do you mean?" Kyle said.

"You know, get my business off the ground there before I transition to a shop."

"Heart Motorcycles? Are you still wanting to do that?"

Faith stood. "Uh, *yeah*. Why wouldn't I?"

"Because you need to get a job. I'm proud of you for taking a chance on that motorcycle shop—"

"Are you? Are you proud? It wasn't two days ago you were laughing at me for it."

"I was still sore over you leaving. That's all. I've been torn up over losing you and I lashed out a little."

"How torn up are you?" she demanded. He hadn't said anything about staying faithful to her.

"I made mistakes, Faith. Haven't you ever made mistakes you wish you could take back? You always said that everyone deserves a clean slate, right?"

"Our problem wasn't that I wouldn't give you a clean slate, Kyle. Our problem was that you never promised to change. You made me think your affairs were my fault."

"Baby," he said, his voice downshifting. "You're so right. I had the perfect woman, and I let you slip through my fingers. What can I do to get you to forgive me? What can I do to get you to come home? We can make a fresh start together, if you'll only let me love you again."

All Faith had ever wanted was a fresh start, but a fresh start here. She'd been chasing relationships that would only let her down, and Kyle was her prime example. She didn't want to hear all the right words. She didn't want empty promises...because she'd had gotten plenty of those in the past.

"That's a really nice offer," she said, covering the heart charm dangling around her neck.

"I want to give you the world, baby," he crooned into the phone. "We could take a second honeymoon in Traverse City and remember all the good times we had. I never should have let you go, Faith. Come back home."

Faith thought of Tully. She knew she would never be good enough to have a man like Tully in her life, but for a magical week or so, he'd respected her and erased the wounds in her soul like no man ever had.

She might not be worthy of John McTully, but she was worthy of a lot more than she ever used to think. Kyle was right. They needed a clean slate, but it was a clean slate apart from each other. She deserved to follow her dream and run full steam at the life she had always wanted. Only now did she wholeheartedly believe she deserved it.

"Kyle, I'm going to tell you this next part slowly, so I want you to listen carefully."

"You got it, baby."

She drew a deep breath. "Don't…ever…call…me…again."

"What? Faith, talk to me."

She didn't care to argue with him or explain why she never wanted to speak to him again. It wasn't her job to convince him of anything. In fact, she'd change her cell phone number in the morning. Her time was better spent focusing on what she did want rather than on listing what she didn't.

With one finger press, she ended the call and dropped the phone on her bed. She stood silently for several minutes, drawing her heart charm along the chain and back again. She had purchased the necklace not too long ago, hoping it would be a reminder of everything she wanted. At the time she'd bought it, she had wanted to believe that life could be different if she could take a chance to start over and make it different.

When she bought the necklace, she wore it out of the store, and it hadn't left her neck since. It was the reminder she needed to keep going, to follow her heart.

It was Caroline who broke her trance.

"What did Kyle want? Please tell me you're not entertaining any thoughts of going back to him."

"I'm not."

"That's a relief."

"I want more, Caroline."

"You deserve more, cousin."

"Yes, I think I do."

"Honey, didn't you already know that?"

"I don't know," Faith said. "I know it now."

"So what are you going to do?"

"I'm going to repair my store window..."

"You said that already."

"And then," she said, smiling, "I'm going to repaint it."

TULLY PARKED HIS truck on the street near Heart Motorcycles. He'd spent the evening thinking about Faith and their time spent together. He'd considered calling her after he'd finished at the station with Miss Jenkins, but he hadn't been able to bring himself to do it. He didn't want her to assume that the only reason he could talk to her now was because she had been cleared as a suspect. But after a couple of days, he had found himself in his truck and driving to her shop before he could convince himself otherwise.

Faith stood on the sidewalk, supervising as a glass company replaced the giant picture window at the front of her store. She glanced at him for only a moment before turning her attention back to the task at hand. He shuffled up the sidewalk and came to a stop beside her.

"I was worried you wouldn't be able to get anyone out here until next week."

"Don't go worrying about me," she said, her voice sharp. He let her comment hang a few beats, recalculating what to say next. She wasn't in the mood to make things easy on him.

"I gather you've learned by now..."

"Miss Jenkins? Yeah, the news has been spreading like wildfire."

"I'm sure it has. It'll be hard on her."

"It'll be hard on you too." She peered up at

him, her expression softening. “A few people have told me know how much she means to you. I imagine that after what happened with your own mother…” Her words trailed off as if sensing that the mere mention of it could cut him. “Anyway, when I learned about Miss Jenkins, my first thought was of you. Did you have to arrest her?”

“It was informal. She wasn’t going to put up a fight. She’s an old woman who got scared and made a series of bad mistakes.”

“Was she remorseful?”

“Of course.” He was used to the people he cared about disappointing him, but he’d never expected such things from Miss Jenkins. “The whole thing wasn’t pretty. The fallout in town, I imagine, will be worse.”

“I really am sorry you had to be the one to do it, John.”

“I avoided The Copper Kettle this morning. I’m not ready to weigh in on what happened, though I know everyone is going to want me to.”

“Funny how I haven’t seen anyone since the news broke yesterday. CeCe used to scurry by here as persistent and annoying as a mosquito buzzing in my ear and now—” She waved her arms on either side of her. “The street in front of my store has gone silent. No apology for Ray Talbert's daughter, not that I was going to hold my breath for one."

"Faith," he began. "I—"

"There's one perk I can cherish, huh? You've finally started calling me Faith. You had to wait until you knew I was innocent to say it but—"

"I never thought you were guilty."

"No?" She locked onto him now, gray eyes brewing. He'd been drawn to her that day at the gas station just as he was drawn to her now. He wanted to lean in, move closer, connect a hand to her cheek and his mouth to hers.

She, however, was not in the mood for connection. She was hell-bent on putting him in his place.

He decided he would help her.

"I might not be the best friend or the best boyfriend or the best son, Faith, but I've always been the best detective. I've dedicated my life to serving and protecting the people of this town. When I met you, I felt a shift in myself that I wasn't prepared for. I thought you were clouding my judgment, and that scared me. Truth be told, I think you're still clouding my judgment."

"I'm not doing anything," she insisted. "I never was, John. I only wanted to—" She whispered as if recalling a sad memory. "All I've ever wanted was to..."

"What?" he said but she shook her head and shifted away from him.

"It doesn't matter now. You work alone, right? Your message has been received loud and clear."

"I never wanted to hurt you, Faith. I wanted us to be friends and be able to—"

"What? Flirt and dance around our feelings for years to come because you can't commit to anything other than your job?"

Now it was his turn to shift on his feet. Was that what he did want? To entertain his feelings for her but at a distance, returning to some version of their past week that didn't involve her getting too close?

She grasped the heart charm hanging around her neck and heaved a deep breath.

"You might not be the best boyfriend or the best son, but you could be, you know. You limit yourself from being those things because you don't want to care too much. You think that if you do, if you let yourself really care and really connect, you'll get hurt again. And guess what. You might. That's the risk, but I believe it's a risk worth taking." She pinched the bridge of her nose and drew a breath. "Your dad is squatting on The Void in some broken shack that I wouldn't let Duke sleep in, but you just let him. Like giving it your all, doing everything in your power to get him home, might backfire on you somehow."

"He's a grown man. He can decide for himself."

"He's your *dad*. He deserves for you to take the risk. And I deserve for someone to take a risk on me too. I deserve better than men who only offer me less. I'd even convinced myself that that was fine for me, for who I was, but not anymore." Her fingers toyed with the charm. He sensed her drawing strength from it like the charge on a battery. Her necklace and store meant a lot to her. He knew it was something deep and everlasting.

"I'm going to reopen my shop and make a name for myself here, and I'll tell you something else, John McTully." She closed the distance between them and placed her hand over the scar on his collarbone. Her eyes flashed, wild and determined, her control of the situation, of him, pulling his focus to her. His skin tightened as her fingers shifted the fabric of his shirt and drove a current through his body, blocking out the scene around them. All that was left was her and him, together.

"Faith…"

"I have loved you for longer than you know. A few days ago, I might have convinced myself that I could settle for something less from you, something less than what I wanted, if it meant being with you. But now I realize that I deserve to be loved fully, heart and body and soul. And you, John…" She slipped her hand under the top of his shirt and pressed her hand firmly to the scar. "You deserve to be loved that way too."

He blinked hard. He wanted to pull her into his arms and never let her go, but he knew she'd have none of it. She didn't trust that he would mean it, even if he did.

Before he could respond, she reclaimed her hand, the sudden absence leaving the spot on his chest cool. She crossed to her shop and disappeared with an urgency that made him think twice about following her.

The guys from the glass repair store continued to work, methodically, no one glancing over. People milling the sidewalk and cars driving by moved with the same speed they had moments before. The sun continued to shine. The morning was as bright and promising as it had been when he'd first arrived. No one reacted to what Faith had said or done. He stood as rigid as a statue, rooted to the ground as if vines had sprouted and wrapped around his feet. Inside, however, his emotions whipped furiously. Watching her walk away left him strangled by his own desires and considering whether he could ever again live a life that didn't have Faith Fitzpatrick in it.

CHAPTER EIGHTEEN

FAITH PARKED HER car behind her shop and lugged a bag of paint containers through the back door. She'd taken Tully's advice and bought more colors to go along with the red, including a rosy pink, baby pink, white and charcoal gray. She'd been reimagining what the store logo would look like all day and now that the new window had been replaced, she was ready to get started.

She kicked the back door closed and fumbled for the overhead light when she heard voices. Through the window, the perfectly polished one that she hoped she'd never have to replace again, she spotted people peering in from the other side.

"Oh, great," she muttered to the empty store. "What do they want now?"

Faith dropped the bag of small paint containers on the counter and made her way to the door, unlocking it and stepping out into the late afternoon sun. A crowd of people stared at her. She shifted uneasily on her feet.

"Can I help you?" she said, aware her tone was defensive and harsh. With nearly two dozen people there, she didn't have another tone in her arsenal that matched the situation. She half expected someone to point a finger at her and declare her the black sheep of Main Street. If this was an intervention on her behalf, she feared what their motivation was and what they hoped the outcome would be. Heath Harrison and a boy she assumed was his son watched, along with Rick Murdock and his wife, Gemma, whom she recognized instantly. She didn't know what to expect and emotionally began readying her armor.

She was about to say something rash, no doubt, just as she spotted Mara Selby and her daughter, Lucy. She and Mara had been on good terms since she'd arrived in town. Officer Stillwater and a pretty blonde, most likely his wife, were there too. Officer Stillwater grinned.

"What is all this?" Faith asked, now scanning the crowd for Tully. He may not want to reciprocate feelings for her the way she'd wanted, but he had been kind and supportive and she knew he would never be a part of a mob mentality against her.

Her heart sank when she didn't immediately find him as his tall frame would be nearly impossible to miss. But when she spotted Caroline and Trig, her stance softened. She blinked several times, noticeably confused but instantly reassured that nothing sinister could be at play with her cousins there. She trusted them. If they were on board with whatever was transpiring on her front walk, she shouldn't have anything to fear.

Trig winked at her and it brought a nervous smile to her face.

CeCe stepped forward, her arm linked with Miss Jenkins's arm.

"I'm sure you're wondering what we're doing here," she said.

"You think?" Trig called, prompting a few laughs from the group. CeCe pretended not to hear him.

"Betty had some things to say, and she insisted on saying them publicly. She's the one who rallied everyone to come here. Go on, Betty."

Miss Jenkins slipped her arm from her friend's. The lace hem of her baby blue dress swished around her calves as she settled in front of Faith.

"Everyone knows by now that I was the one responsible for vandalizing the shops around town." She clasped her hands nervously in front of her. "I let my fear get the best of me and did things I'm quite ashamed of." Red lines forked like spider webs across the whites of her eyes. She spoke to the people on the street like a church mouse campaigning for mayor. Her voice shook like a leaf, but she continued, "My friends have forgiven me, and with time I hope the other shop owners will too." She turned to Faith, her head dipped in shame. "I feel worst about how all this has hurt you, Faith. I didn't want to add to any apprehension you had about returning here, but I think I did. I made everything harder on you. I'm so sorry for that, truly sorry."

Faith stood dumbstruck, glancing from Miss Jenkins to those folks on the street before her gaze landed back on Miss Jenkins. She was apologizing to her *in public*. This was new.

Faith touched her necklace as a lump rose in the back of her throat.

"I don't know what to say. You took me by surprise."

"I hope you won't judge me based on this past week," Miss Jenkins said. "I do want you to stay in Roseley. We all do, don't we?" She held out a shaky hand to the crowd as everyone nodded.

"You didn't have to do this," Faith said, unsure how to handle the crowd, the attention or Miss Jenkins, who was about to dissolve into a puddle of tears in front of her. "This isn't necessary—"

"So you won't forgive her?" CeCe said, stepping forward to wrap an arm around Miss Jenkins's shoulders. Faith tipped her head thoughtfully, studying CeCe's expression. She supposed that question was exactly what she should expect from the busiest of busybodies.

But Faith wouldn't be influenced by other people's impressions of herself anymore. She would blaze her own trail and build a new life the way she wanted it to be. That new life would start with forgiveness, of herself and others. She was done holding on to old grudges and meeting her neighbors with hostility. It was time to set those things down here on the sidewalk, finally.

"Of course I forgive you," Faith answered. "I appreciate your apology. You certainly didn't have to do it in front of half the town—"

"Yes, I did," Miss Jenkins quickly said, stepping forward and touching her arm. "Yes, I did."

Faith nodded, as CeCe held out a black window box, a mailbox similar to the one hanging outside the other shops on the street.

"I need to say something too." CeCe shook the window box to make Faith accept it. "I haven't made your life very easy the past week, and I hope you'll accept this as a token of my—" she cleared her throat as if the words stung like vinegar on her tongue "—apology."

"I smashed yours," Faith sputtered. If these two women could clear the record in front of half the town, then so could she. She wanted to, so much. "When I was a teenager, I smashed up your mailbox and I admit that I enjoyed every second of it."

No one spoke as CeCe stared at her. Faith waited for the stout little woman to yank back the black box and cry that she'd always known Ray Talbert's daughter was a criminal, but instead, CeCe burst out laughing. Her voice cackled loudly, startling Miss Jenkins, who clasped a hand to her chest.

"Water under the bridge," CeCe cried, her cheeks rounding to a rouge. "I probably deserved much worse."

Angelo stepped forward to hand Faith a basket of mini sandwiches as Caroline hurried forward to hug her.

"I think you're officially one of the gang," Caroline whispered as folks began to talk among themselves, taking turns to welcome her to town.

Faith whispered back, "I never thought I'd see the day."

"Glad you decided to stay?"

"Glad I decided to move here in the first place." Trig took her new mailbox and got to work mounting it outside her shop.

"You belong here, Faith," Caroline said. "You've always belonged here. It just took you a while to find your way home again."

"I think…I think I do belong here," Faith admitted, hugging herself as people chatted all around her. For the first time ever, she felt it too.

TULLY AND SAMANTHA climbed out of the truck, prompting yips from Duke. He barreled through the tall grass and came crashing with excitement into Samantha. She held out her hands to try to stop him, but he only took it as an invitation to play.

"Not on my new shorts, Duke," she cried but it was too late. Dusty paw prints, one pressed perfectly to each thigh, were Duke's calling card. His happy tongue waggle had Samantha quickly forgiving him. "Good to see you too, dog breath." She laughed before pushing him to the ground and petting him on the head. "Has Dad been treating you okay? Think he'll be happy to see me?"

His sister directed her questions at Duke, but Tully knew her words were meant for him. He'd had to talk her into visiting Dad, and even though she admitted she *needed* to see him, she hadn't wanted to.

"Dad?" Tully called, making his way toward the shack. He swatted away mosquitoes, as dense as the humid air they swarmed in.

"I hear ya!" Walter called. He emerged from the nearby trees, but slowed his pace when he saw Samantha. "I wondered when you'd show."

"Hi, Dad," she said, her voice now as soft as it had been when she'd been a little girl. "I just got back into town—"

"You've been back for days."

"I'm here now." She crossed to him and held out a brown paper bag.

"What's this?"

"Gifts from my travels."

"What am I supposed to do with souvenirs out here?"

"They're all things you can use up, don't worry. I know better than to get you knick-knacks."

Walter peered into the bag before pulling out a box of chocolate-covered caramels.

"I'll give 'em a try," he said before shoving them back into the bag.

"They're delicious," Tully offered. "Sam gave me a box and it was all I could do not to eat them in one sitting."

"I said I'll take 'em." Tully and Sam exchanged a tense look. "What are you doing back in Michigan?" Walter asked. Samantha removed her sunglasses, channeling nervous energy like she had with her dolls after their mom left.

"I came to see Tully…and you. It's nice to be home for a little while."

"A little while? You leaving again?"

She waved her sunglasses around, punctuating her words as she spoke.

"Oh, you know. I need to get on the road soon or I'll go stir-crazy. There's so much to see and so little time."

Walter scowled. "You're young. You've got all the time in the world."

"Not really," she said, but Walter had turned his attention to Duke, scratching the dog behind the ears and muttering something like Duke was his only true confidant. Samantha rolled her eyes, noticeably irritated at being ignored. Tully could already hear her complaining now about how she'd come to see him and all he wanted to do was talk to the dog. He hoped she didn't take the bait, didn't say something to ignite an argument.

Tully had no sooner opened his mouth to segue the conversation to something pleasant when Samantha boiled over. "How long are you going to stay out here in the middle of nowhere, Dad? It isn't right, you squatting. You have a perfectly nice house in town with a refrigerator and air conditioner and running water—"

"Did ya come here to visit me or to lecture me? Besides, I don't need any of that stuff."

"That stuff? You don't need running hot and cold water?"

"What'dya bring her out here for?" Walter

said, his growing anger now aimed at Tully. "She's just like your mother, always reaching, never satisfied."

"Why do you always say things like that?" Samantha said, her own frustration clear. "You're always coming down on me, but I wasn't the one who left."

"That's enough for today," Tully said, holding up a steady hand. He knew the problems between Sam and his father wouldn't be solved in one visit. There was no use getting everybody worked up in this heat.

"You talk to him," Samantha sighed, turning toward the path. "I'll be in the truck."

Tully rested next to his dad on his sitting logs. Walter and Sam had been like oil and vinegar from as far back as Tully could remember. He assumed his dad saw a lot of his mother in Samantha, and he assumed Sam was always, unsuccessfully, trying to prove the old man wrong.

"She's impossible," Walter said, scratching Duke on the belly. "You know she is."

"She's trying, which is more than I can say for you."

Walter scowled at him. "I didn't ask her to come here."

"No, you left her no choice. You haven't been home in a long time."

"Bah." Walter rummaged through the paper bag, yanking out a handful of chocolate-covered caramels and popping them in his mouth. Tully let him chew for a while and get his hot temper down before continuing. He'd spent a lot of time thinking about what Faith had said to him. He'd thought about how it was time for his dad to come home, and how he was the only person who could really make that happen. The fallout might be hard and possibly ugly, but it had to happen.

"Dad, it's almost time."

"For what?"

"It's almost time for you to come home."

Walter grunted. "You've been hanging around your sister too much."

"You've been spending too much time out here."

"Says who? *You?*"

Tully pictured his dad standing on the ledge of a high building. If it were up to him to coax his dad back inside, into safety, it might feel similar to this.

"The town is going to start developing this land. It's been all over the newspapers for the last year. I won't have you camped out here blocking the bulldozers in protest."

Walter chuckled and ran a hand down his face.

"That would be the day."

"I wouldn't put it past you."

"There's nothing for me in town."

"There's a daughter and son who miss you and old friends who ask about you often."

"I don't need any friends."

"I didn't say you did. I said you belong in town with us."

"What for? I'm a one-man operation and that's how I'm going to stay. No use fighting it if that's what I was always meant to be."

Tully's breath caught, recalling how he'd said something rather similar not too long ago to the one woman whom he had ever had deep feelings for.

"You should come home, Dad, before it gets cold. No more winters out here."

Walter crinkled the brown bag shut and moved to stand. It was his signal that the conversation was over, but Tully wasn't leaving without making his dad understand. "I'll think about it," Walter said, making for his shack.

"October."

"What?"

Tully stood and stared down his father as if he were a hostage negotiator. "You need to come home by October."

"Who's the father and who's the son here?" Walter said, choking out a laugh. "I don't gotta do anything by October."

Tully scratched Duke under the chin. The dog thumped his tail heavily on the ground.

"Duke is coming to live with me in October. If you want Duke, you'll have to follow him home."

Walter wobbled on his feet. His jaw dropped so low Tully thought he might have to catch it.

"Son..." he said.

"You think about it," Tully said, motioning to Duke. "I don't know how we'd explain it to him. I'm sure he'd take it hard." He patted Duke goodbye and walked to his truck. It was best not to get into an argument with his dad, but he didn't mind leaving him something to consider. As Walter would do almost anything for Duke, pondering life without the dog might be all the persuasion needed to get his dad back.

"What did you say to him?" Samantha said when Tully climbed into the cab. "When you left, he looked like a kid learning there was no Santa Claus."

"I gave him some things to think about."

"That's all he does these days."

"I know the feeling." Tully had spent the last few days thinking about what a fool he'd been. He'd met a woman whom he didn't want to live without, and he'd convinced her that he worked best alone.

"I heard Miss Jenkins apologized to Faith," Samantha said as if reading his mind. "I heard the details from folks at The Nutmeg Café."

"I heard that too."

"She's great. I don't know what your problem is."

"Me?"

"Yeah. She's the best thing to happen to you in a very long time. Charlie filled me in on what went down between you two. What's holding you back from fixing things and you know—"

"—dating her?"

"Marrying her. I've seen the way you look at her."

Tully gripped the steering wheel and pressed his foot harder on the gas pedal, hoping the open road might cure what ailed him. He knew he was only lying to himself. The only thing he wanted, the only thing he needed, was Faith.

"It might be too late. I can't show up to a woman like Faith with a measly bouquet of roses, asking her to give me a second chance. It doesn't work like that with her."

"Why not?"

Tully considered what it would take to convince Faith that he loved her, and that he wanted to be with her for a lifetime. Short of moving heaven and earth, he was fresh out of ideas.

"It's not good enough. She's so much more than she realizes, and she deserves everything."

"You have big, bad detective skills. I'm sure you'll come up with a brilliant plan."

"Is that right?" Samantha slugged him in the arm and laughed.

"Yep. You always do."

FAITH HAD FINISHED work for the day. She'd cleaned up her tools, carefully putting everything back where it belonged, then scrubbed the grease from under her fingernails and locked up for the night. The few days since she'd opened her shop had made her hesitantly optimistic. Business wasn't booming by any stretch of the imagination, but she'd had several phone inquiries and had even detailed her first motorcycle. She'd spent a good hour polishing a little Harley-Davidson Softail and had enjoyed every minute of it.

She'd already decided to take a cruise along the lake on her ride home when her cell phone rang. Her cousin's voice sang cheerfully into the line.

"I forgot to mention something when I saw you earlier today," Caroline said. "You can't come to dinner tonight."

"Uh, excuse me?"

"In fact, you can't come back to the house until I say so."

Faith frowned. "Is there something at the house you don't want me to see?"

"Not exactly," Caroline said. "However, tonight is so beautiful, why don't you hang out at your shop, catch the sunset from your rooftop. I really think you should."

"I'd rather watch the sunset from the road, on my motorcycle, but you are welcome to watch the sunset on my roof, if that's what you're after. You know how to climb the fire escape."

"I'm not talking about me, Faith. You should go up there."

"I just locked up for the night, Caroline, and I want to get out of here. Why are you acting strange?"

Caroline whispered, "I'm trying to tell you something."

"You're failing miserably."

"I'm trying to tell you to get your argumentative self to your roof."

"Why?"

Caroline giggled. "Trust me on this one." Before Faith could protest, her cousin ended the call. Faith stared up at the roof of her shop. She hoped her cousin hadn't organized another mob to meet her up there. Being blindsided by a crowd of well-wishers had been touching but was something a person didn't need twice in a lifetime.

Reluctantly, she headed to the outside fire escape and climbed the two stories to her rooftop. She strode across the concrete landing, making her way to the opposite edge, which overlooked Main Street. In the distance the sun was straddling the water. She had just decided that a view this beautiful should be shared with another person when she heard someone climbing the fire escape. She knew who it would be, and it wasn't Caroline.

"John," she said. "What are you doing here?"

"I've been waiting for you to finish work for a while. I need to talk to you, and I wanted to do it here."

"I don't understand. Why?"

He crossed slowly enough that she could watch his every move with laser focus. She had missed him, missed the deep drawl of his voice and the way his hand fit snuggly around hers. She yearned to hold his hand again.

"You said you loved me for a long time. The least I could do was wait for a few hours." He stopped a pace away, though not far enough away for her to hide the blush of her cheek, recalling her embarrassing words. She'd told him about the feelings she'd harbored, because she thought things between them were over. As he'd meant so much to her over the years, she'd wanted him to know.

"That's what you remember from our conversation?" she said, her sarcasm doing little to mask her unease.

"I remember everything about that conversation, but at the time I didn't understand that piece. Did we know each other in high school?"

"You didn't know me."

"But you knew me?"

She smiled.

"Sort of. You were out of my league."

He considered this, then closed the distance between them. Her breath hitched.

"What about now?" he asked.

"You can't be serious," she whispered, shaking her head. "You're still out of my league, though to be fair, I can't think of a woman in this town good enough for you."

He took her hand, turning it over gently. He rubbed a thumb over her knuckles and fingernails that still carried stubborn grease stains. "You've been busy."

"I had my first customer."

"Delicate hands." He pressed her fingertips to his lips, his kiss puckering a soft sound against them. "Strong heart."

"I'm trying."

"So am I."

"I know. Samantha said you saw your dad again." She quickly clarified, "She stops by to chat sometimes. I think it's good you're talking to him. That you both are."

"I have a lot of baggage," he said.

"Everyone does."

"I didn't want to saddle anyone else with it."

"That's not how love works."

"No. Here's the thing, Faith," he said. "*I* don't think I'm good enough for *you*."

"You don't mean that."

"No?" He brought her hand to his throat, pressing it to the place where his pulse fluttered under the skin. "Then why is my heart racing at the thought that this is my one chance to make you understand how much I love you? Why am I terrified you won't believe me?"

She pulled her hand away, thinking he must be mistaken. She'd had a man profess his love once before, but it hadn't turned out to be true. No man had loved her enough to make her believe it. Her father had laid the groundwork of doubt, and Kyle had sealed the deal.

"Men are all words. You say that now, but what about months down the road? Years?" She had her business now, and she'd been making friends. If that was all she had in her life, she could consider herself a happy woman, couldn't she?

Tully went serious. "I remember something else I said to you. I said I work alone. I convinced myself a long time ago that I didn't need anyone and that I certainly didn't *want* anyone. If I had never met you, I might have been quite content believing that. If you hadn't come strutting into my life, I might have convinced myself that I was doing fine alone. But I'm not fine. I'm not okay. Not anymore."

"What does that mean? Does that mean you want to take me out on a date or something?"

"A proper date, yes. I was hoping for a date tonight and tomorrow night and the night after that."

"And then what?"

"Then a date to pick out an engagement ring—"

"I don't wear rings. Grease. See?" She held up her hand, hell-bent on setting things straight. He was getting ahead of himself. Maybe he missed her, but so did Kyle and she wasn't about to go swooning into his arms again.

"John, promises like that don't…"

"Don't mean anything to you anymore."

"They sure don't. They don't stand up, never have. At least, not for me. My father said he'd spend more time with me once work slowed down, once he'd closed the next deal, and you know how that turned out. Kyle promised to change…" She shook her head. "Heck, he didn't even really promise that."

Tully traced a line down to her heart necklace.

"This means something to you, doesn't it? I noticed it one of the first times we talked. What does it mean?"

She closed her eyes, savoring the tenderness of his hand on her skin.

"I bought it to remind myself that I deserve

everything I want. If I don't follow my heart, what's left for me?"

"*Have* you followed your heart?"

"I stayed, didn't I?"

"I'm glad you did. A lot of people want to be here for you, support you, if you let them."

As much as she had appreciated Miss Jenkins's gathering folks to hear her apology and welcome Faith to town, trusting new friends went against all her old instincts. If she wanted a second chance, she needed to give everyone else a second chance too. She had to learn to trust them.

"That's easier said than done, but I'm trying."

"Faith." She blinked, aware that he'd said her name intentionally. "Faith, I want you to try me. Stay with me."

His words were patient, delicate, like snowflakes melting against her skin. He pulled at the collar of his shirt, exposing the scar she'd kissed the night he'd told her about his mother leaving. She had wanted to kiss all his pain away, her lips drawing out the venom that had pooled there since childhood. From this same vantage point on the roof, she had thought that she could be his everything if he would only let her, because all she had wanted that night was him. All she'd ever wanted was him.

As she stared at the spot where his scar had once been, she blinked furiously. Inked over where his mother's abandonment had been logged was a small heart tattoo, identical to hers. It was the same design as the heart charm dangling around her neck, the same as the heart logo she'd painted on her shop window. He'd sealed a connection to her forever, permanently.

When she searched his face for an explanation, she found an intensity she'd never seen on him before. He looked like he could swallow her up whole in one ravenous gulp. Her mouth parted to release an exasperated gasp, and she decided to let him try.

"Stay with me, Faith," he said, drawing her close. "Marry me, and I promise to never cause you a day of pain. I'll protect your heart as I know you'll protect mine."

She would, she thought. Every ounce of her being would protect him, cherish him, love him. She touched the whiskers around his mouth, then ran her fingers through his hair. When she kissed him, her body molded into his embrace, and she could think of no better way to say yes.

EPILOGUE

October had found its way to Little Lake Roseley faster than Faith's Street Glide traveling an open road. When Tully had asked her what kind of wedding she'd always imagined, she'd told him she'd wanted to ride off into the sunset with him. It hadn't been much detail to guide Caroline, who acted as both maid of honor and wedding planner, but it had been all she'd really wanted aside from him.

Nearly every resident within a ten-mile radius was in attendance for the big day. News of John McTully's wedding had traveled far and wide, leading folks to show up to celebrate their favorite hometown son and his new bride.

Set against the foothill of Falcon's Peak, the trees had had a two-week head start, leaves turning to fierce red, golden yellow and sunset orange. The ceremony was short, the receiving line was long and even Uncle Gus, who'd returned to town for the event, couldn't remember a wedding in recent history where the bride and groom had looked more in love. Bonnie had once joked that Faith had given her whiplash with how often she looked at Tully and looked away again. But as Bonnie would fondly tell it later, Faith and Tully hadn't seemed to see anything during the ceremony besides each other. Their unwavering dedication made Bonnie dab her eyes a few times. She was also sure that even Tully's eyes misted when Faith walked down the aisle.

Walter brought Duke and, as agreed, moved back to his house before the ceremony. Tully considered it a generous wedding gift. He also found it fitting that his dad wouldn't wear a tie, while Duke didn't mind his. To sweeten the pot, Tully bought the antique motorcycle and sidecar off the Callahan brothers, who hadn't pressed charges against Miss Jenkins. Faith managed to repair it, and they surprised Walter with it on his first day home. Walter was so pleased, he rode it to the ceremony while his favorite copilot happily rode at his side.

Samantha put together a wedding website for the couple and did such a fantastic job, Faith hired her to do the same for Heart Motorcycles. With Sam's online strategy, Faith found herself with more work than she knew what to do with, drumming up business from neighboring towns too.

Tully had wanted to buy Faith a diamond engagement ring, but after she refused for the last time, he bought her a diamond to add to her heart necklace. In lieu of gold wedding bands, they agreed to get matching tattoos on their ring fingers. CeCe had originally thought the act silly, but when she overheard folks at the ceremony admiring it, she was the loudest champion of the romantic gesture. Over the months, she had become the couple's most passionate champion alltogether.

After the couple exchanged vows and kissed for the first time as husband and wife, the crowd cheered but Tully couldn't hear them. All he could see was Faith. When their reception was still going strong, Faith took his hand and gave him a pleading look. She was ready to ride into the sunset with him.

"Are you sure you can ride in that dress?" he said as they sped for the two motorcycles Charlie and Caroline had decorated for them. Faith winked, kicked off her heels and stepped into her motorcycle boots. He'd known that Miss Jenkins had found Faith a vintage wedding dress, but it wasn't until Faith unsnapped the skirt and slid it to the ground that he realized she had been wearing a pair of blue jeans under it the entire time. She hopped on her Sportster, looking quite pleased with herself. "What about your veil?" he asked.

Faith removed her long veil and slid on her helmet. As he slid on his and they fired up their engines, he couldn't help but stare. She was a sight: white lace bodice, blue jeans, motorcycle boots and the prettiest smile he'd ever seen.

"Where to, Mrs. McTully?"

"How about forever?" she called over the crackle of the engines. Tossing her veil to the wind, she carefully navigated the dirt path until she hit the pavement and accelerated. Tully gave her a short lead before chuckling to himself and giving chase.

* * * * *

For more enchanting romances set in quaint Roseley, Michigan, from Elizabeth Mowers and Harlequin Heartwarming, visit www.Harlequin.com today!